Murder at the Mill

A Redmond and Haze Mystery Book 3

By Irina Shapiro

Copyright

© 2020 by Irina Shapiro

All rights reserved. No part of this book may be reproduced in any form, except for quotations in printed reviews, without permission in writing from the author.

All characters are fictional. Any resemblances to actual people (except those who are actual historical figures) are purely coincidental.

Contents

Copyright 2
Prologue 5
Chapter 1 7
Chapter 2 11
Chapter 3 16
Chapter 4 25
Chapter 5 28
Chapter 6 32
Chapter 7 40
Chapter 8 44
Chapter 9 47
Chapter 10 54
Chapter 11 61
Chapter 12 65
Chapter 13 71
Chapter 14 77
Chapter 15 80
Chapter 16 83
Chapter 17 89
Chapter 18 96
Chapter 19 103
Chapter 20 109
Chapter 21 124
Chapter 22 135
Chapter 23 142
Chapter 24 146

Chapter 25 155

Chapter 26 163

Chapter 27 167

Chapter 28 170

Chapter 29 180

Chapter 30 189

Chapter 31 191

Chapter 32 195

Chapter 33 200

Chapter 34 202

Chapter 35 209

Epilogue 214

Notes.. 219

Excerpt from Murder in the Caravan 220
Redmond and Hazy Mysteries Book 4 220

Chapter 1 222

Chapter 2 228

Chapter 3 241

Prologue

The moon hung low in the nighttime sky, its fat belly skimming the tops of the elms that stood like a row of silent sentinels in the distance. Silvery light bathed the meadow and danced on the inky waters of the river that had once been the source of the family's income but now flowed over the stationary wheel of the mill, gurgling and rushing past, its current as strong as ever. Wooly clouds moved at a stately pace across the star-strewn sky, obscuring parts of the moon and throwing wild shadows on the frostbitten countryside.

Sadie Darrow stopped the dogcart and looked out over the haunting scene, her nerves as frayed as the cuffs of her coat. She'd been alone since suppertime, washing up and then darning shirts and socks by the fire. Frank and the boys had left hours ago, but only Jimmy and Willy had come back, drunk and subdued, and had gone to bed after muttering something about Frank staying for another round.

She should have gone to bed and left Frank to fend for himself; he was a grown man, after all, but something had made her pull on her threadbare coat and worn boots and set off into the night in search of her husband. He hadn't been at the Queen's Arms, nor had she seen him ambling along the lane that led toward their house. So, she'd come to the mill, hoping he'd staggered to the old building to sleep off the drink on the moldy old cot that had been there since the days when the mill had been a thriving concern and not the derelict relic it had become in the last few years.

A thick cloud that had momentarily obscured the moon passed, leaving the meadow and the mill bathed in moonlight. Sadie squinted, her gaze drawn to the wheel. Something was lying across it, something long and thick. Climbing out of the cart, she hurried toward the deserted building, her boots crunching on frosty grass, her gaze glued to the odd shape on the wheel.

A strangled scream tore from her chest as her mind finally accepted what her eyes had been seeing all along. A naked man was strapped to the top of the wheel, his head thrown back, his eyes wide open as if he were stargazing. His skin was bluish with cold, his body arched to fit the shape of the wheel, the stiff rod of his manhood pointing straight at the sky.

    Sadie clapped a hand over her mouth as she stared at her husband's slack face, and then she smiled, ever so slightly, before turning away and going for help.

Chapter 1

Thursday, December 20, 1866

Inspector Daniel Haze shivered, as much from the bitter cold as from the sight that had greeted him when he'd arrived at the mill. Constable Pullman, who'd come to fetch him from Squire Talbot's Christmas ball, stood on one side, Captain Jason Redmond on the other, all three men speechless in the face of the crime scene, for there was no doubt this had been a crime, and a gruesome one at that. A second constable, a young man of about twenty with just a hint of a fair moustache, was stepping from foot to foot and rubbing his hands, having had to stand watch over the body until the inspector and the surgeon had arrived.

"Well, what do you make of this?" Daniel asked as he turned toward Jason, whose head was tilted to the side as if he were looking for something in particular.

"I won't know anything for certain until I examine the body," Jason said quietly, "but I think it's safe to assume this wasn't an accidental death."

Daniel looked around, scanning every inch of ground. There was nothing to see. The grass glittered in the moonlight, the stalks petrified with cold. There were no obvious footprints or signs of struggle. He looked around for the dead man's clothes but couldn't see them anywhere. Perhaps whoever had done this had left them inside the millhouse or had taken them away as a precaution or as a souvenir of the night's events.

"Have you ever met the man?" Daniel asked. "His daughter works in your kitchens, doesn't she?"

"Yes, Kitty's been working at Redmond Hall since September, but I've only ever seen her brothers. They come to collect her on her afternoons off. Nice chaps. Quiet," he added thoughtfully.

"From what I hear, Frank Darrow was anything but quiet, but I never met the man in person."

"Let's get him down, shall we?" Jason said, setting down his medical bag and walking toward the immobile wheel.

"How do we go about it, guv?" asked the young constable, whose name was Ingleby, looking at the corpse with ill-concealed distaste.

"Someone will have to hold the wheel to make sure it doesn't shift, and two people will have to climb up and cut him down. Any volunteers?" Daniel asked, looking from one constable to the other.

"I'll hold the wheel," Constable Ingleby said eagerly.

"I'll go up, but I'll need one of you to help me," Constable Pullman said.

"I'll go," Jason said, but Daniel held up a hand to stop him. "It's my case, it's my responsibility. I'll ask you to hold my things," Daniel said, taking off his woolen coat and top hat. He was still in evening clothes, his white shirt and silk scarf stark against the black broadcloth of his jacket.

"Be careful, Daniel," Jason called out as Daniel walked toward the wheel, followed by the two constables, who disappeared inside the millhouse and emerged a few minutes later, carrying a ladder, which they propped up against the wooden hub of the wheel. Daniel went first, followed by Constable Pullman.

"Hand me the blade," Daniel called out.

Constable Pullman pulled a pocket knife out of his coat pocket and handed it to Daniel.

Taking hold of the knife, Daniel sawed through the rope that bound Frank Darrow at the ankles, then carefully shifted his weight to get easier access to the man's wrists.

"Constable, I will pass him to you headfirst," Daniel said. "Grab him under the arms and carefully begin to make your way down."

"As you say, guv," the constable replied, but the confusion on his face was a testament to the impracticality of Daniel's plan.

Daniel pulled the man by the arm until the upper body was hanging off the wheel. Just as the constable reached for the dead man's torso with his free hand, the body slid downward, knocking both Daniel and Constable Pullman off the ladder and sending all three hurtling to the ground. The constable cried out as the dead body landed on top of him, followed by Daniel, who knocked his head against the dead man's shoulder and banged his knee painfully on the hard ground.

"Are you all right?" Jason exclaimed as he rushed toward the heap of body parts. "Constable?" he called out to the poor man. The constable's helmet had slid forward and was obscuring his vision, which was probably a blessing since Frank Darrow's torso was right in front of the constable's face, his erect penis nearly in the constable's mouth. Constable Ingleby stood off to the side, frozen with horror.

Daniel sprang to his feet and adjusted his spectacles, which were miraculously still intact, if on a bit crookedly, gasped when he saw the position of the body, then grabbed the corpse by the arms and pulled, moving the man's private parts downward just in time for Constable Pullman to push up his helmet and look about.

"Got the wind knocked out of me is all," Constable Pullman grumbled as he crawled out from under the body, leaving Frank Darrow's remains sprawled on the ground.

"I hope our little tumble doesn't interfere with your conclusions," Daniel said as he looked up at Jason, who was trying hard to hide the twitching of his lips and the amusement in his eyes.

"It shouldn't. Let's get him to the morgue," he said, mastering his mirth.

The two constables lifted the corpse by the arms and legs and carried him, with great difficulty and much huffing and puffing, toward the police wagon.

"He's one heavy sod," Constable Ingleby muttered.

9

"A dead weight, one might say," Constable Pullman replied between intakes of breath.

The constables deposited him on the floor and invited Jason and Daniel to follow. They climbed into the wagon and sat on either side of the corpse, Daniel wincing slightly as the door slammed behind them and was locked from the outside. The only source of light was the barred windows, which let in narrow shafts of moonlight that fell on the milky-white body on the floor. Daniel had a strange urge to cover up the body but had nothing save his coat, which he wasn't about to remove. The temperature inside the wagon was as arctic as it had been outside. He looked down at the dead man and pushed his spectacles up his nose as they began to slide downward. "This is my first case as an inspector for the Essex Police," he said dreamily. "Is it wrong to be excited?"

"Not at all," Jason replied. "I have no doubt you'll get justice for Frank Darrow."

"I hope so," Daniel said. "I hope so."

Chapter 2

The morgue, or the mortuary, as the desk sergeant on duty at the station referred to it, was located in the basement of the building. The walls were covered in white tiles from floor to ceiling, and several gas lamps were affixed to the walls at equal intervals, giving off a sickly yellow light. There was a stone table, complete with a hole at the center for drainage, and several cabinets equipped with surgical tools, bowls, and beakers. There were also a washbasin, soap, and a towel provided for the surgeon's use, as well as a coatrack to hang one's coat and hat before getting down to business.

"Dr. Engle left his apron," the sergeant said, pointing to a bloodstained apron that hung on a hook behind the door. "You're welcome to use it."

"Thank you," Jason said, trying not to show his distaste.

Removing his outer garments, he hung them up on the coatrack, then unwound his cravat and stuffed it into the pocket of his coat. He then reached for the apron. It wouldn't do to return to Redmond Hall covered in blood and gore, especially if he happened to come across poor Kitty, whose father he was about to disembowel. As Jason prepared to begin the autopsy, he wondered if Kitty had been informed. She hadn't been at Squire Talbot's Christmas ball, not having been invited along with all the other villagers because she didn't come from Birch Hill.

Kitty Darrow was from Elsmere, a village several miles north of Brentwood. Jason hoped that whoever broke the news to her would be gentle. Kitty was a shy, quiet girl of fourteen who felt the most comfortable with Mrs. Dodson, who was not only both cook and housekeeper but also Redmond Hall's mother hen and treated Kitty more like a daughter than a scullery maid. Jason's young ward Micah was quite fond of Kitty as well. He still admired Fanny, the upstairs maid, whose fair curls and large brown eyes had probably attracted many a young man, but Kitty was closer to his own age, and he tried hard to befriend her and win her approval, as any eleven-year-old boy would.

Kitty had never mentioned her father to Jason, but then their paths didn't often cross, and when they did, Kitty usually mumbled something in response to his greeting and scurried away. Jason would always be an American commoner in his own mind, but to those around him, he was Lord Redmond, master of Redmond Hall and heir to the profitable estate that had been left to him by his titled grandfather. Few noblemen would soil their hands with the blood of peasants, but Jason was a trained surgeon who'd performed countless postmortems during his medical training in New York and then life-saving surgeries near the battlefields of the American Civil War. He was happy to help the police, and especially Daniel Haze, who'd become his closest friend in England.

"I'll stay, shall I?" Daniel asked as he positioned himself at the corpse's feet for a better view.

"Of course," Jason replied. He laid out the supplies he'd need on a small table near the stone slab and turned to the body.

"Are you going to start cutting now?" Daniel asked. He seemed torn between curiosity and apprehension.

"Not just yet. I will see what I can learn from the body's external appearance first."

"Right," Daniel said, visibly relieved. "Eh, Jason, why does his, eh…?" Daniel faltered, but having followed the direction of his gaze, Jason understood the question.

"This is what's known as a death erection," Jason explained. "It happens most frequently when a man dies by hanging, since there's pressure from the noose on the cerebellum, but it's possible that the killer had applied pressure to the back of the victim's neck, producing a similar effect."

"You don't think he was killed while in the act?"

Jason cocked his head to the side, considering the question. "He may have been. I'll know more once I've finished."

Jason carefully examined Frank Darrow from head to foot before rolling the corpse over onto its stomach. Using his fingers to part the hair, he checked for bruises and lacerations to the scalp before making his way down and checking every inch, then returned the body to its original position on its back.

"What do you reckon?" Daniel asked.

"There are no obvious wounds," Jason said. "Not a mark on him save these bruises on his shoulders and back of the neck, but they're not what killed him. The marks on the ankles and wrists are from the ropes and were inflicted postmortem."

"So, how do you think he died?"

"That's what I'm about to find out."

Jason picked up a scalpel and made a Y-shaped incision in the man's chest and stomach, then pulled apart the flesh to reveal the ribcage and the bowels.

A strangled cry came from Daniel Haze. "If you'll excuse me," Daniel choked out. "I'll just wait outside."

Jason chuckled to himself and continued with the autopsy. It'd been a while since he'd performed a postmortem, but some things weren't easily forgotten once learned. He spent the next several hours completely immersed in the process, determined to discover everything he could about Frank Darrow and the life he'd led before winding up on the slab in the Brentwood station mortuary from his remains.

By the time Jason emerged into the corridor, a faint pink haze could be seen through the high window of the basement chamber, the impenetrable black of the night replaced by a murky gray that was growing lighter by the minute. Jason pulled out his watch and checked the time. It was just past seven in the morning, and he'd been awake for more than twenty-four hours.

Daniel, who'd been dozing in a hard wooden chair beneath the window, woke with a start and stared at Jason, his eyes clouded with confusion.

"Good morning," Jason said softly, giving Daniel a moment to recollect exactly where he was and why.

"Good morning. Are you finished, then?"

"Yes."

Jason was just about to share his findings with Daniel when Detective Inspector Coleridge, Daniel's superior, appeared at the end of the corridor, still dressed in his coat and hat. Snowflakes dusted the shoulders of his dark-gray coat and luxurious fur collar and decorated the brim of his bowler hat.

"Gentlemen," Coleridge boomed as he approached. "I've just been informed. Extraordinary," he said, shaking his head. "Nearly thirty years as a policeman and I've never heard of such a thing."

"Someone certainly has a good imagination," Jason said, recalling the sight of Frank's naked body glowing in the moonlight.

"Do we have a cause of death?" Coleridge asked as he yanked off his gloves.

"Frank Darrow died by drowning."

"What?" Haze and Coleridge asked in unison, their mouths agape with shock.

"He died by drowning."

"What brings you to that conclusion?" Coleridge demanded.

"The victim did not have any visible wounds on his body except for some bruising along the shoulders and the back of the neck, and his lungs were full of water. My theory is that someone held him down in the river until he drowned. After death occurred, they undressed him, tied him to the wheel, and then shifted the wheel so the body was positioned along the top and more clearly visible, which I think was the objective."

"But why?" Daniel asked, his mouth forming a moue of distaste.

"To kill him wasn't enough. The murderer clearly intended to humiliate him as well," Jason theorized.

"Was he in good health otherwise?" Daniel asked.

"Judging by the state of his liver, he was a heavy drinker, and he'd ingested quite a bit of ale immediately before his death. Otherwise, he was in fine health."

"How long has he been dead?" Detective Inspector Coleridge inquired.

"It's hard to say, given that he was left out in the cold, but if I had to guess, I'd say about three hours."

"Who found the body?" Coleridge asked.

"His wife, Sadie Darrow, arrived at the mill sometime before midnight. Seems she had been out looking for her husband. Then the oldest son, James Darrow, reported the crime to the sergeant on duty about half past twelve."

"Well, Haze, this is what I believe they refer to as a trial by fire," Detective Inspector Coleridge said, a smile of amusement just visible beneath the waxed moustache. "Your first official case with the service, and it's a corker."

"I won't let you down, sir," Daniel said, drawing himself up to his full height and squaring his shoulders.

"I have every faith in you. Now, go home, change out of those clothes, have some breakfast and a strong cup of tea. You have a long day ahead of you."

"Yes, sir," Daniel replied.

"Constable Pullman will take you gentlemen home in the police wagon. It's snowing out there, so you'll have a deuce of a time finding a hansom to take you all the way to Birch Hill."

"Thank you, sir," Daniel said. "Shall we?" he addressed Jason.

Jason nodded, too tired to speak.

Chapter 3

"Daniel, where have you been?" Sarah exclaimed when he finally walked into the house, his coat and hat dusted with snow and his shoes leaving wet tracks on the polished floor. "I was so worried."

"I'm sorry, my dear, but there's been a murder."

Sarah's hand flew to her mouth. "A murder? Where? Was it anyone we know?"

"At the old mill near Elsmere. A man by the name of Frank Darrow. His daughter, Kitty, works as a scullion at Redmond Hall."

"Oh, that poor girl," Sarah said. "How dreadful to lose a parent so suddenly and violently. How was he killed?"

"He was drowned," Daniel said, intentionally omitting the racier details. There was no need for Sarah to know the rest, at least not this morning. "I'm afraid I must go out again as soon as I've changed and eaten."

"Of course," Sarah said, nodding. "I understand. I'll tell Cook we're ready for breakfast."

"Haven't you eaten?"

"I was waiting for you," Sarah said shyly. "Would you like your eggs fried or boiled?"

"Fried. Are there any kippers?" Daniel asked.

Sarah made a face of distaste at the mention of the kippers. "I'll tell Cook to make some. You must be exhausted," she said, laying a hand on his chest. "My poor dear."

"I am rather tired," Daniel admitted, smiling down at her. "Who brought you home from the ball?"

"Captain Redmond's driver brought mother and me home. It was a tight squeeze in the brougham, what with Mr. Sullivan, Miss Talbot, and the vicar, but we were grateful for the ride, as I am sure was Miss Talbot. Trudging home in satin slippers would not have been pleasant."

"No, I don't suppose it would be," Daniel said, trying to suppress a yawn.

"Go on. I'll tell you the rest later," Sarah promised.

Daniel sighed and nodded wearily. He had no interest in village gossip but was glad to see Sarah so animated. It hadn't been that long ago that she'd spent her days reading or staring out the window, her mind trapped in the recurring nightmare of their son's death. He'd happily listen to her recite the day's menu or a list of preserves in the pantry just to hear her speak and to know that she was engaged with the world, and their life. They would forever mourn Felix, who'd been nearly three at the time of his death, but life went on, and now, three years later, they were finally beginning to repair their fractured relationship and find their way forward.

Daniel made his way upstairs, where he shaved, washed his face, and combed his hair. He then changed into a clean shirt, put on his favorite suit of brown tweed, and returned downstairs. Sarah was already in the dining room, a cup of steaming tea before her.

"Come and sit down," she invited. "Tea?"

"Please."

Daniel accepted a cup of tea, added milk and sugar, and sighed with contentment after taking the first sip. He hadn't realized how thirsty he'd been. A few moments later, Tilda brought in a tray laden with two plates of fried eggs, toast, butter, marmalade, and a dish of kippers.

"Can you tell me more about the case?" Sarah asked as she buttered her toast.

Daniel shook his head. "I'd really rather not talk about it. It's bizarre, to say the least, and the details would only upset you."

Sarah lowered her knife and fixed him with an accusing stare, one eyebrow raised in astonishment. "Surely you won't keep the details from me, now that you've told me that."

"Sarah, it's gruesome. Do you really wish to hear the rest?"

"Indeed, I do," Sarah replied, lowering the eyebrow marginally.

Daniel quickly filled Sarah in on the particulars, leaving nothing out. It helped to talk about it, since it was a way to organize his thoughts, but he still thought Sarah would have been better off not knowing the grisly details.

"Good Lord," Sarah exclaimed. "That must have taken some doing."

"Yes. I think it's safe to assume this wasn't a random attack. The man must have truly infuriated someone to elicit this kind of a response."

"Is that what this is? A response?" Sarah asked.

"It must be. If you were to murder someone, why would you go through the trouble of taking off their clothes and mounting them up on that wheel?"

Sarah nodded. "If it is a response, it's one of Biblical proportions."

"I'll say. Except our murderer is not divine. He's just a man who was angry enough to go through the trouble of humiliating Frank Darrow, even in death."

"Where will you start?" Sarah asked as she took a bite of her toast.

"I'll start with the family. See if they can shed any light."

Daniel finished his breakfast, gulped the rest of his now-tepid tea, and got to his feet. "I have to go," he said apologetically.

"Will you be home for dinner?"

"I hope so," Daniel said. "That all depends on what leads the family can provide."

"Thank you, Tilda," Daniel said to the servant, who handed him his coat, hat, and gloves. He grabbed his walking stick from the stand near the door and headed out into the overcast morning.

Elsmere was a typical English village, similar in appearance and layout to Birch Hill. The two most important establishments of the village stood directly opposite each other, separated only by the village green. Daniel decided to forgo the church for the moment and stopped into the Queen's Arms, where Frank Darrow must have worshipped regularly, given the state of his liver and his level of inebriation at the time of his death. The barkeep looked up as Daniel walked in, as though surprised to see a customer so early in the day.

"Good day to you," Daniel said. "I'm Inspector Haze of the Brentwood Constabulary. Would you kindly direct me to the Darrow house?"

The barkeep looked furtive for a moment, then forced a smile onto his craggy face and nodded. "Of course. It's about a mile from here. Just follow the road westward. You can't miss it. So, it's true, then?" the man asked, his eyes dancing with morbid curiosity. "We heard Frank was found dead, but Sadie is keeping mum, and no one has seen the boys yet this morning."

"It's true that Frank Darrow is dead," Daniel replied. He wasn't about to offer up any further information. Not yet. "Thank you for your help."

He'd question the barkeep later, once the public house officially opened for business and the regulars began to speculate, doing some of the legwork in Daniel's stead. They'd know something of Frank Darrow's life and associates, and their theories, even the barmy ones, could prove useful, particularly since Daniel had not known Frank personally and would have to rely solely on the say-so of others.

Daniel followed the man's directions and drove the dogcart west until he saw a shabby two-story farmhouse in the distance. A thin plume of smoke wound into the nearly white sky, and several chickens pecked in the yard, trying to find something to eat beneath the thin layer of snow. A mangy dog barked wildly when Daniel turned off the road and drove into the yard, stopping before the door. A slim young man of about twenty stepped outside.

"What ye want 'ere?" he asked rudely. He looked pale and tired, and his eyes were red-rimmed, as if he'd been crying.

"I'm Inspector Haze," Daniel said as he climbed down from the cart. "I am investigating your father's death. Are you James Darrow?"

"I am," the young man replied. "Come in, Inspector."

Daniel followed the young man into the house. The smell of bacon and toasted bread filled the small space, making Daniel wish someone would open the window and air the place out. A woman he presumed to be Mrs. Darrow sat by the window, darning a shirt, while another young man, this one a bit younger than James, sat at the table, a book open in front of him.

"Good morning," Daniel said awkwardly, knowing it was anything but a good morning for this family. "I'm Inspector Daniel Haze. I'm very sorry for your loss."

"Thank you, Inspector," the woman said.

"Mrs. Darrow, I presume?" Daniel asked.

"I'm Sadie Darrow, and these are my boys, Jimmy and Willy. Please, have a seat, Inspector."

Sadie Darrow was probably no older than forty, but she could have easily passed for someone much older. Her brown hair was liberally threaded with gray, and her dark eyes looked sunken and dull, her skin sallow. She wore a threadbare gown of faded brown wool, and her boots were scuffed and probably worn through. Her hands, which might have been delicate had she been born a lady, were red and work-roughened, the nails bitten to the quick.

"Thank you." Daniel took a seat at the table, across from Willy, and waited for Mrs. Darrow to join them. Jimmy remained standing but moved toward the hearth, where Daniel could see him.

"Mrs. Darrow, can you tell me what happened, starting with the last time you saw your husband alive?"

Sadie Darrow nodded. "Frank and the boys came 'ome 'round 'alf past six."

"Where did they come from?"

"Since the mill closed—that'd be five years ago now—they've been working for Graham and Sons Coal Dispensary. From eight in the morning till six in the evening, six days a week. And I char for the Sawyer family, the other side o' the village, three days a week," Sadie added, even though Daniel hadn't asked her about herself. "So, as I were sayin', they came 'ome 'round 'alf past six and we 'ad supper. After supper, Frank and the boys went to the Queen's Arms. That'd be the last time I saw Frank alive."

Daniel turned to Jimmy. "What happened when you got to the Queen's Arms, Jimmy?"

"Nothin'," Jimmy said, shrugging. "We had us a few pints, chewed the fat with a couple o' mates, and gone 'ome."

"And your father?"

"'E stayed behind."

"Why?"

"Said 'e weren't ready to go 'ome. His mate, Elijah Gordon, offered to stand 'im another round."

"What time was this?" Daniel asked.

"'Round nine or thereabouts. Right, Willy?"

"Yeah, 'bout that," Willy agreed. He looked a lot like his brother but was a little stockier and shorter that Jimmy. Both young men had the look of their mother about them.

"What happened then?" Daniel asked.

"We got back and went to bed. Ma was gettin' ready for bed too," Jimmy said.

"What made you go out and look for Frank?" Daniel asked. "Did you normally go looking for him if he failed to come home by a certain time?"

"No, but Elijah Gordon 'as always been bad news. 'E'd stand Frank a pint, then expect one in return, and so it went until Frank had run up a tab it'd take him months to pay off. Then 'e'd come 'ome so drunk, 'e wouldn't be able to go to work the next day and lose wages. And Mr. Graham, that's 'is employer, 'ad already threatened 'im with dismissal."

"So, you went to fetch him home?" Daniel asked.

Sadie nodded. "When I got to the Arms, Tony Parks told me Frank had left an 'our or more since. Elijah were still there, but 'e were too far gone to talk to."

"So, what did you do?" Daniel asked.

"I 'adn't seen Frank walking down the lane, so I went to the mill."

"Why?" Daniel asked. He couldn't begin to fathom why a man who'd been drinking for several hours would go to a derelict mill in the middle of the night rather than make his way home.

"Because 'e went there sometimes. 'Specially when 'e were drunk. He missed the place. It'd been in 'is family for generations before 'e were forced to close it. Sometimes 'e even slept there."

"When you arrived at the mill, did you see anything out of the ordinary?"

"Ye mean besides my 'usband strapped to the wheel with his prick pointing skyward?"

"I mean like evidence of a struggle or someone still in the vicinity," Daniel amended patiently.

"Nah, nothin' like that."

"What did you do then, Mrs. Darrow?" Daniel asked softly, feeling guilty for forcing the woman to relive what had to be one of the worst moments of her life.

"I returned 'ome, roused Jimmy, and told 'im to go get a policeman right quick."

Daniel turned to Jimmy. "Is there anything you wish to add?"

Jimmy shook his head. "I went straight to Brentwood, to the station."

"Can you think of anyone who might have wanted to harm Frank?" Daniel asked, looking at all three Darrows in turn.

"Frank was not what ye'd call an amiable man," Sadie said, "but I can't think of anyone who'd do that to 'im. It were awful, seein' 'im like that."

"So, what kind of man would you call him?" Daniel asked.

"Selfish," Sadie replied instantly.

"Jimmy? Willy?" Daniel prompted.

The young men shook their heads, but not before Daniel noticed the sheepish look on Jimmy's face.

"Jimmy, I need to know the truth," he said sternly.

"Well, I don't think this 'as got anythin' to do with 'is death, but Mr. Graham sacked 'im last night."

"What?" Sadie cried. "Why?"

"'Cause 'e were insolent to the overseer. Called 'im a worthless sod, and worse." Jimmy looked at his mother apologetically. "Sorry, Ma, but we didn't want to upset ye."

"I can't be any more upset than I already am," Sadie replied. "What about ye two? Ye still got a job to go to?"

"We're all right," Jimmy said. "We'll go to work on Monday."

Sadie nodded, and Daniel could almost feel her relief. This was not a family that could afford to lose wages.

"What about Kitty? Has she been told?" Daniel asked.

"Kitty doesn't know, unless someone else told 'er," Jimmy said.

Sadie suddenly looked up, searching Daniel's face as if she'd thought of something important. "How'd 'e die, Inspector? Surely 'e didn't freeze to death."

"He drowned, Mrs. Darrow."

"Drowned?" she echoed.

"Yes. There was water in his lungs."

"Ye cut 'im open?" Willy cried.

"I'm sorry, but yes. We needed to know what killed him."

"Ye had no right," Willy sputtered, color rising in his cheeks as he looked from his mother to his brother. "Ma, tell 'im. They 'ad no right!"

"What's it matter now, Willy?" Sadie said, laying a hand over her son's.

"It matters. It's wrong to butcher a man as if 'e were a sheep carcass," Willy protested.

"It's all right, son," Sadie said, her tone soothing. "It's all right."

"Is there anyone I can speak to who might know what Frank had been up to in the days leading up to his death?" Daniel asked.

"Talk to the barkeep at the Arms," Sadie muttered. "Tony Parks saw a lot more of my 'usband than I did."

"Thank you," Daniel said, rising to his feet. "I will keep you apprised of our progress on the investigation."

Sadie nodded. "Do that," she said. Her sons remained silent, their gazes unbearably sad.

Chapter 4

Having left the Darrows to their grief, Daniel returned to the Queen's Arms to speak to Tony Parks, who, judging by his expression, had been expecting him to return sooner rather than later. A few people had made their way to the pub while Daniel had been at the Darrow house and were now sitting in a tight knot, whispering urgently. Daniel was sure they were discussing the murder, and he would have loved to hear what they were saying, but the men grew silent, watching him with apprehension.

"Can I get ye a drink, guv?" the publican asked as Daniel leaned against the bar. "On the 'ouse."

"Sure, why not?" Daniel said. He was thirsty, but his main reason for accepting the drink was to seem friendly and unpretentious. Most people were put off by the police and withheld even the most basic information for fear of somehow being implicated. Having a half pint of ale wouldn't prevent Tony Parks from clamming up, but it wouldn't hurt.

"Mr. Parks, you have seen a lot of Frank Darrow over the years," Daniel said, not bothering to phrase the inquiry as a question.

"I have," the man replied. "Frank was a regular."

"Was he a heavy drinker?" Daniel asked. He already knew the answer, but it was as good a place to start as any.

"More so in recent years."

"Why was that, do you think?" Daniel asked.

"Mourned the mill, Frank did. Frank liked being his own master."

"Why did the mill close?"

Tony Parks shrugged. "You can't stop progress, Inspector. Things change, and if you don't change with them, you die."

Daniel nodded wisely, but he didn't quite agree. Not everything changed. He was sure business at the Queen's Arms went on as usual, progress or not. "So, Frank Darrow's milling process became outdated. Is that what you mean?"

"I reckon so. Don't know much about milling."

"What can you tell me about Elijah Gordon?" Daniel asked. He could see the other patrons leaning forward, eager to hear the conversation.

"Not much. Elijah's a cooper. Does all right for himself."

"Does he live in the village?"

"Lives 'bout two miles north of here," Parks said, gesturing in the direction of Gordon's house.

"Was Frank Darrow at odds with anyone? Did he have enemies?"

"Frank was easily provoked when in his cups, but I'd say he was generally liked."

"Sadie Darrow said he wasn't an amiable man," Daniel said, watching Tony Parks for a reaction.

"She's not a very amiable woman," Parks replied. "Always has a face like curdled milk. What man would want to come home to such a drab?"

Daniel finished his drink and set the cup on the bar. "Thank you, Mr. Parks. I may need to speak to you again."

"I'm here every day."

Before leaving, Daniel approached the group of men, who were now pretending not to see him and stared into their tankards as if they could see the glimmer of gold shining from the bottom.

"I'd like to ask you a few questions," Daniel said.

"Ye a rozzer?" one of the men asked.

"I'm an inspector with the Brentwood Constabulary," Daniel replied.

The men nodded. "What ye want to know, guv?" a grizzled character in his sixties asked. He seemed to be the leader of the group, so Daniel directed the question to him.

"What can you tell me about Frank Darrow?"

The men exchanged glances and shrugged, as if on cue. "Frank were a good fellow," the man replied. The others nodded in agreement.

"Did any of you see him last night?"

"That we did. 'E came most days. Jimmy and Willy was 'ere too."

"And did Frank act like his normal self? Did he argue with anyone or appear angry or upset?"

"'E were just Frank," the leader said. The others nodded. "'E started drinkin' at the bar, then settled at that table over younder when Elijah Gordon came. Those two, thick as thieves since they was children."

"Did Frank leave on his own?"

"Aye, 'e did. Said 'e wanted 'is bed."

"Did he mention his intention to go to the mill?" Daniel said, losing hope of learning anything of interest.

"No. 'E said 'e were goin' 'ome."

"Thank you," Daniel said. "If you think of anything you consider relevant, please send word to the Brentwood police station. I'll be happy to come back to speak to you."

"Sure thing, guv," the grizzled fellow said. "Sure thing. Ye can count on us."

Daniel left the Queen's Arms and climbed into the dogcart. He hadn't learned much, but at least he had the name of someone who could tell him more not only about last night, but about Frank Darrow the man.

Chapter 5

By the time Jason woke, it was well past noon and he was hungry. He washed and shaved, got dressed, and made his way downstairs, hoping Micah was at his lessons and wouldn't ask him a thousand questions about last night, but luck wasn't on his side.

"Captain! Thank God you're finally up," Micah cried as he exploded from the library with his tutor trotting after him. "Was the poor sod really naked and tied to the waterwheel? Jesus, Joseph, and Mary, I wish I could have seen that!" Micah exclaimed.

"I'm sorry, Captain, but he was desperate to speak to you," Shawn Sullivan said, his fair skin turning a mottled pink with embarrassment at not being able to control his pupil.

"It's quite all right, Mr. Sullivan. I know how determined Micah can be when he wants something," Jason replied in his most reassuring manner.

Shawn Sullivan was an excellent tutor but a rather emotional young man who was easily upset. He was also a flamboyant dresser, a fact that drove Dodson batty with disapproval. Today, he was wearing his favorite green puff tie matched with a crimson waistcoat, probably in honor of Christmas, and a brown suit. His auburn hair was brushed back from his forehead, and his dark-blue eyes were anxious.

Turning back to Micah, Jason shook his head in disapproval. He didn't even bother to ask how Micah knew about the murder. Everyone in Birch Hill knew everything, and their information was usually frighteningly accurate. He only hoped Micah hadn't taken it upon himself to inform poor Kitty.

"Is Kitty here?" Jason asked, keeping his voice low.

"She's down in the kitchen with Mrs. Dodson," Micah replied.

"Does she know about her father?" Jason asked, addressing the tutor.

"I can only assume that she does," Shawn Sullivan replied. "Is it true, then?" he whispered. "Was he truly naked?"

"You're as bad as Micah," Jason snapped. "Yes, it's true."

"May God have mercy on his soul," the tutor said under his breath.

"I'm going to go speak to Kitty," Jason said.

"I'm coming with you," Micah announced.

"I would like to speak to her in private," Jason said. "I think it's time you got back to your lessons."

"Yes, Captain," Micah said with an exaggerated groan.

Jason took a calming breath and headed for the green baize door that separated the rest of the house from the servants' quarters. He walked down a narrow passage, then turned left and entered the kitchen. It was pleasantly warm, the yeasty smell of fresh bread and the succulent aroma of roasting meat filling his nostrils. He really was hungry.

Mrs. Dodson looked up from the potatoes she was dicing, her gaze anxious.

"Mrs. Dodson, can I trouble you for a cup of coffee and something to eat?" Jason asked.

"Of course, Captain. I can fix you a proper breakfast, if you like."

"Whatever you have on hand."

"There's a slice of cottage pie left over from last night's supper." The Dodsons had opted not to attend the Christmas ball and had remained at home, enjoying a night off from their duties. Mrs. Dodson would never have served him cottage pie, thinking of it as peasant food, but she'd obviously made one for herself and her husband.

"Cottage pie would be wonderful," Jason said. "May I speak to Kitty for a moment? Where is she?"

Mrs. Dodson blushed like a young girl. "Kitty went to the necessary."

"I see. I'll wait, then."

Kitty returned a few minutes later. She looked surprised to see Jason in the kitchen and instantly averted her gaze.

"Good afternoon, Kitty," Jason said gently.

"Good afternoon, yer lordship," Kitty muttered. Jason had asked her to call him Captain, but Kitty insisted on using his rank as a sign of respect.

"May I have a word with you in private?" Jason asked.

Kitty's eyes opened wide, her anxiety palpable. "Did I do something wrong?" she whispered. "Am I to be dismissed?" Even if she were, Jason wouldn't be the one doing the dismissing, but he hated that she felt so nervous around him that she instantly assumed the worst.

"No. No, of course not. Come into the butler's pantry with me," Jason invited.

Kitty looked like she was about to faint, but she followed him into the pantry and stood by the door, looking like she was about to bolt. Jason had considered closing the door but changed his mind, stepping behind Dodson's desk instead to give Kitty some space.

"Kitty, I'm very sorry to have to tell you, but your father is dead," Jason said. He wished he could have phrased things more elegantly, but dead was dead, and there was no easy way to tell someone.

"Dead?" Kitty whispered, looking him full in the face, her nervousness forgotten.

"Yes. He's been murdered."

"Murdered?"

"Yes. The police are trying to discover who is responsible," Jason assured her.

"'Ow was 'e killed?" Kitty asked. Jason couldn't help noticing that she seemed more curious than upset.

"He drowned, but not accidentally."

"I see," Kitty said, nodding, her head dipping.

"I'm very sorry for your loss. Would you like Joe to take you home? You can spend some time with your family. You don't have to come back until you're ready, and please, don't worry about your wages. You will be paid in full," Jason added, knowing that was always a consideration.

"Thank ye, yer lordship. That's most kind of ye."

"Kitty, if there's anything you need—"

"I 'ave everything I need, yer lordship. Thank ye."

"Go on, then. Get your things. Joe will have the carriage ready in a few minutes."

Kitty sucked in her breath. "The brougham? Oh, I couldn't, sir."

"Of course you can. I insist. And please pass my condolences to your family."

"Thank ye, sir," Kitty whispered. Her hands were trembling, and she looked alarmingly pale.

"Kitty, are you all right? Would you like some water? Or maybe you should have something to eat before you go," Jason suggested.

"I'm fine, sir," Kitty whispered, and fled.

Chapter 6

As Daniel pulled up in front of Elijah Gordon's house, he reflected that the man had to be doing well for himself. The red-brick house looked solid and spacious, with a freshly painted green front door and shutters, and heavy velvet curtains at the windows. Carefully trimmed shrubs grew beneath the windows, and the outbuildings looked well maintained.

The door was answered by a young female servant, who informed him that she would announce him to the mistress and left him to wait on the doorstep. When the door opened again, it was by a woman of middle years who had to be the mistress of the house. She smiled pleasantly, her head tilting to the side as she waited for him to state his business.

"Good day to you, madam," Daniel said. "I'm Inspector Haze, and I need to speak to Mr. Gordon."

"Yes, of course. Is this about the murder?" she asked in a hushed tone, but her eyes sparkled with curiosity, and her lips were slightly parted in anticipation of his answer.

She was very attractive. Her gown, made of fine dark-blue wool, was trimmed with a bit of lace and adorned with a silver brooch, and her hair, still dark and abundant, was curled at the front and gathered into a low knot at the nape. Her face was surprisingly smooth for a woman of her years and as rosy as a young girl's. She had to be about the same age as Sadie Darrow, but the difference in their appearances and stations was marked.

"I'm afraid it is. Your husband was one of the last people to have seen Mr. Darrow alive."

"Dear me. How dreadful. I do hope Elijah had been kind to him, at least. Those two were always arguing."

"Were they? What about?" Daniel asked, curious.

"Oh, this and that. Isn't that what happens when you bring two opinionated men together and add ale?"

"Is it?"

"It was with Elijah and Frank. It was good-natured, though. They were friends."

"Is your husband at home, Mrs. Gordon?"

"Elijah's in the workshop. That's it over there," she said, pointing to a large barnlike structure. "Elijah is devastated," she added sadly. "He could barely take any breakfast this morning. Do be gentle with him, Inspector."

"I'll do my best," Daniel assured her.

He walked over to the workshop, where Elijah Gordon and his assistant were hard at work.

"Mr. Gordon," Daniel said as he entered the woodsy-smelling space.

"Yes?" Elijah Gordon looked much like one of his barrels: squat, stout, and barrel-chested. He appeared to make up for the thinning hair on his head with thick, wooly muttonchops and a voluminous moustache that obscured his mouth almost entirely. He seemed friendly though, which was always a good start. Daniel explained the reason for his visit and watched the man's face cloud with sadness.

"I saw Frank only last night. We had a few pints. Had I known that was the last time I was going to see him..." Elijah's face drooped like a melting candle.

"How long had you known Frank Darrow?" Daniel asked. He'd already been told that Frank and Elijah had been lifelong friends, but he liked to verify the information for himself.

"Why, all my life. We both grew up in Elsmere."

"Were you always close?"

"More so when we were young men, but in recent years, our friendship was limited to sharing a few jars at the Queen's Arms now and again."

Daniel noted that compared to the Darrows, Elijah Gordon's speech was more educated and his manner more refined.

Beneath his apron, he wore a silk waistcoat, and his boots looked relatively new and were polished to a shine.

"How did he seem to you last night, Mr. Gordon?" Daniel asked.

"He seemed fine."

"What time did he leave?"

"Around ten."

"And did he plan on going straight home?" Daniel asked.

"Yes, he did," Elijah Gordon replied.

"Mr. Gordon, can you think of anyone who might have wished him harm?"

Elijah Gordon absentmindedly twirled the end of his moustache, clearly deep in thought. "I don't. Frank was a bit quarrelsome and had something of a temper; I'll admit that, but his anger never lasted long, and he readily made amends if he thought he had been in the wrong."

"Was he often in the wrong?"

"Sometimes. He took offense easily, but I could always see his side of things."

"Could you?" Daniel prompted.

"Life hadn't been kind to him, Inspector," Elijah Gordon said wryly.

"No? In what way?" Daniel knew a few people to whom life had not been kind, but they weren't all described as quarrelsome and hot-tempered.

"He lost the mill. His family had operated that mill for generations. Since the seventeen hundreds, I think."

"Mrs. Darrow said he'd been delivering coal these past few years," Daniel said.

"Yes, he had. He didn't mind the work but hated the overseer. Said he was a persnickety halfwit with a fist as tight as his arse. Wouldn't give Frank a pay increase, no matter how many times he asked. But they got on," Elijah Gordon hurried to add. "There was no bad blood between them."

"Jimmy Darrow said his father had lost his position."

"Oh, really? I didn't know that. I'm sure he would have found something in the new year," Elijah Gordon said. "Frank needed to support his family. He was a man who understood his responsibilities."

"So, he didn't drink his wages at the Queen's Arms?"

"A man deserves a pint of ale from time to time, Inspector. That's not the same as drinking your wages, is it?"

"It is if you don't know when to stop," Daniel pointed out.

Elijah Gordon nodded, as if understanding had just dawned. "Sadie told you that, no doubt. She couldn't forgive Frank for losing the mill. She liked being the miller's lady. It wasn't just the profit Frank had lost, but the status that went with being the proprietor of a thriving concern. He let her down, and she never let him forget it."

"But it wasn't a thriving concern, was it?" Daniel asked. "Was it Frank's fault that the mill had to close?"

Elijah Gordon shrugged. "Who's to say? I suppose there are measures he could have taken to prevent the worst, but, like I said, Frank was a bit quarrelsome and pig-headed. Wouldn't take advice from anyone. If someone had tried to help him, he'd probably have sent them packing, and with a few choice words at that."

"Well, thank you, Mr. Gordon," Daniel said.

"Anytime, Inspector."

As Daniel approached the dogcart, the door to the house opened again, and Mrs. Gordon appeared on the step. "Inspector," she called out. "Won't you come in? I've just made a pot of tea."

Daniel was about to refuse, but quickly changed his mind. He had no immediate leads to pursue, and he was cold and tired after his sleepless night. A cup of strong, hot tea would be most welcome.

"Thank you, Mrs. Gordon," Daniel said as he came inside.

"Here, let me take your things," Mrs. Gordon said, and held out her hands for Daniel's coat, hat, and gloves. There was no sign of the maidservant. "Come into the parlor and make yourself comfortable."

Daniel stepped through the doorway and found himself in a well-appointed room decorated in shades of apple green. A merry fire blazed in the grate, and the smell of something freshly baked wafted from the kitchen.

"Do sit down," Mrs. Gordon invited. "I'll just get the tea."

"You're very kind," Daniel said as he settled before the hearth and felt its warm embrace.

Mrs. Gordon returned a few moments later, carrying a tray laden with a teapot and two cups and saucers, a plate of seedcake, a bowl of sugar cubes, and a small jug of milk.

"How do you take your tea, Inspector?"

"Milk and two sugars," Daniel replied automatically.

Mrs. Gordon poured out and handed him his cup before pushing the plate of cake toward him. "Help yourself to a slice. I just made it this morning. Elijah has such a fondness for cake," she added playfully. "But I'm sure you've already figured that out. Don't need to be a police inspector to detect that a man likes to eat."

Mrs. Gordon didn't look like the type of woman who'd do her own baking, but her skill in the kitchen wasn't relevant to the investigation, and the cake did smell appetizing. Daniel helped himself to a slice and took a small bite. It was delicious, and he nodded in appreciation. "I can see why he has a weakness for your cakes, Mrs. Gordon."

She smiled and took a piece of cake for herself, breaking off a tiny piece with her fingers and delicately putting it in her mouth. "I do get lonely here sometimes," she said. "Elijah spends his days in the workshop, and I'm here alone, rattling around this big house," she complained.

"Do you have children?" He made no mention of the servant. The lady of the house wouldn't think of the maid as her companion.

"Oh, yes," she said, nodding. "We have a daughter. Clara is newly married and expecting her first child," she added, lowering her voice as if she were sharing a confidence. "I do hope we'll get to see the child from time to time. Clara's husband is a good man, but he's not one for visiting or being hospitable to his wife's parents. We rarely see her these days."

"I'm sorry to hear that," Daniel said. He took a sip of tea and studied Mrs. Gordon over the rim of the cup. He hadn't planned on questioning her, but this was too good an opportunity to miss, and as both his wife and mother-in-law often pointed out, women were vastly more observant than men and certainly more forthcoming. "Mrs. Gordon, did you know Frank Darrow well?"

"Well enough," she replied noncommittally.

"You didn't like him," Daniel said, watching her carefully.

"There wasn't much to like. He was pugnacious and bitter. Always blaming everyone and everything for his misfortunes except the one person truly responsible."

"You think he was responsible for what happened to him?" Daniel asked, secretly glad that Mrs. Gordon didn't have any qualms about speaking ill of the dead.

"Of course, he was. He was too short-sighted and stubborn to read the writing on the wall, so to speak."

"What writing was that?"

"Frank's father worked hard all the days of his life to keep the mill going. He was a good man and a loyal friend to his neighbors. His son, on the other hand, had always been one to cut corners wherever he could find them. Oh, he was doing all right for himself the first few years after his father passed, but then the Grenvilles began to make trouble for him."

"And who are the Grenvilles?" Daniel asked.

"The Grenvilles own the mill in Elton. That's about eight miles from here," Mrs. Gordon explained. "Not only had they made improvements to their milling process, but they had offered the farmers a slightly higher price for their grain, luring most of Frank's customers away within a year."

"Why would local farmers travel eight miles to sell their grain, especially if the price is not significantly higher?" Daniel asked. He knew nothing about milling, only that grain was milled into flour, which was then used in baking.

"Clearly, you don't do the baking in your house," Mrs. Gordon teased. "Most mills offer two different processes: low milling and high milling. Low milling produces coarse, brown flour. High milling results in finer, whiter flour that's sold to the bakeries at a higher price. Some customers wish to sell their grain, while others only want to mill some grain for their personal use," Mrs. Gordon explained. "If you're selling one bag of grain, the difference in price might not be significant, but if you had reaped an entire field of wheat—" She let the sentence hang, leaving him to calculate the difference in profit.

"Ah. I see what you mean," Daniel replied, surprised to discover that Mrs. Gordon was so knowledgeable. He couldn't help wondering if Sarah knew this much about milling grain.

"My father was a farmer," Mrs. Gordon said, correctly guessing at his thoughts. "I used to help him balance his ledgers. He was hopeless with figures."

"You must have been a great help to him," Daniel said. "Do you assist your husband as well?"

"Elijah won't let me anywhere near his books," Mrs. Gordon replied. "He thinks a wife's duty is to see to her husband's needs and look ornamental."

"So, the Grenvilles drove Frank Darrow out of business?" Daniel asked, redirecting the conversation back to the case.

"In a manner of speaking. See, Frank could have made improvements, tried to match the price the Grenvilles were offering, but he was too tightfisted to spend the money, so his custom began to dwindle. Besides, that wheel was always getting stuck. Imagine bringing your grain to be milled and being told you must come back another time and take the chance of it still not being fixed. Would you return, or would you go to a mill that was sure to be working?"

"So, you're saying it was Frank Darrow's fault that the family fell on hard times?"

"I am. And speaking of family, the man never had a kind word to say to any of them. Sadie was pretty once, and clever. She had other suitors, but she chose Frank, because he was handsome and charming and stood to inherit the mill and the land the house stood on outright. Sadie thought she was set for life, but now she must char for her neighbors to make ends meet. I would have hired her myself, but it'd be too awkward to have her here."

"Mrs. Gordon, can you think of anyone who might have hated Frank enough to kill him?" Daniel asked. According to the Gordons, Frank Darrow hadn't been business savvy or easy to get along with, but that was no reason to kill him and leave him tied to a waterwheel wearing nothing but an expression of shock.

"I think Frank got himself involved with something dodgy," Mrs. Gordon said.

"Dodgy in what way?"

"Illegal. I reckon that's why he was sacked. I'd speak to his employer if I were you. I wager he can point you in the right direction."

"Thank you, Mrs. Gordon. I will." Daniel finished his tea and rose to his feet, ready to leave. He'd learned all he could from the Gordons, and now that he was fortified with tea and cake, he was ready to continue with his inquiries.

Chapter 7

Having seen Kitty off, Jason retreated to the drawing room to consider the case, but his mind kept straying to last night's ball. He'd left without offering an explanation to Katherine Talbot, leaving her without a partner for the quadrille, which he had been looking forward to. In the six months he'd been in England, he'd come to care for Katherine, first as a friend, and then as a woman. Katherine wasn't the type of woman he would have found himself attracted to a few years ago. She wasn't beautiful in the way Jason's former fiancée had been, nor was she rebellious, spontaneous, or willing to use her feminine wiles to get what she wanted. Katherine was loyal, compassionate, and kind, and, to Jason, all the more beautiful for being a woman he could trust not only with his sometimes-unorthodox thoughts, but with his heart.

For all her beauty, his former fiancée Cecilia had been frivolous and changeable, and had married Jason's friend Mark Baxter while Jason had been incarcerated at Andersonville Confederate Prison in Georgia, a hellish place that still haunted his nightmares. After the prison had been liberated and Jason returned home, weak and emaciated after months of near starvation, Cecilia had never even bothered to call on him or apologize in person for turning her back on him when he'd needed her most. They hadn't spoken in person since he'd joined the Union Army, and he'd found that once he was over the shock of her betrayal, he had been relieved to no longer be bound to her and grateful to her for saving him from making a terrible mistake. Now, he was a free man, and he'd choose more wisely.

Jason wished to court Katherine openly, but she had begged him not to make their budding relationship official. Being a dutiful daughter, she felt it her responsibility to look after her father, Reverend Victor Talbot, who was happy to treat Katherine as his cook and housekeeper and never stopped to consider that she might be entitled to a life of her own. Had this been Cecilia, she would have simply got herself engaged and presented her father with a fait accompli, but Katherine loved and respected her father, and needed his approval and blessing more than she cared to admit.

Despite her obvious feelings for Jason, they had yet to even kiss, an omission that left him burning with longing and frustrated desire.

He could have a woman easily enough if he had a mind to go that route. Even Moll from the Red Stag would be more than willing to satisfy his needs, but Jason was not a man who thought of sex as something to be taken or paid for. He'd had his share of casual encounters when he was a medical student and had been introduced to women who were only too happy to give the young doctor an education he wasn't likely to get at the university, but now he was nearly thirty and he wanted to lie with a woman he loved, a woman he could easily imagine as the mother of his children and a companion for his old age.

Jason sighed and peered out the window for the umpteenth time. It was snowing lightly, the world beyond a study in white and gray. He didn't think the roads would be impassable but had no way of knowing if it was snowing heavier elsewhere.

"Why do you keep looking out the window?" Micah asked as he walked into the room, a book under his arm.

"I like the snow," Jason lied. He couldn't tell Micah the truth; it would spoil the surprise.

"No, you don't. You hated the snow back in New York."

"Well, it looks prettier here," Jason replied, hoping to put Micah off the scent. The boy had the nose of a bloodhound. "Where's Mr. Sullivan?"

"He had a headache and went to lie down."

"And are you responsible for him having a headache?" Jason asked, a smile tugging at his lips.

Micah shrugged. "I don't like translating from the Greek. It's tedious."

"Yes, it is."

"So, why must I do it? When will I ever need to know Greek?" Micah asked petulantly as he settled across from Jason.

"You need to be proficient in certain subjects in order to get into a good university," Jason replied.

"What if I don't want to go to university?"

"So, what will you do instead?"

"I can be a farmer like my pa was," Micah said defiantly.

"Yes, you can, but is that what you really want?"

"I don't know what I want," Micah said, his face drooping. "Sometimes I feel like I don't belong anywhere."

Jason could understand only too well how Micah was feeling. He'd felt the same way after he'd returned home after nearly a year of captivity. His parents had died while he was away fighting, Cecilia had turned tail, and most of his friends had either been dead or were still recovering from their wartime experiences, as he had been. Everything had changed, but he had changed the most. Micah, who'd been left orphaned after his father and brother died at Andersonville, had become Jason's reason for being in those first few months. Jason had dedicated himself to searching for Micah's sister, Mary, who seemed to have fallen off the face of the earth after the Donovan farm in rural Maryland had been burned to the ground.

"What are you reading?" Jason asked, nodding toward the book Micah was holding.

"*A Tale of Two Cities*," Micah replied. "Have you read it?"

"I have. It's very good. Are you enjoying it?"

Micah nodded. "May I lend it to Tom after I'm done?" Micah's only real friend in Birch Hill, Tom was the son of a gamekeeper on the Chadwick estate who happened to be the brother of Jason's groom and coachman, Joe Marin.

"Of course."

"It might take him a long time to read it," Micah said. "Tom is a slow reader, and he doesn't know many posh words."

"Tom doesn't have the benefit of Mr. Sullivan teaching him," Jason replied.

42

Shawn Sullivan, whom he'd hired three months ago during an investigation into the death of Elizabeth Barrett, had not only proved to be a competent tutor but become something of a friend to Micah. Coming from a similar background, Shawn Sullivan had forged an instant bond with his pupil, and with Jason as well. They never alluded to his homosexuality, but Jason suspected that Shawn had a lover in London whom he saw on his days off. Jason had offered Shawn the use of the carriage to take him to and from the railway station but asked no questions about where the young man was going. It was Shawn's private business as far as Jason was concerned.

"Looks like it's going to be just the two of us for Christmas," Micah said wistfully.

"I'm sorry. I know you miss celebrating Christmas with your family," Jason said softly.

"You're my family, Captain," Micah said, and blessed Jason with a smile of such pure devotion that it nearly made him cry. Jason looked away for a moment to hide his emotion, but Micah had seen it.

"We'll always be together, you and I. Won't we?" Micah asked.

"Always."

Or maybe not, Jason thought miserably. *That all depends on what happens within the next few days.*

Chapter 8

The snow had stopped, leaving the countryside draped in a quilt of glittering white velvet. An unnatural hush had settled over the land, the only sounds the snorting of Daniel's horse as it trotted along and the crunch of wheels on the freshly fallen snow. Even the birds were silent, hunched on their perches in the trees, their wings dusted with snowflakes. Daniel tried to focus on the questions he wished to put to Mr. Graham, but his thoughts were muddled, and his eyes were beginning to close of their own accord. He hadn't slept in what seemed like days, and his usually sharp senses were dulled by fatigue.

Instead of returning to Brentwood, Daniel decided to head home. He needed to kip for a few hours, then consider the facts with a clear head before proceeding with the investigation. He also wanted to speak to Jason Redmond. The captain wasn't just a skilled surgeon, he had a keen mind and often saw things from a different perspective, pointing Daniel in a hitherto unconsidered direction.

Less than an hour later, Daniel crawled into bed and allowed sleep to overtake him, his mind mercifully keeping away from images of the dead man and his pale body against the black vastness of the night.

**

It was just after four o'clock by the time Daniel awoke, and he lay in bed for a few minutes, watching the lavender hues of twilight deepen into rich shades of violet, deep shadow encroaching on the fading light of the winter afternoon and blunting the objects in the room.

It was winter solstice—the shortest days of the year—a time when families came together and celebrated Christmastide. It should not be a time for hatred, murder, or unspeakable humiliation. Death, especially untimely death, was awful to be sure, but to be trussed up like a chicken, stripped naked, one's most private parts left on display, was a fate worse than death, in Daniel's opinion. When his time came, he hoped he'd die in his own bed, surrounded by people he loved—Sarah and their children. And he never wanted to be the subject of a postmortem. He couldn't imagine anything more dehumanizing than being carved up like an animal carcass, one's organs removed and examined, and every little vanity that one had held on to in life stripped away.

Daniel sighed. He couldn't bring Frank Darrow back to life, but he could bring him a measure of justice. He could discover why someone had done what they'd done and maybe impose the truth onto the scandalous tale that would follow Frank's memory for decades to come.

Daniel left the cozy confines of the bed, dressed, and presented himself downstairs. Sarah and her mother, Harriet were in the drawing room, their faces soft in the glow of the gas lamps and the leaping flames of the coal fire.

"Daniel, the tea is still hot," Sarah said. "Come and have a cup. You must be famished."

"I am, actually," Daniel said as he sat next to Sarah and accepted a cup of tea.

Sarah reached for a plate and served him a thick slice of sponge.

"Hmm, delicious," Daniel said as he took the first bite.

"I made it myself," Sarah said, smiling shyly.

"That makes it even more wonderful," Daniel said with feeling. Sarah had always enjoyed baking, but as far as he knew, this was the first time she'd baked something in years.

"Do you really like it?" she asked.

"I like it so much, I'm going to have one more slice," Daniel said, reaching for another piece of cake.

"Have you had a productive day?" Harriet asked. She loved hearing about his cases and was often helpful in her own way, but Daniel wasn't ready to discuss the day's events.

"Not as productive as I would have liked. I hope you two will excuse me," Daniel said as he ate the last of his cake and drained his teacup, "but I must speak to Captain Redmond."

"What? Now?" Sarah asked, her gaze flying to the carriage clock on the mantel.

"I'll be home in time for dinner. I promise. We can talk then."

"Take the cart, Daniel," Sarah suggested, correctly surmising that Daniel was planning to walk. "You'll catch a chill."

Daniel shook his head. He'd consumed four slices of cake since breakfast. He needed to walk. And he needed to think. "I'll be fine, my dear. I'll wear woolen socks and an extra muffler."

Sarah shook her head in dismay, but Harriet smiled at him, amused. "No one has died of too much fresh air or exercise," she said, addressing her daughter. "It's a fine evening out there. I almost wish I could come with you. I so seldom leave the house after dark these days. And I miss walking in the snow."

"Then let's go," Sarah said, springing to her feet. "Let's bundle up and go walk in the snow, Mother."

"Really?" Harriet exclaimed, her face spreading into a youthful grin. "Yes. Let's. We can escort Daniel part of the way."

"That sounds like an excellent plan," Daniel said, thrilled to see the sparkle in Sarah's eyes.

Chapter 9

Daniel breathed a sigh of relief when the warm lights of Redmond Hall came into view. Normally, his shoes crunched on the gravel as he approached the stately manor house, but today, his steps were silent, all sound muted by the fluffy snow. Sarah had been right in her prediction. His feet felt numb, and his nose and cheeks burned with cold. Daniel smiled at the thought of sitting by the fire, a drink in hand, as he shared his worries about this case with his friend.

"I'd like to see the captain," Daniel said when Dodson opened the door to his knock.

"Of course, you do," Dodson said, his drawl annoyingly judgmental. Dodson would never say anything outright, but he visibly disapproved of Lord Redmond, one of the wealthiest noblemen in the county, involving himself in solving gruesome murder cases like a common bobby. Giles Redmond, Jason's grandfather, would never have countenanced such a thing and would have given his grandson a dressing down worthy of the patrician old trout he had been during his lifetime. Daniel could understand only too well why Jason's father, Geoffrey Redmond, had absconded to America and married the woman of his choice, a young lady his father had not approved of and had forbidden him to marry.

"Daniel," Jason said, smiling warmly. "What a pleasant surprise. Do come in. Scotch or brandy?"

"Brandy, I think," Daniel said as he settled in the comfortable wingchair by the fire. Jason poured them both a drink and sat opposite him, crossing his long legs at the ankles, his feet dangerously close to the fire.

"Thank you," Daniel said, and took a sip. The fiery liquid blazed down his gullet and settled in his stomach, warming him through instantly and making him feel pleasantly relaxed.

"Have you been able to learn anything useful?" Jason asked as he took a sip of his own drink.

Daniel sighed. "Not really. I spoke to the family, who seem to have no idea who might have wished Frank harm. I also spoke to the publican at the Queen's Arms and Frank's good friend Elijah Gordon and his wife."

"And?"

"The impression I got was that Frank was not a pleasant man. Mrs. Gordon described him as bitter and angry, a man who blamed others for his own shortcomings and had been too shortsighted to preempt the decline of his family's business."

"Not a flattering description," Jason observed.

"No, but hardly a reason for murder. This crime is like nothing I've ever seen in all my years as a peeler and then a parish constable. This wasn't just about getting rid of someone. This was truly a crime of passion."

"Not passion—rage," Jason argued. "Whoever killed Frank Darrow would not be satisfied with simply ending his life. The killer must have burned with hatred for him to have first killed him, then stripped him naked and tied him to the wheel. He wanted to humiliate him and destroy him completely. From this day on, the only thing anyone will remember about Frank Darrow is the manner of his death. A hundred years from now, the inhabitants of Elsmere will tell tales over a pint of how the man had been left naked, his stiff phallus pointing at the moon."

Daniel tried to suppress a smile. "You must admit, it is a tale worth telling."

Jason nodded. "Not something I'd want said of my own demise. But there's something else as well."

"What?" Daniel asked, instantly more alert.

"Whoever killed Frank Darrow couldn't bring himself to watch him die," Jason said.

"I don't follow."

"Think about it, Daniel. Here is a man you despise so much, you will risk going to the gallows for murder if apprehended. Yet, instead of sticking a knife in him and watching the light go out of his eyes, or shooting him at close range and enjoying the surprise on his face as the bullet tears its way through his body, possibly leaving him to bleed out, you choose to lure him toward the river and hold his head down as he drowns. Surely that's less satisfying. Even to have hanged him would have been more in keeping with the scenario. Unless the neck is immediately broken, it can take a man some time to die. If it's his suffering you're after, then that would be a definite option."

"I agree, but what are you suggesting?"

"I think that the person who killed Frank Darrow was consumed with hatred, but this was not the work of someone who enjoyed the killing. Drowning Frank was a means to an end, not the ultimate goal."

"You think the ultimate goal was to degrade him and strip him of all dignity."

"Yes, I do."

"What would make someone hate so fiercely?" Daniel asked.

"Perhaps Frank had humiliated the killer or cheated him of something very dear to him."

"So, you don't think this is about money?"

"It could be. If someone had lost their livelihood because of Frank Darrow, I could easily see how that could whip them up into a murderous frenzy. Or, of course, it could be over a woman. That might explain the urge to strip him naked."

"Despite his difficult character, Frank Darrow was a fine-looking man," Daniel said. "His wife, on the other hand, looks like a hag, the poor woman. I've no doubt life with him wasn't easy."

"So, he might have kept a mistress," Jason said, nodding.

"It's certainly possible."

"Who are you going to interview next?" Jason asked.

"I was going to start with Robert Graham, Frank's employer, who, incidentally, dismissed him from his position only yesterday."

"What had he done to lose his job?"

"I don't know, but I mean to find out. Then, I will have to question the vicar. He may have got wind of an adulterous affair," Daniel said.

"You'd be better off talking to the vicar's wife, if he's got one. It's usually the women who are keenly aware of village gossip."

Daniel nodded. "You are right there. Mrs. Gordon was a lot more forthcoming and honest, I daresay, than her husband, who painted Frank as a good man and a loyal friend."

"I have a suggestion," Jason said as he set his empty glass on the small table between the two chairs. "I can go speak to Mrs. Darrow."

"What do you hope to discover?" Daniel asked, intrigued. Jason always had excellent ideas.

"I'm not a policeman. I'm the surgeon who handled her husband's remains. She might be more forthcoming with me and let something slip."

"I would very much appreciate that." Daniel leaned back in his chair and studied the captain's firelit profile. He was always charming and easygoing, the latter a byproduct of his American upbringing, but there was tension in his shoulders, and he seemed to be clenching his jaw as he stared into the leaping flames.

"Are you quite all right, Captain?" Daniel asked. "You seem—I don't know—worried, I suppose."

Jason turned to face and him and offered up a tired smile. "I've been a little anxious these past few days."

"Anything you care to talk about?"

Jason's shoulders slumped, almost as if he'd been waiting for Daniel to inquire about what was going on. "When Micah and I returned to New York after our release from Andersonville, I hired a private investigator. I may have mentioned it before."

"Yes. I recall. To track Micah's missing sister," Daniel said. Jason had mentioned the disappearance of Mary Donovan when he'd shared his wartime experiences with Daniel, but he hadn't mentioned her in some time. Daniel had assumed there was nothing to tell and hadn't asked for an update on the search.

"Yes. Mr. Hartley had encountered a dead end, but a few months ago, he wrote to me to say that a woman who'd known Mary might have a lead on her whereabouts."

"Did she?"

"She must have because I received a wire from Mr. Hartley several weeks ago. All it said was, 'M.D. sailing on the *Glendevon* December 1'."

Daniel leaned forward, confused by the brevity of the message. "Did he not follow up with a letter? Is Mary traveling alone?"

"I don't have any further details. At first, I was excited, anticipating Micah's joy when Mary turned up in time for Christmas, but I'm beginning to worry, Daniel."

"Why? She might still arrive. Does she have funds?" Daniel asked. He didn't wish to be indelicate, but Mary would need to find her way to Birch Hill.

"I had instructed Mr. Hartley to pay for Mary's ticket, should she wish to come to England, and provide her with enough funds to assure her safe and comfortable journey. The *Glendevon* is a White Star vessel, which was due to arrive in Liverpool three days ago. Mary would have been here by now had she indeed been on it."

"I think you're worrying needlessly. The vessel might have been delayed by the weather. It's not abnormal for ships to arrive a few days later than expected, especially in winter."

Daniel could understand Jason's worry all too well. Numerous ships were lost during transatlantic crossings, especially during the winter months. It was a dangerous journey, and a long one, and it would be some time before information finally reached friends and family if there had been a tragedy at sea.

"At least she survived the epidemic," Jason said.

"What epidemic?"

"There was a cholera outbreak in New York this past summer. Many casualties, most of them Irish immigrants."

"Didn't you say the Donovans had lived in Maryland?"

"Yes, but I don't know where Mary might have been since leaving the farm. She may very well have been in New York. People tend to flock to areas that are populated with people they can relate to and feel comfortable with."

"And you think Mary had fled to New York?"

"It's possible," Jason said. "And she would have sailed out of New York, if the information Mr. Hartley provided is accurate. I would have sent Joe to Liverpool to collect her, but since I didn't know the exact date of arrival or what Mary even looks like, it would have been likely that Joe and Mary's paths would never have crossed. It seemed more logical to provide for her passage and wait for her to come to us."

"You did the right thing," Daniel assured Jason. "Just be patient. If Mary was on that ship, she'll get here."

"I'm glad I didn't break the news to Micah in my excitement. He'd be devastated to lose her all over again, should anything happen." Jason smiled sadly. "I'm sorry. I'm not usually so pessimistic, but Micah and I have lost too many people over the past few years to simply expect things to work out."

"Your anxiety is understandable, but keep the faith and try to stay busy. I find that always helps in times of uncertainty. I can really use your help with this case."

"You have it. I will call on Mrs. Darrow tomorrow morning."

"Thank you, Jason. I really must get going."

"Would you like to stay for dinner?" Jason asked.

"I'd love to, but I promised Sarah I'd come home."

"Of course. You mustn't keep your wife waiting. Shall I ask Joe to drive you?"

"Thank you, but I'll walk," Daniel said as he set down his empty glass and stood to leave. "Captain, would you like to join us for lunch tomorrow?" Daniel asked.

Sarah had been on him for ages to invite Jason to dine with them, but some stubborn, foolish part of Daniel had been reluctant to pass on the invitation. It wasn't due to the gap in their station; Jason always treated him like an equal and had invited him to dine many times since they'd first met in June.

Daniel supposed it was that some part of him wanted to keep Jason to himself. Daniel had had many friends growing up, but those friendships had cooled once he'd left Birch Hill to become a policeman in London, and by the time he'd returned, shortly after Felix's death, his friends had moved on with their lives and felt awkward around a man charged with keeping the peace, which they tended to violate from time to time. Jason was the first friend Daniel had made in years, and he supposed he was reluctant to share him, even with Sarah.

"Thank you. I'd be honored," Jason replied, hiding his surprise behind a warm smile.

"See you at one o'clock, then."

Chapter 10

Friday, December 21

Upon his arrival in Elsmere, Jason asked Joe to let him out by the Queen's Arms and walked the rest of the way. To roll into the Darrows' yard in his grandfather's sleek brougham seemed gauche and was sure to put Mrs. Darrow off talking to him. He'd dressed simply, wearing the tweeds of a country doctor rather than the fine broadcloth and expensive silk associated with the wardrobe of a Victorian gentleman.

A large dog of an unknown breed came bounding toward Jason as he approached the house, but he pulled off his glove and held out his hand to the animal, allowing it to sniff at its leisure. The dog seemed satisfied and trotted away, no longer interested in the stranger. The same couldn't be said for Mrs. Darrow, who stood in the doorway, eyeing him warily.

"Good morning, Mrs. Darrow," Jason said as he approached the door. "I'm Captain Redmond. I've come to offer my condolences on the death of your husband, if that's all right," he added. He didn't want to make the woman feel obligated to let him in if she had no wish to do so, but Mrs. Darrow wasn't fooled by his use of his military rank rather than his title.

Her eyes opened in shock, and she practically jumped aside in her eagerness to welcome him. "Please, come in, yer lordship. Ye honor us," she gushed.

Jason entered the house and accepted the proffered seat. Mrs. Darrow stood before him, kneading her hands nervously, as if unsure what to do. She looked around the room furtively, as if deeply embarrassed by the shabby parlor with its lumpy cushions and faded curtains, a crimson blush creeping up her neck into her sallow cheeks.

"Please, sit down," Jason said softly, ashamed for putting the woman in this uncomfortable position at a time when she had enough to deal with. "I don't want to put you to any trouble. I only wanted to express my sympathies in person."

"Thank ye, my lord. And thank ye for sending our Kitty home to us. She's better off with her family at a time like this. Can I offer ye some tea? Ye must be chilled to the bone," she added, probably only just realizing that she hadn't seen a carriage, only the man, and that he was calling on her at the socially inappropriate hour of ten in the morning.

"Tea would be lovely," he said, hoping she wouldn't offer him the last of the tea and sugar. He'd have to speak to Mrs. Dodson about increasing Kitty's wages.

Mrs. Darrow left him in the parlor while she busied herself with making the tea. Except for the sound of Mrs. Darrow moving about in the kitchen, Jason heard no other noises. There were no footsteps coming from the bedrooms above, no male voices, or the murmur of Kitty's shy tones. It was a workday, but Jason didn't think James and William Darrow would have gone in the day after their father's death.

"Where are your children?" Jason asked once Sadie Darrow returned to the room with a tray that held an old brown teapot, two cups and saucers, a small bowl of sugar, and a jug of milk.

"Kitty is upstairs, asleep. She's not been well since 'earing the news. And the boys 'ave gone to Brentwood, to the police station, sir."

"Why? Have they some new information to report?" Jason asked, pricking his ears for something useful.

"No. They only wanted to ask when we might 'ave Frank's body back for the burial."

"I'm afraid the body won't be released for a few days yet," Jason said. "Probably not until after Christmas."

Mrs. Darrow nodded. "I told them as much, but they needed to see their da. They're devastated."

"Were the children close to their father?" Jason asked.

55

The question seemed to take Mrs. Darrow by surprise. "I s'pose ye could say that. The boys 'specially. They used to go fishing in the river by the mill every summer. They were good times."

"Did they still go fishing after the mill closed down?" Jason asked.

Mrs. Darrow shook her head sadly. "No. Not then."

"Mrs. Darrow, was there anyone who held a grudge against your husband? Anyone who might have really hated him?"

"Not that I can think of. Frank got on with everyone in the village, even after they stopped coming to the mill."

"He didn't blame them for taking their custom elsewhere?" Jason asked.

"'E did. But 'e kept his feelings to 'imself. Most of the time, at any rate," Mrs. Darrow added.

"Was Frank ever away from home for any length of time? Did he have dealings with anyone outside the village?"

"Well, 'course 'e did. 'E worked in Brentwood and the surroundin' areas. But 'e came back at night. Always."

Jason took a sip of his tea, considering his next move. He was getting nothing useful, and this was his only chance, since he couldn't very well find an excuse to come back again.

"Mrs. Darrow, did you ever suspect your husband of infidelity?"

Jason hated to ask. He wasn't the police, and Sadie Darrow was under no obligation to speak to him, even if he was her daughter's employer. The question was rude and invasive, but since she couldn't very well throw him out, she'd be forced to answer or at least do her best to avoid answering, which would be telling.

Mrs. Darrow stared at him across the table, her face going pale with shock. She reached out and wrapped her fingers around her teacup, as if the warmth could somehow comfort her, but her hands shook so badly that she spilled some tea, wetting the cuffs of her gown and scalding her hands. She yelped and yanked her hands away, but her gaze never left Jason's face.

"Are you all right? Did you burn yourself?" Jason asked.

"I'm fine," she snapped. "It's nothin'."

The woman looked down at her lap, but not before Jason noticed the spark of fear in her eyes. "Why would you ask me that, a woman so newly widowed?" she finally asked, her voice barely audible. "That's cruel, my lord, if ye don't mind me saying so."

"I'm sorry, Mrs. Darrow. It was completely inappropriate. I was only trying to ascertain if there might have been a jealous husband or son who may have wanted to revenge himself on your husband."

Mrs. Darrow looked up, her expression brimming with scorn. "I'd thank ye to leave the investigatin' to the police, yer lordship. Now, if ye don't mind, I 'ave chores to be getting on with."

"I'll leave you in peace, then," Jason said, setting down his cup. "If there's anything I can do for you or for Kitty, please don't hesitate to ask."

Mrs. Darrow nodded but didn't say anything more before Jason walked out of the house and into the brilliant light of the winter morning. His boots crunched on the snow as he strode through the open gate and into the lane. Despite Sadie Darrow's obvious anger, he was pleased with the morning's work. He didn't get much, but enough to have made the visit worthwhile. Frank Darrow had definitely been up to something, most likely with someone's wife, and betrayal and jealousy were always a motive for murder.

Instead of returning to the carriage, he walked to the church, which was almost an exact replica of the one in Birch Hill. If he didn't find the vicar inside, he'd try the vicarage next. The clergyman was under no obligation to speak to him, but vicars were notoriously sycophantic and wouldn't refuse to speak to a nobleman, even one who wasn't of their parish.

Jason found the vicar outside, speaking to a shabbily dressed middle-aged man who stood leaning on his shovel, his ungloved hands red and raw, his face florid with either cold or a love of drink. Probably both. A shallow grave yawned in the pristine whiteness of the snow, a small pile of earth rising to one side.

"Ye'll have to delay the funeral till tomorrow, vicar," the man was saying angrily. "The earth's near frozen. I can't 'ave the grave dug in time."

The vicar was about to reply when he saw Jason striding down the path. He was around Jason's age, but his balding pate, receding chin, and bushy whiskers gave him the staid appearance of a much older man. He smiled in a friendly way when Jason approached, and turned his back on the disgruntled gravedigger.

"Good morning, sir," the vicar said.

"Good morning. I'm Jason Redmond of Redmond Hall," Jason said, giving the vicar a few moments to process the information and come to the appropriate conclusion.

"My lord," the vicar exclaimed, "it's an honor to make your acquaintance."

"And you are?" Jason prompted after the man failed to introduce himself.

"Ahem. I'm sorry. Silly of me. Of course," the vicar blathered on. "Reverend Smalls, at your service, sir." He gave Jason a questioning look. There was absolutely no reason for Jason to be there, but the vicar was too polite to ask him the purpose of his visit.

"I have just paid a condolence call on Mrs. Darrow. Catherine Darrow is in my employ," Jason explained imperiously.

"Yes. Of course. I did know that. Very kind of you to give our Kitty gainful employment, sir. Very kind, indeed."

"I would like to ask you a few questions about Frank Darrow, Reverend Smalls. Shall we go inside? It's positively arctic out here."

The vicar balked visibly but followed Jason into the church, probably because he could no longer feel his extremities.

"I'm not at liberty to discuss my parishioners, my lord," Reverend Smalls said once Jason turned to face him, looking at him expectantly.

"Yes, of course. I completely understand. Your discretion does you credit," Jason assured him. "It's only that I wouldn't want to feel compelled to dismiss Catherine because of what happened, you understand," Jason said. He felt like the worst kind of blackguard for implying that he would sack an innocent girl because of her association with the murder, but he needed answers, and he meant to get them.

"Sir, Kitty is a young woman of excellent character," Reverend Smalls exclaimed. "Please, the Darrows need her wages."

"Yes, I'm sure they do," Jason drawled, and waited.

"What was it you wished to know?" Reverend Smalls asked, capitulating. Jason was gratified to see that he cared enough about Kitty and her family to bend the rules. It immediately elevated his opinion of the man.

"Did the Darrows have a happy marriage?" Jason asked.

"As happy as any," Reverend Smalls replied noncommittally.

"And did Frank Darrow have a reputation for tomcatting around?"

Reverend Smalls colored. "He did have an eye for the ladies, yes, but I'm not aware of any specific liaisons, if that's what you're getting at."

"Do you know if Frank Darrow had ever cheated anyone in the village out of money he owed them?"

"If he did, I've never heard as much. Now, if you will excuse me, my lord, I have a bereaved family to visit. It seems they won't be burying their son today," Reverend Smalls said irritably.

"Just one more question, Reverend Smalls. Are you married?"

The vicar looked like Jason had just asked him if he liked to expose himself to unsuspecting females. "I am not," he sputtered. "What's my marital status got to do with the murder?"

"Absolutely nothing," Jason replied, smiling in his most charming manner. "I thought I'd make the acquaintance of your lovely wife, since I was already here." He tipped his hat and walked away, leaving the man gaping after him.

Chapter 11

Being a well-known figure in Brentwood, Robert Graham had not been difficult to find. Daniel approached him just as Graham and his wife left their elegant house, heading toward the waiting carriage.

"Mr. Graham, I'm Inspector Haze of the Brentwood police, and I would like to ask you a few questions about Frank Darrow," Daniel said, effectively blocking the man's path.

"You're really going to do this now?" Graham asked irritably. He was a tall, thin man whose angular face was softened by a neatly trimmed beard. The hair beneath his hat was cut short and sprinkled with gray, and his dark eyes snapped with impatience.

"This is as good a time as any, and probably preferable to me calling on you when you're at the table."

"Just answer his questions, Robert," Mrs. Graham said. She smiled at Daniel indulgently as if he were a child behaving unreasonably.

"What do you wish to know?" Robert Graham inquired archly.

"Anything you can tell me about Frank Darrow, for starters."

"Boorish, lazy, opinionated, and sly as a fox."

"I see you really liked him," Daniel quipped, unable to stop himself. So far, not a single person had said anything even remotely flattering about Frank Darrow.

"Not much to like. His sons are good lads and hard workers, but Darrow didn't get the job to haul coal."

"Why did he get it?" Daniel asked, surprised by Robert Graham's comment.

"He got it because it gave him access to people's homes."

"How do you mean, sir?"

"For many years, Graham and Sons Coal Dispensary was the only company that served the Brentwood area, but in sixty-two, a competitor opened its doors, making it harder to obtain new custom and retain established clients since Millbank's had set out to undercut our prices. So, my wife had a good idea." He smiled at his wife, obviously proud to have given her credit for her initiative. "We began to offer free chimney cleaning to our customers twice a year. Frank was too big of a man for the job, but his boys were still thin enough to get down the chimney. The three of them usually went out as a team."

"I'm sorry, sir, but I don't follow," Daniel said.

"After a time, some of our customers began to report that items were missing from their homes. Nothing obvious at first, just little things like an enamel snuff box, an expensive card case, or a silver needle holder. Things that were small enough to stuff in one's pocket while in the room."

"And you think it was Frank Darrow that took them?"

"The thefts seemed to coincide with his presence in the house and had escalated over the past year. An emerald ring was reported missing a few days ago by a prominent Brentwood family."

"Why did you not report Frank Darrow to the police, Mr. Graham?" Daniel asked.

"Because I didn't have any solid evidence, only my suspicions. After the first few reports, I had everyone turn out their pockets when they returned from their deliveries, but as you and I both know, the items could have been hidden or passed on to someone who was situated along the route to our warehouse. So, I dismissed Darrow and withheld his wages. There's no shortage of men who need work, and delivering coal doesn't require skilled labor."

"How can you be so sure his sons weren't involved?" Daniel asked.

"I pride myself on being a good judge of character, Inspector. Those lads are as honest as the day is long, but it's not out of any misguided sense of honor, you understand. They simply lack the intelligence and the imagination to do anything other than menial labor. But that doesn't answer your question, does it? I know because they never went inside the house. They did their work from the rooftop and Frank handled the inside. When delivering coal, they only had access to the coal chutes. They had no call to ever enter the premises."

"What do you think Frank Darrow did with the stolen goods?" Daniel asked.

Robert Graham gave him a contemptuous stare. "What do you think he did, Inspector? He sold them to a fence. He could hardly display them in his house and hope to avoid being arrested for theft."

"There has been a spate of burglaries in the area," Daniel said. "Did any of the burgled houses belong to your clients?"

"Several, in fact," Robert Graham admitted, his expression shifting from annoyance to obvious unhappiness.

"And do you think Frank Darrow might have had something to do with the burglaries?"

"Why would he bother to steal pocket-sized items from the house if he knew there'd be a bigger payoff at the end?" Graham asked.

Because he wouldn't have to share the profit with his accomplices, Daniel thought, but refrained from pointing this out to Robert Graham.

"Now, if you don't have any more questions, Inspector, we'll be on our way. Come along, my dear."

"Good day to you," Daniel said to the Grahams' retreating backs.

Daniel sighed and returned to the dogcart. He would have liked to speak to Detective Inspector Coleridge, but as the inspector had an appointment in Colchester and wasn't expected at the station until the following morning, his questions would have to keep. Daniel climbed into the cart and took hold of the reins.

He'd better hurry. Sarah would have his head if he was late and didn't have time to change before luncheon.

Chapter 12

Luncheon was a pleasant and intimate affair. Sarah and Harriet fussed over Jason as if he hadn't eaten in days, and Jason was gracious and charming, not that Daniel would expect anything less. He had to admit that it was nice to have Jason there in a social capacity, and he hoped this gathering would be the first of many.

"Captain, do tell, is it true that the corpse was found in a rather, shall we say, awkward predicament?" Harriet asked, blushing like a young girl. Daniel had omitted some of the more distasteful details when telling Harriet about the case, so she must have heard it from someone else, most likely Tilda, who'd had it from some tradesman.

"Yes, it's true," Jason replied, "but you didn't hear that from me."

"Mum's the word," Harriet said, nodding gravely while trying to hide her amusement.

"Really, Mother," Sarah exclaimed. "A man was murdered in cold blood and strung up like a partridge, and you're making merry at his expense?"

"Strung up like a plucked partridge," Harriet corrected her daughter. "And I'm not poking fun at his predicament. What happened to him is awful."

"Why would anyone go to such lengths?" Sarah asked, looking from Daniel to Jason. "Surely they could have just thrown him into the river and let the current do the rest."

"I don't believe that was their intention," Daniel said. "They wanted the body to be found, hence the dramatic display."

"But why strip him naked and tie him to the wheel? It makes no sense."

"It makes no sense because we don't yet know the motive," Jason interjected. "Whoever killed Frank Darrow had a point to make, and they made it, quite dramatically."

"What possible point could they have wished to make?" Sarah persisted, clearly more disturbed by the treatment of Frank's remains than his actual death.

"They wished to humiliate him so thoroughly that no one would ever mention Frank Darrow without recalling the circumstances in which he'd been found," Jason said.

"Such unnecessary cruelty," Sarah muttered under her breath.

"According to Robert Graham, Frank Darrow was stealing from the houses he visited in the course of his duties. There have also been several break-ins in the past few months. It's quite possible that the man had some sort of a dispute with his accomplices and they killed him and displayed his body to teach others a lesson."

"I suppose that's a possibility," Jason said, his expression thoughtful. "I am not familiar with criminal organizations in England; perhaps they're more sophisticated in their methods, but had the man cheated his cronies in New York, they'd have simply cut his throat and tossed him in the East River or left his body in some alleyway. They wouldn't have bothered with the theatrics."

"Whoever did this certainly has a flair for the dramatic," Harriet said. "They wanted their handiwork to be remembered for years to come."

"Yes." Daniel nodded. "You've hit the nail right on the head, Harriet. This was a performance of sorts. A play put on for the benefit of the villagers and the police."

"We know who was cast in the lead role, but now we have to discover who the other players were and who directed this performance," Jason chimed in. "Whoever did this must be very proud of the stir they caused."

"If they are, they're savoring their triumph in silence," Daniel said.

"I think we've had enough talk of death," Sarah said reproachfully. "Captain, are you pleased with your ward's tutor?

Mother and I have come across him several times while taking a walk, and he seems a most pleasant young man."

"Mr. Sullivan is an excellent tutor, and Micah is very fond of him. In fact, he's also teaching Micah to paint, being something of an artist himself."

"Does Micah have any artistic talent?" Harriet asked.

"I wouldn't go so far as to call it talent, Mrs. Elderman, but Mr. Sullivan believes it's a way for Micah to express his grief at losing his family, and I must agree that a certain amount of rage comes through in his work."

"Rage?" Harriet echoed. "Surely Mr. Sullivan should not encourage that."

"On the contrary. If it helps Micah come to terms with his loss, then a few streaks of paint on canvas will prove most beneficial. After all, what's the harm?"

"What is he painting?" Sarah asked.

"Scenes of battle, wounded men, a drummer boy sitting beneath a tree, crying," Jason said sadly. "The paintings would be jarring to someone not familiar with Micah's history."

"Poor child. The things he must have seen in his short life," Sarah said with a great sigh. "What kind of parent would take their son to war?"

"I can't justify his father's reasoning, but I do know Micah's father loved him dearly. I knew Liam Donovan well, and he was a good and caring man."

"Even good and caring men can often be tragically misguided," Harriet said.

"I agree with you wholeheartedly, Mrs. Elderman," Jason said.

"I do believe we're ready for pudding, my dear," Daniel said in an effort to navigate the conversation away from the suffering of children, which would inevitably lead Sarah to memories of Felix's agony after the accident.

"Yes, of course. Cook has made us a lovely treacle tart," Sarah announced. "I hope you'll like it, Captain."

"I've never met a tart I didn't like," Jason replied graciously.

"And I've asked her to brew a pot of coffee. Daniel mentioned that you prefer coffee to tea."

"A cup of freshly brewed coffee is one of life's greatest pleasures."

"It's a pleasure I can happily live without," Harriet said, "but I do like the way it smells. So much more fragrant than tea."

"Indeed," Daniel agreed, glad to have steered the conversation toward calmer waters. "I think I'll join the captain in a cup of coffee. It's quite enjoyable when taken with cream and sugar."

The rest of the meal passed in pleasant discourse, Jason and Sarah comparing the various Christmas traditions they'd grown up with.

"The servants always look forward to Boxing Day," Sarah said.

"Boxing Day?" Jason asked, his brow furrowing in confusion. "Do people have boxing matches on that day?"

"No." Sarah laughed merrily. "Boxing Day is the day after Christmas. Traditionally, it was the day the servants celebrated the holiday because they had to wait on their masters on Christmas, so they were given the next day to rest. It was also the day they received gifts from their masters, and since many of the gifts came in boxes, it came to be known as Boxing Day."

"I see," Jason said, looking relieved. "I have prepared gifts for the staff. Should I give them the gifts on December twenty-sixth, then?"

"That's entirely up to you. I'm sure they will appreciate your kindness regardless of which day you choose to reward them," Sarah said. "Would you like more coffee, Captain?"

"No, thank you. I really must be going. This has been delightful. I thank you for the invitation, Sarah."

Sarah beamed at Jason. "Do say you'll come again soon," she said.

"It would be my pleasure," Jason replied as he rose from the table.

"I'll walk you out," Daniel said.

"Is there anything else I can help you with?" Jason asked as he accepted his coat, hat, and gloves from Tilda. He'd related his conversations with Sadie Darrow and Reverend Smalls while they had waited for luncheon to be served, disappointing Daniel with the lack of anything concrete to pursue.

"I wish there were. Except for Frank Darrow's alleged theft, I have nothing to go on. Besides, you have your own affairs to attend to just now. I think it's best you're on hand, should your guest finally arrive."

"Yes. I believe you're right. Please, send word should you learn anything new or have need of my assistance."

"I will," Daniel assured him, and went to join the ladies in the drawing room.

"He's so charming," Harriet said, smiling wistfully. "And so single."

"Now, Mother," Sarah began, but her glance strayed to Daniel. "Is it true he's sweet on Miss Talbot?"

"My lips are sealed," Daniel said, refusing to gossip about Jason's private life, or lack thereof. He was aware of Jason's feelings for Miss Talbot and couldn't begin to understand why the vicar's daughter didn't encourage his suit.

"Miss Talbot has been harangued into submission by her despot of a father," Harriet said. "I suppose she thinks she'd be betraying the old goat if she married and left him to fend for himself. I'd be surprised if he even noticed her absence," Harriet speculated.

"How can a man of God be so oblivious to the feelings of those around him?" Sarah asked. "Surely he must realize that Katherine is ripe for marriage. Another few years and she'll be considered a spinster."

"Some would call her a spinster already. What is she, twenty-three?" Harriet asked. "The romantic in me hopes Captain Redmond and Katherine Talbot will make a match of it, but were I his mother, I wouldn't be too pleased to see him casting his sights on a vicar's daughter. Why, with his fortune and good looks, he can have his pick of eligible young ladies."

"Perhaps he's not ready to marry," Daniel snapped, annoyed by the direction the conversation had taken. "He was betrothed to a woman back in New York. Things ended badly. He might still be smarting."

"It's the women who suffer the consequences of a broken engagement, not the men," Harriet said.

"He wasn't the one who broke it off," Daniel retorted. "She left him."

"Now that is one foolish woman," Harriet said, shaking her head at Jason's fiancée's obvious idiocy. "When you catch a man like Jason Redmond, you hold on to him with both hands."

"And feet, if necessary," Sarah added with a giggle.

"Oh, not you too," Daniel groaned.

"I'm sorry, my dear, but I must agree. Jason Redmond is quite a catch. And he is very handsome." Sarah's blush made Daniel irrationally jealous.

"Ladies, if you will excuse me," Daniel said, unable to bear any more of this silliness. "I have a case to solve."

Daniel walked out of the drawing room, but not before he heard his mother-in-law waxing poetic about Jason's gray eyes and beautiful smile.

70

Chapter 13

Upon arriving at home, Jason was informed that Master Micah and Mr. Sullivan had gone out for a walk, so he retired to the drawing room and settled before the fire. He'd meant to finish the book he'd been reading but couldn't concentrate, so he gave up and stared into the flames instead, memories of past Christmases marching through his mind. There were all the joyful holidays he'd spent with his parents, and his maternal grandparents while they had still been alive, and the Christmas he'd spent camped out with his regiment in Virginia, which had been surprisingly festive because he hadn't known then that his parents were already gone.

He chose not to recall the past two Christmases, the first one spent in prison and the second back in New York. A deep silence had descended on the house that Christmas after the servants had gone home to celebrate with their own families and Micah had fallen asleep, still weak from his ordeal and grieving the loss of his family. It had been the loneliest Christmas of Jason's life, and he hoped never to experience its like again. But here he was, two years later, still alone, and still lonely.

Jason stood abruptly and strode from the room, the solution suddenly obvious. If he left now, he could catch Katherine before evensong. Six months was long enough to get to know a person and determine whether the path to happiness lay in that direction. He knew his own heart but had yet to confirm how Katherine truly felt. All her excuses about seeing to her father's many needs were just that—excuses. He would not pressure her to give him an answer immediately, but he would declare himself and let her decide how she wanted their relationship to progress. Katherine would either agree to make their courtship public, which would be a prelude to an engagement, or she would reject him once and for all and, in her own way, set him free.

"Are you going out, sir?" Dodson asked as Jason nearly collided with him outside the drawing room.

"Yes, I am."

Jason waited impatiently for Dodson to fetch his hat, coat, gloves, and walking stick, and almost sprinted for the door. His mind was made up, and he couldn't wait another second to set his plan in motion. He stepped outside and took a deep breath, enjoying the chill freshness in the air. He thought it might snow again. There was still about an hour of daylight left, but the faint outline of the moon was already clearly visible, the translucent orb riding just above the bare branches of the tall trees beyond the parkland. Jason's boots crunched on snow-covered gravel as he set out. His body thrummed with excitement and anxiety. What happened within the next hour would change the course of his life.

Jason was jolted out of his reverie by the appearance of an unfamiliar carriage. It rolled through the open gates at the end of the drive and headed for the house, the coachman's gaze fixed on Jason once he'd spotted him. The man tipped his hat and slowed down, waiting for Jason to step out of his path. Jason stood off to the side, his heart thumping with relief as the carriage drove past and pulled up before the front door. This had to be Mary Donovan. At last. The coachman jumped off the box and approached the door of the conveyance.

"Allow me," Jason said as he reached the carriage.

"As you wish, guv," the man said, and stepped aside. Jason opened the door, the smile of welcome freezing on his face when he saw the person within.

"Hello, Jason," Cecilia said as she took his hand and stepped down from the vehicle. Jason had every intention of responding, but the words seemed to stick in his throat.

"Aren't you going to invite me in?" Cecilia asked. She'd always been playful and self-assured, confident of her beauty and place in society, but now she sounded wary and uncertain of her welcome. Given their history, she had every reason to be.

"Yes, of course. Forgive me," Jason said woodenly. "Please, come in."

Dodson had already opened the door, his features at war as he tried to look bland despite his curiosity.

"Dodson, this is Mrs. Baxter, an old friend from New York. Please ask Mrs. Dodson to prepare a room. But we'll need some tea first."

"Eh, yes, sir."

"And please see to the coachman. Surely, it's too late for him to return tonight. The cost of lodging at the Red Stag and supper should do it."

"Of course, sir."

Dodson took their things, and Jason escorted Cecilia into the drawing room. From the window, he could see Joe taking charge of Cecilia's trunk. The shadows of twilight were painting the lawn and parkland in shades of dusky purple, the moon now glowing like an oil lamp.

"I'm sorry to come unannounced," Cecilia said as she settled before the fire.

Jason took a seat opposite her. He didn't mean to stare, but he hadn't seen her since he'd enlisted, never imagining when he'd said goodbye to her that she'd marry Mark less than a year later. She was still beautiful, but Cecilia was no longer the girl he'd fallen in love with. A new maturity radiated from her, and an unfamiliar reserve that put Jason on his guard even more than her unexpected arrival.

"Cecilia, what are you doing here?" he asked, unable to wait any longer to hear the reason for her visit.

Cecilia stared into the fire, the flames reflecting in her pupils and giving her a somewhat demonic appearance. "They're dead, Jason."

"Who's dead?"

Cecilia sighed with her whole body, her shoulders slumping in defeat. "Mark and George, our son. He was only eight months old." She began to cry softly and buried her face in her hands.

"I am so sorry, Cecilia." Jason handed her his handkerchief, and she dabbed delicately at her eyes.

"I can't bear it, Jason," she said hoarsely. "I just can't."

"When did it happen?"

"September. Mark had been exposed to cholera at the hospital. He'd infected Georgie. They were gone within two days. Just like that. One day they were there, and then they weren't."

"Did you not get ill?"

"I had sent Georgie and the nanny home from Newport. We'd been there the whole summer, but everyone was leaving, and Mark said it was safe to return to New York. I stayed a few extra days to close up the house."

Cecilia started crying again, racking sobs rocking her delicate frame. "I sent him to his death. My poor little baby. He was so sweet. So loving."

"And Mark?" Jason asked softly.

"I hadn't seen Mark since May," Cecilia replied, still sniffling. "We were having some problems, but I was determined to get our relationship back on track once I returned from Rhode Island. I did love him, Jason."

Jason nodded. He still didn't quite understand why Cecilia had decided to show up on his doorstep, but now wasn't the time to ask. Fanny entered with the tea tray and set it down on the low table, her inquisitive gaze never leaving Cecilia's tear-stained face. Jason poured a cup of tea and handed it to Cecilia, who accepted it silently but didn't drink. She held the cup between both hands, cradling it as if it could save her from grief somehow.

"I'm sorry to show up like this," she finally said. "I can't imagine what you must think, but I was desperate to get away from that empty house. I'd wake in the night, thinking I heard Georgie crying or Mark coming in from a shift at the hospital, and for one moment, I'd be so happy, until reality reasserted itself and I felt like I'd lost them all over again. I needed to get away, but I couldn't bear to go traveling on the Continent by myself."

"You can stay as long as you like," Jason said, knowing he didn't mean that. He felt desperately sorry for Cecilia. She looked and sounded broken, but she'd broken him, and her presence in his house was awkward, to say the least. What did she hope to gain by coming to him? Did she think he could take away her pain? Make her forget? Did she hope to pick up where they'd left off?

"Do you mean that?" she asked, her gaze searching his face.

He nodded, unable to speak the words.

"Jason, I'm so sorry for the way I've treated you. I was selfish and stupid. I suppose I was terrified of getting left behind, stuck in a limbo of waiting for word of my missing intended while all my friends got on with their lives. I should have waited," she whispered. "It was never the same with Mark."

"Cecilia, please…"

Jason never got to finish the sentence because Micah burst into the room, likely in search of a cup of tea and a slice of cake. His eyebrows rose dramatically as he took in the scene.

"Cecilia, this is Micah Donovan," Jason said. "He's my ward."

"Oh." Cecilia stared at the boy in surprise. "It's a pleasure to meet you, Micah."

"Likewise, I'm sure," Micah said formally.

"Please, excuse us, we didn't mean to interrupt," Shawn Sullivan said, giving Micah a meaningful stare as he followed him into the room. "We'll just leave you in peace. Come, Micah. We can have our tea in the schoolroom."

"Apologies, Captain," Micah muttered, and followed the tutor from the room.

"Ward?" Cecilia asked. She hadn't said the words out loud, but Jason could almost hear the question. Everyone assumed Micah was Jason's illegitimate son, despite the difference in their coloring. Micah's flame-colored hair and blue eyes were assumed to have come from his mother, which they had, but Jason had never met the woman.

"Yes. He's my ward. I gave his father my promise that I would look after him. We knew each other in the war."

"I see," Cecilia said, her relief obvious. Her reaction irritated Jason, as did her presence. He felt pity for her and deep sadness at the thought of Mark and George's deaths, but Cecilia was no longer his concern. She was the past, and he hoped Katherine was the future.

"It's a beautiful house," Cecilia said, looking around the room. "And you're a lord now. Lord Redmond. That has a nice ring to it."

"I prefer to go by Captain Redmond," Jason said.

"The war is over, Jason," Cecilia said.

And so are we, Jason thought. "Would you like to rest before dinner?"

"Yes. Thank you," Cecilia said, setting down her still-full cup. "I won't be able to sleep, but a hot bath would be just the thing. It was so cold in that damn carriage; I'm still shivering."

"Of course. Dodson will see to it."

Cecilia reached out a hand and laid it on Jason's forearm, looking at him with tear-filled eyes. "I couldn't bear the thought of being alone on Christmas, Jason. Thank you for letting me stay."

Jason nodded, embarrassed by her obvious gratitude. If not festive, this Christmas certainly promised to be interesting.

Chapter 14

After several buckets of hot water had been lugged up to Cecilia's room by a disgruntled Henley, who felt he'd been demoted from the position of gentleman's valet to maid-of-all-work, and a fire had been laid in the grate, Cecilia finally went upstairs, leaving Jason to ponder what the hell to do about her unexpected arrival and obvious intention to stay. He felt genuine sympathy for her, but the love he'd felt for her in the past was long gone, stamped out by her callous behavior toward him.

After his return from Andersonville, Cecilia hadn't even written to him, much less visited him to see how he was and explain her decision to marry Mark. She had blithely gone on with her life, seemingly content in her marriage and probably complaining nonstop about the pregnancy and the limitations it placed on her daily life. Jason had heard about her from friends who'd come to call, but he hadn't seen her in person. Not once. And now she was here, certain in the knowledge that he would help her and possibly even harboring hopes of rekindling their romance.

Jason sighed with frustration. Had his mother still been alive, he'd have talked to her about his predicament, but now, the closest thing he had to a mother figure was Mrs. Dodson, and he found that he welcomed her counsel. She'd be busy with dinner preparations, but she'd spare him a few minutes. She always did.

Mrs. Dodson was whipping something pink in a bowl but stopped what she was doing and looked at him expectantly when he came in. Jason sat down at the scrubbed wooden table and peered into the bowl.

"Salmon mousse?" Jason asked.

"Would you like a taste?"

"I'll wait for dinner," he replied. Cecilia would like it, he reflected. It would appeal to her love of all things plummy, as Shawn Sullivan liked to say.

"Find yourself in a bit of a pickle, do you?" Mrs. Dodson asked nonchalantly. Jason wasn't surprised by the question. Having shared a few middle-of-the-night cups of tea with the housekeeper, he'd confided in her and had allowed her to advise and comfort him when he'd needed it most.

"I don't know what to do about Cecilia," Jason said, assuming Mrs. Dodson already knew all about Cecilia from her husband. He sounded like a little boy who'd come crying to his mommy, but he really had no idea how to handle the prickly situation.

"What would you like to do?"

"I would like to show her the door. Right now," Jason replied, not having realized that was how he really felt until the words left his mouth.

"Then do. You owe her nothing, given how shabbily she treated you."

"Her husband and baby son are dead," Jason said softly, an imagine of a laughing Mark, drunk as a skunk after a night of carousing with their friends, vivid in his mind. "Cholera."

"That's regrettable, but that doesn't excuse her behavior toward you. Nor her all-too-obvious plans."

"What plans?" Jason asked, but he already knew what Mrs. Dodson would say.

"I reckon she sees the obvious benefits of rekindling your feelings for her. What better remedy for heartbreak than a new marriage, and a rich estate and title thrown into the bargain?"

Jason was about to reply when Kitty came in through the side door, her cheeks rosy with cold and a bucket of water in her reddened hands. She froze when she saw Jason, her gaze panicked as she stood rooted to the floor.

"Kitty, what are you doing back?" Jason asked, equally surprised to see her. "I thought you were going to spend a few days with your family."

Kitty set the bucket down and looked at him, her eyes wide with apprehension. "I wanted to come back, sir. I thought it'd be all right."

"It is all right, if that's what you want, but you shouldn't have come back on my account. I will pay you for whatever time you need," Jason reiterated.

"It ain't 'bout the money, sir. May I stay? Please?"

"Of course, you may, but if you change your mind, feel free to go see your family for as long as you like."

"Thank ye, sir."

"Fetch me some butter from the larder, Kitty," Mrs. Dodson said. "I reckon she wants to get away from all that grief," she said to Jason as soon as Kitty was out of earshot. "Some folk cope by moping and crying, others take themselves off and don't weep until they're ready to."

"Yes, I agree with you there, Mrs. Dodson," Jason said as he rose to leave.

He returned to the main part of the house and continued to his room, where he changed into the clothes Henley had laid out for him. He had no desire to dine with Cecilia. In fact, he wasn't hungry at all. What he really wanted to do was speak to Daniel. Something about his brief encounter with Kitty had left him feeling uneasy, despite Mrs. Dodson's sensible explanation. Why was she so reluctant to be with her family at a time when they needed her most? And why had she seemed so frightened when he'd asked her about it? Was this the form her grief was taking, or was there something she wished to get away from and saw Redmond Hall as a safe haven?

Chapter 15

Saturday, December 22

Saturday morning found Daniel at the police station, waiting to speak to Detective Inspector Coleridge. Sergeant Flint and Constable Pullman were out front, reminiscing about past Christmas dinners and debating the merits of plum pudding versus mince pies. Daniel would have liked to share their holiday spirit but couldn't get the Frank Darrow murder off his mind. The who and the why of it had kept him awake nearly all night.

Detective Inspector Coleridge finally arrived at ten o'clock, his cheeks pink with cold. He pulled off his gloves and stuffed them into his pockets, removed his coat and hat and hung them on the coat rack, then invited Daniel to follow him into his office after asking one of the constables to fetch him a cup of tea. Having settled behind his desk, Coleridge offered Daniel a seat, then tilted his head to the side and interlaced his fingers, resting his hands on his sizable paunch.

"What have you got for me, Haze?" he asked.

"I have a lead, sir, but I require some assistance."

"Go on," Coleridge said.

"According to Robert Graham of Graham and Sons Coal Dispensary, Frank Darrow was stealing small objects of value from the homes of the clients."

"How would he gain access to their homes? Was he not delivering coal?" Coleridge asked.

"It seems that Graham and Sons now offer free chimney cleaning to their loyal customers. Frank Darrow handled the inside end while his sons were on the roof. Given the number of chimneys a well-to-do home has, that gave Darrow access to several rooms without anyone becoming suspicious of his presence."

"I see. And you think he sold these items on."

"He had to have. Also, according to Robert Graham, some of the recent break-ins targeted the houses of Graham and Sons customers. Is there a way to check how many?"

Inspector Coleridge considered the question for a moment. "Given that Graham and Sons is the biggest distributor of coal in the Brentwood area, it stands to reason that some of the victims had to be their clients. Do you think Frank Darrow could have been involved—on a bigger scale, I mean?"

"I think it likely. And once the houses were burgled, the stolen items would have to be disposed of. I was wondering if you might point me in the direction of known fences."

"There are several duffers known to us who deal in stolen goods, but I don't think Frank Darrow would be foolhardy enough to dispose of the stolen property here. Brentwood is not London, where a man can cloak himself in anonymity and lose himself in the dimly lit alleyways and smoke-filled public houses no policeman would be brave enough to enter after dark. Were he to peddle his loot here, we'd get word of his activities right quick."

"So, how would he go about disposing of his loot?" Daniel asked, taken aback by Coleridge's response.

"He might seek out someone with a wide range of connections."

"Such as?"

"Such as Dickie Stokes."

"And who is he?" Daniel had never heard the name.

"He's the proprietor of the Pump House Inn in Warley. The proximity of the inn to the Warley Barracks ensures that there's lots of custom from military personnel and much coming and going. There's even a coach stop outside the inn."

"Are you suggesting that this Dickie Stokes is smuggling out stolen goods right under the nose of the army?"

"I am, indeed. Dickie is a clever fellow, and very popular with the soldiers, who often get themselves into a spot of bother they need help getting out of. He's the man to see if you want to raise funds discreetly."

"I see," Daniel said. "I'll go and see him today, sir."

Coleridge nodded. "Do that, but don't get your hopes up. Dickie is a slippery character. He won't tell you anything he doesn't want you to know."

"I won't, sir," Daniel reassured him. There was a sinking feeling in the pit of his stomach. Detective Inspector Coleridge was right. Even if Frank Darrow's murder was in some way connected to the thefts, he didn't expect someone brazen enough to break the law in full view of the army to fess up to the crime.

Chapter 16

Daniel was admitted to the Pump House by a short, thin man, whose weasel-like appearance went hand in hand with what Daniel expected a man named Dickie Stokes to look like. The man squinted at him from beneath sparse lashes, taking his measure in return.

"We're still closed, sir," he said reprovingly. "'Tis not even noon yet."

"I'm not here to drink, Mr. Stokes. I'm Inspector Haze of the Brentwood Constabulary, and I'd like a word, please."

The man laughed, a phlegmy sound that made Daniel wonder if he might be consumptive.

"I'm not Mr. Stokes. Wait 'ere."

It wasn't lost on Daniel that the man hadn't offered his name. He disappeared through a door to the left of the bar and returned a moment later, a sly smirk on his face.

"Right this way, *Inspector*," he said, pronouncing the word as if it were an insult.

Daniel rounded the bar and entered a surprisingly spacious office. He'd expected a scarred desk and a rickety chair, but the desk and chairs were mahogany, their design modern and handsome, and the carpet was thick and expensive, the rich pattern adding a splash of color to the windowless room. The man who stood to greet him was a surprise as well. He was tall and broad, his clothes well-tailored and his coat made of the finest broadcloth. His dark hair was threaded with silver, and there was a spark of amusement in his intelligent gray eyes. In fact, he bore such a strong resemblance to Jason Redmond that Daniel wondered if Dickie Stokes might be a cousin or an uncle, born on the wrong side of the blanket.

"Good morning, Inspector. What can I do for you?" Dickie asked, surprising Daniel with his clipped tones. This was no small-time thief who did his business in dark alleys and back rooms of taverns. This man had presence, and to Daniel's great amazement, charisma.

"Good morning, Mr. Stokes. I'd like to ask you a few questions regarding a case I'm working on," Daniel said.

"Please, sit down," Stokes said as he resumed his seat behind the desk. "Drink?"

"No, thank you."

"How can I help you, then?"

"Did you know a man named Frank Darrow?" Daniel asked.

"We'd met on occasion. I was sorry to hear about the manner of his death." Dickie didn't bother to hide his mirth, his lips stretching into a grin. But his gaze was watchful.

"But not about his actual death?" Daniel asked, taken aback by Stokes' choice of words.

"We all die sooner or later."

"Did you and Mr. Darrow do business together?" Daniel asked.

"And what kind of business would that be, Inspector?"

"He brought you items to fence," Daniel said bluntly.

Dickie Stokes smiled sadly and put a hand over his heart. "You wound me, Inspector. Fencing is such a dirty word. I'm an honest businessman."

"Who deals in stolen goods."

"If something I buy or sell happens to be stolen, I'm certainly not aware of it. My relationship with my clients is based on trust."

"And how, exactly, does such a relationship work?" Daniel asked, trying to rein in his dislike of the man.

"It's very simple, really. Say a man loses heavily at cards and needs to raise funds to pay off his debt. He might have a family heirloom he'd like to sell, like his long-dead grandmother's antique ring, for example. I will happily buy the ring from him, for a discounted price, of course, and furnish him with the cash that will restore his honor."

"How very noble of you," Daniel interjected acidly.

Disregarding the comment, Stokes continued. "I then might have another young man who'd like to buy his lady love a betrothal ring but can't afford the type of bauble her father would approve of, so he comes to me, and lo and behold, I have just the thing he needs."

"The long-dead grandmother's antique ring," Daniel supplied.

"Exactly, which I will sell to him at a profit, as any self-respecting businessman would."

"So, you have helped one man avoid ruin and another man to impress his future father-in-law," Daniel concluded.

"All very legitimate, I assure you, and I must admit highly rewarding, given how often I am able to help those in need," Dickie Stokes said, smiling at Daniel innocently.

"You are a veritable saint."

"Why, thank you, Inspector. I wouldn't have said that of myself, but coming from a man such as yourself, it's doubly flattering."

"So, did Frank Darrow sell you any of his grandmother's jewelry or his grandfather's silver snuff boxes?" Daniel asked, playing along.

"He sold me an item or two, but he told me they were his to dispose of, and I believed him."

"Where are the items now?"

"Long gone, Inspector. Long gone. There's a market for family heirlooms, particularly in London."

Daniel felt anger bubbling away inside his chest but willed himself to remain calm. He'd get nowhere by threatening a man like Dickie Stokes or demanding answers. Besides, he was positive

Dickie didn't do his own dirty work. He had people like the weasel outside to do his bidding. If he couldn't sell something locally—after all, how many young men needed rings to impress their future fathers-in-law? —he'd send the stolen goods to London, possibly even with the London coach that made a stop in front of the tavern. He'd either entrust the items to the coachman, who might be eager to help for a cut of the proceeds, or send one of his men to an associate in London, who'd fence the goods there and send Dickie what was due him. In short, everyone won.

"Mr. Stokes, let us say that while selling his family heirlooms, or his mark's silver, Frank Darrow ran afoul of someone. Would that someone then have killed him?"

Dickie Stokes smiled again. He had very good teeth, Daniel noted. "Inspector Haze, in my experience, when someone runs afoul of someone, as you so delicately put it, they generally find themselves on the wrong end of an enthusiastic beating, meant to remind them what will happen if they don't make things right and pay their debts. If they still fail to get the message, they'll get their throat slit in a dark alley or get thrown in the river. It's faster and much less personal. Simply business. The way Frank was dispatched was highly personal, but then again, if he'd cheated his partners of what was rightfully theirs, that would make it personal indeed."

"Did Frank have partners?" Daniel asked, hoping Stokes would put him onto someone who'd know more of Frank's activities.

Dickie Stokes shrugged. "One would have to assume so, given that the houses he worked at got thoroughly cleaned out."

"How is it possible to break into the house of a wealthy individual?" Daniel mused. "One would assume that the servants would instantly raise the alarm."

Smiling at Daniel's naivete, Dickie Stokes leaned back in his chair and assumed the position of a man deeply in thought.

"You pose a good question, Inspector. If I were a chimney sweep and had access to the house, especially the bedrooms, I might just leave a window unlocked somewhere, wouldn't I. Many a wealthy family goes up to London for the Season, leaving their private quarters empty during the night. A body might get into the house through the unlocked window, help themselves to the family silver, and get out the same way, with the servants snug in their beds in the attic and none the wiser until it's time to polish the spoons."

"And you think Frank Darrow did this?" Daniel asked.

"I was only offering a plausible scenario," Dickie Stokes said. "I didn't know the man well enough to know what he was up to, but I'd speak to his associates."

Daniel inclined his head in agreement. "That's sage advice, Mr. Stokes."

"I'm glad you think so." Dickie Stokes looked pointedly at the door. "I'm a busy man, Inspector."

"Thank you for your time," Daniel said as he stood to leave. "By the way, does your inn offer female company, should a young man who'd lost heavily at cards wish to drown his sorrows, using some of the money he'd made off his long-dead grandmother's antique ring?"

Surprise flickered in Stokes' gray eyes. He clearly hadn't expected the question. "Given the inn's proximity to army barracks, we get many wives and mothers in need of a room while visiting their loved ones. It simply wouldn't do to run whores from the premises."

Which didn't mean that Stokes wasn't running a brothel at another location. Daniel wasn't sure why that mattered, but Dickie Stokes did strike him as a man who wouldn't pass up such an obvious business opportunity. Daniel sensed that the man knew more of Frank Darrow's death than he was saying, but as Inspector Coleridge had warned, Dickie wasn't about to tell him something he had no wish for him to know.

"I see. Thank you for your candor. Good day, Mr. Stokes."

"Good day, Inspector."

Daniel left the inn, climbed into the dogcart, and drove away, his mind on Frank's hypothetical accomplice. It stood to reason that Frank had been dealt with by some thug he'd crossed, but who would know the identity of the man, or men, who were now no more than murky shadows in Daniel's mind? Brentwood wasn't London, where rival gangs carved up the streets and controlled the population of the seedier neighborhoods by using rough justice against anyone who dared to speak or act against them. Brentwood was a peaceful town with no known criminal element. But someone was out there, someone who was looking to make Brentwood their patch and wasn't afraid to go up against a man like Dickie Stokes, who played at being an honest businessman but probably had his fingers in many different and illegal pies.

Daniel had meant to return to the station but changed his mind and headed to Birch Hill instead. He needed to speak to someone who wouldn't judge him as Detective Inspector Coleridge would, given that the man had vouched for him to his own superiors, and who might help him organize his thoughts and arrange the information he had to date into a discernable pattern.

Chapter 17

Daniel arrived at Redmond Hall around lunchtime. He was hungry, cold, and disheartened, and hoped the captain would help with all three. He was admitted by Dodson, who directed him to the drawing room. Daniel's greeting froze on his lips when he saw a beautiful woman sitting across from Jason and occupying what Daniel had come to think of as his chair. She smiled pleasantly, her dark gaze appraising him openly as Jason stood to greet him.

"Daniel, do come in," Jason said. One didn't need to be an inspector to detect Jason's tense expression. "Allow me to introduce Mrs. Baxter, an old friend from New York. She's come to stay for a few days."

The woman rose to her feet and came forward, her head tilted to the side playfully as she smiled at Daniel. "Inspector, what a pleasure to meet you. Jason was just telling me that you are one of his dearest friends here in Birch Hill. What a charming village this is," she remarked, still watching him. "It's such a contrast to the hustle and bustle of New York City. I can feel the tranquility soaking into my very bones."

"I'm glad you like our little corner of the world," Daniel said. "The captain has come to appreciate it."

"I never would have imagined Jason living the quiet life of an English nobleman, but here he is," she said, smiling up at Jason as if he'd done something exceptionally clever.

"Yes, here I am," Jason replied, his own expression not nearly as serene.

"I expect you two have much to discuss, so I'll just make myself scarce," Mrs. Baxter said, looking from one man to the other. "I think I'll go for a walk and explore the grounds. I could use some fresh country air."

"It's rather cold out there," Daniel replied.

"You are sweet to worry, Inspector," she said, dimpling at Daniel. "I brought stout boots and my fur-lined cape, which came in very handy on the crossing, I must say. After the bitter wind howling off the Atlantic, this weather is positively spring-like. I will be very toasty, I think."

With that, she glided from the room, leaving both men to stare after her. Jason sank into the chair he'd vacated earlier and sighed dramatically, shaking his head in dismay. "She just showed up," he said miserably.

"I take it you're not pleased?"

"Would you be pleased if the woman you'd been engaged to, who married your best friend without so much as bothering to confirm whether you were alive or dead, appeared on your doorstep?" Jason retorted.

Daniel gaped at him in astonishment. He hadn't for a moment suspected that the lovely Mrs. Baxter was Cecilia, the faithless fiancée. "Why is she here?"

"She lost her husband and infant son to the cholera epidemic in New York," Jason said. "She's running away from her misery, and although I sympathize and grieve the loss of my friend and his baby son, Cecilia coming here was ill-advised."

"I'll say!"

"Anyway, enough about Cecilia. Tell me how the investigation is progressing," Jason invited. "And I hope you'll stay for luncheon."

"Are you sure I won't be intruding?" Jason's raised eyebrows made Daniel laugh. "Well, if you're in need of a chaperone, I'll be happy to stay and guard your virtue," he quipped, finally making Jason smile.

"Tell me what you've discovered."

"Not a whole lot," Daniel confessed. "Frank Darrow was handsome, lazy, and according to some, sly. He'd allowed his family's business to fail due to his lack of ambition and foresight and then used his position with Graham and Sons to supplement his income. To what degree, I'm not yet sure. It may be that he was nothing more than a petty thief who helped himself to small, valuable items, or he might have been part of a larger operation that targeted homes of the wealthy, particularly those who were out of town at the time of the chimney cleaning. Having gained admittance to the house, Frank could have left a window unlatched, therefore making it that much easier for someone to enter the house quietly and help themselves to whatever valuables were to be had without waking the servants."

"Petty thievery can be a one-man job, but robbing a house would require an accomplice, unless Frank himself returned to finish the job," Jason suggested. "He might have involved his sons."

Daniel shook his head. "Somehow, I don't think he did. You've seen the Darrow house. There were no signs of prosperity. Looks might be deceiving, but I'd say the Darrows lead a hand-to-mouth existence."

"What did he do with his share of the proceeds, then?" Jason asked.

"Perhaps he had the money on him the night he was killed, and it was taken off him."

"So, it's your theory that Frank was either set up or killed by his accomplice?"

"It's a definite possibility, except I've no notion who he may have been working with. Finding his partner or partners would certainly help in identifying suspects."

Jason leaned back in his chair, his head tilted to the side as he considered Daniel's dilemma. "Given that Frank worked with his sons, I'd start with them. They might not have been in on their father's plans, but they knew whom he met with. I'd even venture to suggest that plans are best laid over a pint, so Frank's regular watering hole might prove a useful place to start."

Daniel nodded. "You have a point there, Captain."

"Perhaps." Jason's gray eyes were thoughtful as he considered their theory. "Despite Frank Darrow's criminal activities, I really don't think he was killed because he'd cheated an accomplice or had stolen from the wrong person."

"Go on," Daniel prompted.

"The idea I keep coming back to is that this was a crime committed by someone Frank had wounded deeply," Jason suggested. "But I don't think Frank had hurt this person directly."

"I don't understand," Daniel said, leaning forward in his eagerness to comprehend Jason's reasoning.

"Frank Darrow knew and trusted his killer. He wouldn't have put his trust in someone he'd wronged."

"How did you arrive at that conclusion?" Daniel asked, surprised by Jason's observation.

"If you recall, the only bruising to occur antemortem was around the neck and shoulders, meaning that before Frank was held down beneath the water, he hadn't struggled or tried to fight off his attacker. His nails weren't broken, nor were there any other defensive wounds on his hands or forearms, as there would have been had he tried to fight back or break free. I think Frank had arranged to meet someone at the mill, someone he knew well. The attack was unexpected, giving him no time to defend himself."

Daniel nodded. "Yes, I think you're right, but that doesn't rule out an accomplice. Frank might not have realized that his accomplice knew of his betrayal and had gone along willingly, so as not to arouse suspicion. Or, if we go with the notion that this was someone he'd wounded on a personal level, he may not have known that the husband he'd cuckolded knew of the affair."

"Do you have any concrete evidence that Frank had been unfaithful to his wife?"

"I do not, but I wouldn't rule anything out until there's clear evidence against it. I need to re-interview the family," Daniel said. "If her husband had been unfaithful, Sadie Darrow is sure to know, and if Frank had a trusted associate, his boys might be able to shed some light."

"I asked Sadie Darrow point blank if her husband had been unfaithful. She pretended to be deeply offended by the question but never actually replied," Jason said.

"Perhaps she really was offended," Daniel argued. "What woman wouldn't be, especially if she had believed her husband to be devoted to her?"

Jason smiled. "You have a point there. We have a few minutes before lunch is served. Maybe this would be a good time to speak to Kitty."

"Come with me," Daniel urged, rising to his feet.

"I'm not sure if that's a good idea. Kitty seems to find me intimidating," Jason replied. "Perhaps it's best if you speak to her on your own."

"All right."

Daniel left the drawing room and made his way to the kitchen, where Mrs. Dodson was putting the finishing touches on lunch. Her eyebrows rose in an unspoken question when she saw Daniel.

"I'd like to speak to Kitty," Daniel said.

"What? Now?"

"Surely you can spare her for a few minutes."

Mrs. Dodson nodded, but her expression was still disapproving. Kitty, who'd been scrubbing a pot, wiped her hands on her apron and turned to face Daniel. She looked frightened.

"Kitty, may I ask you a few questions?" he asked, gentling his tone.

She nodded, her gaze fixed on the tips of her shoes.

"Can you think of anyone who might have wanted to hurt your father?" Daniel began.

"No," Kitty mumbled.

"Did you ever see him speaking to someone you didn't recognize?"

Kitty shrugged. "Not in Elsmere. I know everyone there."

"Did your father go to the mill often?" Daniel asked, groping for something else to ask the girl. She didn't seem to know

93

anything, and he could hardly ask her if her father had been seeing women behind her mother's back.

Kitty seemed to shrink into herself at the mention of the mill, but that was understandable given that her father's body had been found there. "'E went there sometimes. 'E missed it, 'e said."

Daniel seized on that. "Did he ever meet anyone at the mill?"

Kitty looked up, her eyes flashing with anger. "Yes, 'e did."

"Whom did he meet?" Daniel asked.

Kitty looked away. "I don't know. I only know someone 'ad been there."

"How do you know? Did you go to the mill too?"

"Not by myself," Kitty replied.

"Whom did you go with?"

Kitty suddenly blanched, her hand going to her stomach. "I'm sorry, Inspector," she cried, and bolted from the kitchen.

"Now, you've gone and upset her," Mrs. Dodson said. "That poor girl. Hasn't she been through enough? It's clear she doesn't know anything."

"Sometimes people know more than they think," Daniel replied.

"Oh, go on with you," Mrs. Dodson said. "Lunch is ready."

Daniel returned to the main part of the house and rejoined Jason and Cecilia, who had returned from her walk

"Were you able to learn anything?" Jason asked as they took their seats at the table.

"Not really. Kitty became ill when I asked her about the mill."

"She's an impressionable girl," Jason said. "She's taken her father's death very badly."

94

"She said he'd met with someone at the mill," Daniel said, paying little attention to Fanny, who served him soup. "Perhaps he used the mill to meet with his associates."

"Did you find any evidence at the mill that would help you identify the person Frank Darrow had been meeting with?" Jason asked.

Daniel shook his head. "There was nothing there besides an old cot, table and chair, and the stub of a candle. The mill is a dead end," Daniel said with a heavy sigh.

"I think the mill is at the center of this mystery, but unless you stumble on a viable clue, you'll never discover its significance."

"I'm afraid I have to agree with you there," Daniel said.

"I do hope you're not going to talk about murder the whole time I'm here," Cecilia said, visibly annoyed. "Really, Jason! Is that how you spend your time these days?"

"I didn't realize I had to account for how I spend my time, to you of all people," Jason replied, his eyes narrowing in irritation. Cecilia stared into her soup, chastised, the color rising in her cheeks.

"I do beg your pardon, Mrs. Baxter," Daniel said, wishing he had declined the invitation to lunch and gone home instead. "The fault is entirely mine."

"Not at all, Inspector," Cecilia replied graciously. "I'm afraid it is I who's intruding. Serves me right for assuming I would be welcome." She gave Jason a sidelong glance, which he pretended not to notice.

Daniel sighed inwardly and turned his attention to the quickly cooling soup, eager to avoid the awkward silence that descended on the room.

"Forgive me, Cecilia. I didn't mean to be rude," Jason choked out, earning himself a beatific smile from Cecilia.

"There's nothing to forgive," she said smugly and patted her mouth with the serviette. "Nothing at all."

Chapter 18

Sunday, December 23

Daniel had meant to speak to the Darrows the previous afternoon, but the luncheon at Redmond Hall had lasted longer than expected, and by the time he'd finally climbed into the dogcart, it was nearly dark and too cold to venture to Elsmere, nearly an hour away. He'd decided to postpone the interview until morning and spent a pleasant evening at home, reading a newspaper by the fire as Sarah and Harriet played a game of piquet.

Immediately after the Sunday service at St. Catherine's, which neither Jason nor Mrs. Baxter had attended, Daniel set off to pay a call on the Darrows. He had a vague hope of solving the murder before Christmas but realized it wasn't a realistic expectation, not when the investigation wasn't yielding results. He knew he wouldn't lose his position as inspector if he failed to apprehend the killer. Not every case was solved, but he needed to prove to himself that he was worthy of this elevation and the trust Detective Inspector Coleridge had shown in him by vouching for him to the Commissioner.

Daniel lacked suspects, but what he really needed to move the investigation along was a concrete motive. Once the reason for the murder became obvious, the suspects would be easier to identify. Why would someone want to kill Frank Darrow and display his body in such a shocking way? As he drove along snowy lanes toward Elsmere, Daniel's mind kept coming back to the same conclusion. Someone had wanted to humiliate Frank Darrow because to kill him just wasn't enough. Whatever Frank had done had been so beyond the pale that to simply end his life had seemed insufficient to the person he'd wronged.

Daniel tied the horse to a post and walked across the yard, ignoring the dog snarling at him from the shed. His knock was answered by Sadie Darrow, who seemed surprised to see him on her doorstep again so soon.

"Good afternoon, Mrs. Darrow. May I come in?"

"I s'pose," Sadie replied, and stood aside to let Daniel into the house.

The aroma of Sunday lunch filled the small space, making Daniel feel a little guilty for troubling the victim's family on the Lord's day. Jimmy and Willy sat at the table, which had already been set.

"I apologize for disturbing you, but I have a few more questions to put to you. I won't keep you long," Daniel promised.

He could sense annoyance emanating from Sadie Darrow and Jimmy, but Willy looked at him eagerly, perhaps wrongly assuming that Daniel now had an idea of who'd killed his father.

"May I sit down?" Daniel asked.

"Might as well." Sadie sat across from him and met his gaze, her expression closed.

"Mrs. Darrow, did you know your husband was stealing from Graham and Sons' customers and that was the reason for his dismissal?" Daniel asked bluntly. He was curious to see what Sadie would say when asked outright but kept his eye on the boys' reactions as well.

Sadie looked defiant for a moment, but then her shoulders sagged with resignation. "Yes, I did. Frank hated delivering coal and thought it his God-given right to help himself to whatever happened to lie in his path."

"Did he have any accomplices?"

"I don't know nothin' 'bout any accomplices. Frank didn't like to share," Sadie retorted.

Daniel turned to Jimmy, whose narrowed gaze was guarded. "Jimmy, did you know your father was helping himself to items from the houses you visited?"

Like his mother, Jimmy looked like he was about to deny the charge, but then nodded. "We suspected. 'E never said outright, and we wasn't inside to see for ourselves. Were we, Willy?"

"We never came inside," Willy confirmed.

"Did your father have any associates? Someone he may have passed the goods on to sell, or perhaps someone who was interested in a bigger job?"

"What ye mean?" Jimmy asked.

"Several houses in Brentwood have been burglarized over the past few months. Some of those houses belong to clients of Graham and Sons."

"That don't make Da guilty," Jimmy snapped.

"I didn't say he was guilty, but perhaps he'd unwittingly told someone the owners were away or mentioned items of value," Daniel suggested, moderating his tone to sound less accusing.

"He never spoke to no one while on the job," Willy said. "Liked to keep 'is 'ead down."

Daniel took that statement with a grain of salt. If the boys never went inside, they couldn't know if he'd spoken to anyone while in the house.

"Was there anyone you saw him with frequently?" Daniel tried again. "Like when he went to the Queen's Arms?"

"He was friendly with the barkeep, and always 'ad a jar with Mr. Gordon," Willy said. "They go back a ways."

"Yes, Mr. Gordon told me that. Friends since boyhood."

"Those two were as different as chalk and cheese, but always loyal to each other," Sadie said. "Frank would 'ave trusted Elijah with 'is life."

"Did Frank have any other particular friends?" Daniel asked. "Someone he may have met recently?"

"Da went to see Dickie Stokes a time or two," Willy volunteered. "But they was 'ardly what ye'd call friends."

"Yes, I've met Mr. Stokes. I don't think he's anyone's friend," Daniel said, keeping an eye on Jimmy. "Have you met him, Jimmy?"

"Just the once."

"Did he speak to you?"

Jimmy shrugged. "'E did, as it 'appens. Just as we was leavin'. Said 'e always 'ad need of enterprising young lads and I should come and see 'im should I get tired of shoveling coal."

"Did you consider his offer?" Daniel asked.

Jimmy scoffed. "I might 'ave no proper schoolin', Inspector, but I ain't no fool. Men like Dickie Stokes need someone to do their bidding so they can keep their own noses clean. They got an army of grunts dead-lurkin', dippin', and pinchin' bobs. I ain't no thief, I told 'im as much, so 'e said 'e could use me as an 'eavy at one of 'is brothels, shaking up punters who refuse to pay or get too rough with the merchandise, or hauling bodies of coves who get too fond of the pipe in 'is opium dens and never come to before they give up the ghost. I ain't going to the big 'ouse or getting boated to protect the likes of 'im."

"Boated?" Daniel asked. He wasn't familiar with the term.

"Shipped off to Botany Bay," Jimmy said, baring his teeth in derision. "Surely ye've 'eard of it, guv."

"It's not a pleasant voyage, from what I hear," Daniel said.

Daniel studied Jimmy's angry face. For someone who proclaimed to keep his nose clean, he certainly was intimately familiar with criminal slang, some of which Daniel had picked up while walking the beat during his peeler days in London. "Dickie Stokes might have an army of petty thieves, but does he go in for breaking a drum?" Daniel asked, hoping he got the term right for breaking into a house with the intention to rob it.

"Nah. Dickie's a duffer, not a cracksman," Jimmy said.

"You certainly seem in the know," Daniel pointed out.

Willy smiled proudly. "Jimmy and I, we like to read *Illustrated Police News*," he announced.

"I didn't realize it was sold in Brentwood," Daniel said. He was familiar with the London newspaper and held a dim view of the sordid and often exaggerated details of London's most outrageous crimes, the stories accompanied by graphic pictures that were meant to shock and sometimes titillate.

"Jimmy has a mate as works in London," Willy explained. "'E always brings us a stack of *Illustrated News* and some penny dreadfuls when 'e comes to visit 'is mam. We 'ave to pay 'im, o' course," Willy added, his brow furrowing. "But it's worth it. Ain't it, Jimmy?"

Jimmy nodded, finally allowing himself something resembling a smile. "Worth every penny. Best bit of entertainment a bloke can get without gettin' the clap."

Sadie got to her feet and went to stir the pot, the contents of which were beginning to burn, if Daniel's nose wasn't deceiving him. She pursed her mouth and glared at him. Daniel took the hint but wasn't ready to end the interview quiet yet.

"Mrs. Darrow, would it be possible for me to speak to you alone for a moment?" Daniel asked politely.

"Go get washed up. Dinner is nearly ready," Sadie said. Jimmy and Willy looked mutinous; they were clearly hungry but obeyed their mother and stepped outside.

"What was it ye couldn't ask me in front of my boys?" Sadie asked. She didn't seem angry, just curious.

"Mrs. Darrow, I don't mean to be indelicate, but did Frank ever pursue other women?"

"Ye mean, did 'e 'ave a piece on the side? I might as well tell ye. 'E did. Wedding vows meant little to Frank."

"Might he have been assaulted by the woman's husband?"

Sadie shrugged. "Why don't ye ask Elijah Gordon? Frank was tuppin' Eleanor, 'is wife, for years."

"Frank and Mrs. Gordon were lovers?"

"Ain't that what I just said?" Sadie asked without heat.

"Was there anyone else he may have been involved with?"

"I wouldn't be surprised if 'e were. Frank were a charmer when 'e wanted to be. 'E liked to be admired and fawned over. 'E sure as heck weren't getting no admiration from me these past few years."

"So, I take it you didn't have a congenial marriage?"

"Congenial?" Sadie Darrow scoffed. "I could barely stand the sight of 'im most days, and 'e weren't exactly treating me like 'is queen."

"Did he have a good relationship with the children?"

"They got on. Kitty were fond of 'im. Jimmy and Willy butted 'eads with 'im something fierce these past few months. Thought 'is thieving ways would be the end of us all."

"But he dismissed their concerns?"

"'Course 'e did, like 'e dismissed everything else 'e didn't care to 'ear. Frank was a law onto 'imself, Inspector, and it's that arrogance that got 'im killed."

"Thank you, Mrs. Darrow. I'll let myself out."

Daniel stepped out into the chill afternoon and nearly collided with Jimmy, who'd been about to open the door. Willy still stood next to the barrel of rainwater they'd used for washing.

"May we 'ave our dinner now, Inspector?" Jimmy asked, his mouth twisting into a wry grin.

"Of course. I'm sorry to have put you out."

"Ye can put us out anytime," Jimmy said. "'E weren't perfect, not by any stretch, but 'e were our da, and we want to know who'd done for 'im."

"We want to see justice done," Willy said, coming up behind his brother. "'E didn't deserve to go the way 'e did. It near broke Ma finding 'im like that. She don't let on, but she's hurtin'," Willy said, his large brown eyes filled with sadness. "She loved 'im, and so did our Kitty. She's so heartsick, she can't even bear to be 'ere. Would rather go back to work. To keep busy, she said."

"Losing a parent is never easy," Daniel agreed. "I'll let you get on."

He walked toward the cart and climbed onto the seat, which was ice cold beneath the thin wool of his coat. Except for the affair with Mrs. Gordon, which he had yet to confirm, he hadn't learned anything new. Sadie Darrow's anger and resentment were understandable enough. Frank had not only lost the mill, he'd lost his interest in her, and that probably hurt more than anything else. And most young men didn't see eye to eye with their fathers. If the boys were as honest as Robert Gordon believed them to be, then Frank's criminal activities would have been a point of contention between them, especially when their own livelihood depended on keeping on the right side of Robert Graham.

Daniel consulted his pocket watch. It had just gone one, and he was expected home for Sunday dinner, but he had one more stop to make before he headed for home. He hoped Sarah wouldn't be too angry with him for being late.

Chapter 19

The Brentwood police station was as silent as a tomb on this last Sunday before Christmas. It was as if the police and the criminal element had agreed to a holiday truce, giving each other a few days off to enjoy the glad tidings of the season.

Sergeant Flint was behind the desk, his pomaded hair gleaming in the light of the gas lamp. He was a man of middle years who always took care with his appearance, waxing his moustache into sharp points that could probably do some serious damage to whoever decided to get too close. Daniel wondered if the sergeant was married but quickly put the thought from his mind, deeming it unworthy. It was none of his affair.

"Inspector Haze," Sergeant Flint said, giving him a pointed look. "What brings you in on a Sunday afternoon?"

"I have a few questions, if you can spare the time," Daniel said. Sergeant Flint didn't seem to be occupied with anything other than watching the door, but one didn't want to presume.

"Of course. How can I help?"

"How many houses have been burgled in Brentwood over the past three months?" Daniel asked.

"I'll have to check."

The sergeant turned to a cabinet tucked into an alcove behind the desk and consulted several files before returning to his post.

"Three. One a month."

"And when was the last one done?"

"December fourteenth."

"So, just over a week ago," Daniel said.

"Yes. What does that prove?" Flint asked, looking at Daniel curiously.

"Nothing, really. Who reported the break-in?"

"Mr. Grills, the butler. Seems he interrupted the robbery and managed to wound the intruder. Clever old sod, Mr. Grills. If I had me a butler, I'd want one just like him," Flint said, baring his teeth in what was meant to be a smile. "Too bad he didn't kill the miscreant or clobber him good enough to give us time to make an arrest."

"And who does the house belong to?"

"Mr. Adler. A Jew," Sergeant Flint added with obvious distaste. "He'd gone away recently to visit family. In Austria, I believe. Mr. Grills mentioned some heathen holiday he was meant to be celebrating at his sister's house."

"What heathen holiday?" Daniel asked, genuinely curious.

"Henka or Hannika, or some such nonsense. Seems they light a candle every night for eight days using some specially made candelabra. Festival of Light, they call it." He scoffed at the notion. "Probably celebrating the death of our Lord, and right around the time of his birth too. Seems significant."

Daniel felt a stab of annoyance at Flint's attitude. Antisemitism was nothing new, but any kind of hatred based on little more than the fact that someone was different didn't sit well with him. It smacked of ignorance and fear, and the desire to persecute. Sergeant Flint might look smart with his sleek hair and waxed moustache, and authoritative in his blue uniform with its shiny brass buttons, but beneath the insignia of the Essex Police beat the heart of a street tough who wouldn't think twice about picking on someone he thought weak and vulnerable.

"What does Mr. Adler do for a living?"

"What do you think?" Flint demanded, scoffing louder this time. "He's a banker. A moneylender. Aren't they all?"

"No, I don't believe they are," Daniel retorted, now growing angry. Mr. Adler was the victim in this instance, not the perpetrator, and he deserved every respect. At any rate, Daniel was done speaking to Sergeant Flint. Being new to the station, he didn't relish the prospect of making enemies. Flint would nurse his prejudices regardless of what Daniel said, and he was in no mood to get into an argument.

"Can I have the address, please?" Daniel said instead.

Sergeant Flint scribbled the address on a scrap of paper. "Much good it will do you. The trail has grown cold—not that there was ever a trail to follow, other than a few bloodstains that led to the window."

"Thank you, Sergeant," Daniel said, and stuffed the paper into his pocket. He'd call on Mr. Grills first thing tomorrow.

Daniel returned home to find Sarah and Tilda decorating the house for Christmas. Pine boughs wound around the banister and were secured with red velvet ribbons, and a small fir tree stood on a round table by the drawing room window, its branches still bare. Sarah beamed at him as he entered the room, savoring his shock at seeing the tree. They hadn't decorated for Christmas since Felix's death, and he'd assumed that this year would be no different despite Sarah's improved state of mind.

"Isn't it lovely?" Sarah asked as she invited Daniel to admire the tree. "John Caulfield brought it by. Seems he's selling trees as well as growing apples."

"Eh…yes," Daniel agreed. "It's very pretty."

"Will you help me decorate it?" Sarah asked. She'd prepared red bows and about a dozen small white candles, and a box of ornaments her parents had accumulated over the years stood on the low table where Tilda usually served tea. Daniel walked over to the box and lifted out an angel made of white satin and tulle and decorated with tiny beads. Felix had loved the angels. He'd traced his little fingers over their wings, smiling happily when Daniel had lifted him up high enough to place the angel on the tree.

Sarah laid her hand over his arm, her gaze tender. "He loved the angels," she said, echoing Daniel's thoughts.

"Yes."

"He's the angel now," Sarah said softly.

Daniel didn't argue. It was easier for her to think of their little boy as an angel rather than a small skeleton lying in a wooden box in the nearly frozen earth of the graveyard.

"Yes," he said again.

"Go on. Put it up there," Sarah urged.

Daniel did as he was asked, torn between gratitude that Sarah was finally accepting their loss and unbearable sadness. Sarah held out another ornament to him, and he placed it on the tree with numb fingers, wishing it didn't hurt so much to move on.

"Felix loved decorating. Remember?" she asked wistfully as she handed Daniel the next ornament. "I think all children do. It's so festive. Even the youngest children seem to understand that something special is happening."

"I think they just like shiny objects," Daniel replied as he affixed a bow to a low branch.

"You'll have help decorating next Christmas," Sarah said softly.

"You can help me now," Daniel replied, wondering why she looked at him in that enigmatic way, a small smile playing about her lips. Sarah tilted her head and her smile widened, her eyes glowing with happiness.

"As much as I like shiny objects, I think our baby will enjoy them more."

"Oh! Oh!" Daniel repeated stupidly. Some detective he was. "Really? Are you sure? When?"

"Mid-May."

Sarah smiled wider as Daniel took a moment to work backward, and he grinned back at her, recalling those perfect, intimate nights in Scotland when they'd finally found their way back to each other after three years of solitary anguish.

"Oh, Sarah, I'm so happy," Daniel whispered into her hair as he pulled her close. "Is everything all right? Are you feeling well?"

"I feel wonderful," she said. "Buoyant."

"I can't wait," Daniel said softly as he allowed his hand to settle on her slightly rounded belly. He should have noticed, should have seen the changes in her, and maybe he had, but he'd been too afraid to ask outright or to hope too fervently. "I can't believe this is really happening," Daniel mused as he held her close. "We've been given another chance, and I'm so grateful."

"Let's keep the news to ourselves for now," Sarah said. "Mother knows, of course, and so does Tilda, but I'm not ready to tell anyone else."

"Of course. Whatever you say," Daniel agreed. He was floating on a bubble of happiness, his earlier frustration at the lack of progress on the investigation forgotten. "Oh, Sarah," he said again, and kissed her tenderly.

Their moment of affection was interrupted by Harriet, who'd quietly come into the room. She coughed delicately, chuckling with amusement as Daniel and Sarah broke apart and both stared into the box of ornaments, as if choosing the next ornament was of the utmost importance.

"May I help?" Harriet asked. "I do love decorating for Christmas. It brings back such memories of when your father and I decorated our first tree. You were six years old," she said, smiling at Sarah wistfully, "and we didn't have any baubles. It was all so new then."

"We didn't have a tree until I was six?" Sarah asked, her brow furrowing in confusion.

Harriet shook her head. "It was in 1848 that *The Illustrated London News* published a drawing of the royal family decorating the tree. It was the first time any of us had seen anything like it. It was Prince Albert's doing, of course. He'd brought the tradition from Germany. Some people grumbled and called it heathen, but most of us embraced it. It was so lovely, so festive. After that first year, your father bought an ornament every year and gave it to you on Christmas Eve, so that you could put it on the tree. Do you remember?"

"I remember this one," Sarah said, lifting out a pale pink silk orb with a beaded tassel. "He gave me that one when I was ten. And he got the angel for Felix's first Christmas," Sarah said, her voice barely audible.

"Yes, I remember." Harriet smiled sadly as she reached out and gently touched a tulle wing.

"We're not going to be sad, not this year," Sarah said, her tone resolute. "This year we have much to celebrate."

"We certainly do, my darling," Harriet said, smiling at her daughter. "You've done us proud, Daniel."

Daniel wasn't sure if she was referring to the coming baby or his new post as an inspector, but felt a blush creeping up his cheeks regardless.

Chapter 20

Monday, December 24

Christmas Eve dawned crisp and bright. Daniel slid out of bed, careful not to wake Sarah. She looked so peaceful. Daniel was tempted to kiss her but changed his mind, not wishing to disturb her sleep. Instead, he grabbed his clothes, including long woolen underwear to put on beneath his tweed trousers, and tiptoed from the room, washing and dressing hastily in the spare bedroom, where Tilda always kept a full pitcher of water just in case he should need to leave early. Downstairs, the preparations for their Christmas Eve dinner were already in full swing. Cook was rolling out the dough for mincemeat pies and Tilda was mixing the filling.

"Good morning, Mr. Haze," the two women said in unison.

"Good morning. Can I trouble you for some tea and toast?" Daniel asked.

"Of course, sir," Cook said as she washed her hands in a basin of water and dried them on her apron. "Shall I do ye an egg?"

"If it's not too much trouble."

"Oh, go on with ye," Cook said, smiling at him indulgently. "We won't send ye out into the cold without a proper fry-up."

"Thank you." Daniel took himself off to the dining room to await his breakfast. He had police work to attend to, but he could spare time for a proper breakfast. Daniel picked up yesterday's evening paper and settled himself at the table. He hadn't had time to read it last night, and it would help pass the time. He sighed with frustration when he saw the headline.

POLICE FAIL TO APPREHEND WATERMILL KILLER.

Daniel folded the paper and tossed it onto the table, angry not only with the reporter who'd written the piece, but with himself for feeling so helpless. What did these people expect? It had been only three days since Frank Darrow's body had been discovered. Unless the police caught the killer red-handed, which didn't happen that often, they were groping in the dark. *He* was groping in the dark. He was missing something vital. He was sure of that. Frank had done something awful, something unforgivable, but to whom?

Daniel was distracted from his unpleasant thoughts by the arrival of Tilda, who skillfully balanced a full tray bearing not only his breakfast but a pot of tea, a jug of milk, and a sugar bowl. He poured himself tea, buttered a slice of toast, and dug into the food. He always thought better on a full stomach.

"Tilda, Mrs. Haze will take breakfast in bed today," Daniel said, hoping Sarah would enjoy the treat. She thought of breakfasting in bed as overindulgent, a habit fit for wealthy ladies who had nothing to do but moon about the house and annoy the servants, but she deserved a morning off, and he wanted her to know that he'd been thinking about her before he left for the day.

"Of course, sir," Tilda replied, giving him a conspiratorial smile. "I'll see to it."

"And include a mince pie, if you have a batch ready," Daniel added. "She'd like that."

Once finished, Daniel accepted his coat, hat, woolen muffler, and gloves from Tilda and walked out into the frigid morning, glad to see that Thomas had already hitched the horse to the dogcart and had it waiting for him by the door.

"Thank you, Thomas," Daniel said to the young man, whose breath was coming out in white puffs as he blew on his ungloved hands to warm them.

"Do you not have gloves?" Daniel asked.

"No, sir. My mam knitted me a pair last Christmas, but I lost 'em and don't 'ave the 'eart to tell 'er."

"Shame," Daniel said, resolving to give Thomas a pair of gloves for Boxing Day. He had a new pair stashed away in case he lost the ones he had, but he could certainly spare them.

Daniel climbed into the cart and took up the reins, eager to get going. He would start with Eleanor Gordon, then pay a visit to Mr. Grills. Despite his earlier frustration with the news, Daniel enjoyed the ride. The fields shimmered with frost, and the bare branches of the trees painted an intricate pattern against the nearly white sky, the weak winter sun shining through the latticework. It was quiet and peaceful, and very beautiful.

Daniel grinned to himself as he replayed the conversation with Sarah in his mind. A baby. A new baby. What joy. The good Lord had truly blessed him this year, and it was all thanks to Captain Redmond. Had Jason not helped him solve Alexander McDougal's murder, he and Sarah might not have reconciled, and he certainly would not have been offered the position of inspector at the Brentwood Constabulary had he not been able to bring in Elizabeth Barrett's killer. He felt so lucky and so blessed that he resolved there and then that he wouldn't allow his failure to catch Frank Darrow's killer in three days to ruin Christmas.

The Gordon property looked picturesque in the early morning light, snow glittering on the tiles of the roof and sunshine reflecting off the windows. Since he'd last been there, a small wreath made of pine boughs and holly had been hung on the door, the velvet bow blood-red against the green paint.

Daniel lifted a hand to wave to Elijah Gordon, who'd come out of his workshop. He wore a brown leather apron tied around his ample middle. His apprentice walked next to Elijah, listening intently to whatever the man was saying. Elijah must have issued some instruction because the lad hurried away toward the shed behind the workshop. Daniel noticed him limping, grimacing with pain every time he put weight on his right leg. He hadn't noticed the limp before, but then the young man had been standing behind some barrels, so it wouldn't have been obvious.

It was kind of Mr. Gordon to hire a lame apprentice, Daniel thought as he approached the door. Life was hard, but it was that much harder for anyone with a disability, be it physical or mental. He'd visited a lunatic asylum once as part of his duties and had suffered from nightmares for a fortnight after, still hearing the screams of the insane and seeing their crazed eyes in his dreams.

Even if the person was only mildly disturbed when they entered such a place, they were sure to completely lose their wits after being there for even a short time. He knew he would. *No human being should be treated so cruelly*, Daniel thought as he knocked on the door.

Eleanor Gordon smiled winsomely as she stood aside to let him in. "Inspector, what a pleasant surprise. Do come in. I don't think you'll say no to a cup of tea," she teased.

Some part of Daniel wanted to refuse, especially since he was still full from breakfast, and this wasn't a social call, but the chilled-to-the-bone part of him readily agreed. "Thank you. Tea would be most welcome."

"Make yourself comfortable. I won't be a moment. The kettle has just boiled. I find I have no appetite for food in the morning, but I can't start my day without a cup of tea," she said. "What a pleasure it will be not to take it alone."

"Does your husband not take breakfast with you?" Daniel asked.

"No. Elijah likes to get an early start. By the time I get up, he's been beavering away in his workshop for hours, and he doesn't come in until nearly suppertime. I do get lonely here all on my own," she said with a pout.

When he'd previously spoken to her, Daniel had taken Eleanor Gordon's manner for one of friendly hospitality, but now he wasn't so sure. Was she making a play for him now that her lover was dead? Did she treat every man who crossed her path with such playful charm?

Eleanor returned a few moments later, carrying a tray laden with all the usual tea things and a plate of scones. There was a dish of jam as well as one of clotted cream. The scones smelled wonderful.

"Help yourself," Eleanor Gordon said as she poured out. She remembered how Daniel took his tea and smiled at him as she handed him his cup.

Daniel wasn't even remotely hungry, but some unseen force compelled him to reach for a scone. He sliced it in half and spread each half generously with cream and jam. They ate in silence for a few moments, then Daniel recalled why he was there.

"Mrs. Gordon, how would you define your relationship with Frank Darrow?"

"Whatever do you mean, Inspector?" Eleanor asked, her eyes widening in surprise.

"I mean, were you having an affair with him?" Daniel asked bluntly, watching the woman for a reaction.

"I wouldn't call it that," Eleanor Gordon replied defensively.

"What would you call it?"

"An occasional roll in the hay," she said. "Frank Darrow was a good lover. Does it shock you, Inspector, that a woman should wish to enjoy the act?"

"Your husband..." Daniel began, but wasn't quite sure what he meant to say.

"My husband doesn't know his arse from his elbow when it comes to pleasuring a woman. It's the wood for his barrels that he strokes affectionately, not me. He hasn't kissed me since our wedding day."

"So, you found what you were missing with Frank?"

Eleanor laughed. "Hardly, but he was willing to scratch the itch, if you take my meaning."

Daniel felt acutely embarrassed by the direction the conversation had taken, then annoyed with himself for allowing the woman to rattle him. He was an inspector of the Essex police, a man of the world, not some inexperienced schoolboy who was mortified by the mention of sexual relations between consenting adults, adulterous though they may be. "Er, yes, I do. Was your husband aware of your arrangement?"

"I doubt it."

"And if he were, would he do anything about it?"

"Like what? Like drown Frank in the river and hoist him up naked onto the mill wheel? If you knew my husband at all, you'd see how ludicrous such a notion is. The only hoisting Elijah is interested in involves a jar of ale and his lips."

"Where did you and Frank meet for your trysts?"

"At the old mill. It was the only place discreet enough in a village where everyone knows everyone's business. We managed to meet on the sly for years."

"Sadie Darrow knew," Daniel pointed out.

"She would, wouldn't she. A wife always knows."

"Mrs. Gordon, was there anyone else Frank was involved with?" Daniel asked. He hadn't known Frank in life, but he didn't sound like the type of man who'd be faithful to his mistress, if Eleanor Gordon could be classified as such.

Eleanor refreshed her tea, took a delicate sip, then set her cup down. "There was someone else," she said at last. "But I don't know who. I think it began about a year ago. Frank became distracted, less available, and when we did manage to come together, less attentive."

"Why do you think it had to do with another woman?" Daniel asked, wondering if Frank had got himself into a situation he couldn't get out of and possibly feared for his life.

"Because nothing else had changed in his life," Eleanor replied. "He did like to talk, mostly about himself."

"Mrs. Gordon, did you know Frank was stealing from the people he delivered coal to?"

"He never said so outright, but I suspected he was up to something. He wasn't exactly what you'd call flush with coin, but he did seem to have more money of late."

"Do you think Frank might have crossed someone or cheated them out of their share?" Daniel asked.

Eleanor shook her head, her gaze thoughtful. "Frank wasn't the type of man to risk his neck. He may have nicked little things here and there, but I can't see him going in for a big job, especially if it involved accomplices. That would be too unpredictable and too dangerous. He could be charming when it suited him, but he trusted few people, especially where money was concerned."

"I will have to speak to your husband," Daniel said.

"You mean you're going to tell him about me and Frank?" Eleanor appeared truly nervous for the first time.

"I'm sorry, but your relationship with Frank Darrow gave your husband a motive for killing him. That's not something I can ignore."

"But Elijah didn't enjoy that side of things," Eleanor said. "He wouldn't have minded."

"Mrs. Gordon, you are your husband's property under the law. Even if he took no pleasure in your marital relations, it doesn't mean he'd want someone else to stand in for him. Jealousy is not a rational emotion; it's an instinct that can drive even the mildest-mannered person to commit murder."

"Please, Inspector, can't you speak to him without revealing my secret?" she implored.

"It's not my job to keep your secrets."

"No, it's not your job, but you're a good man, and a loving husband, I wager," Eleanor said, looking at him desperately. "Surely you can understand a person's need for affection, even if it's obtained from the wrong quarter."

Daniel recalled his own loneliness after Sarah had withdrawn from him after Felix's death. He could understand the need for affection only too well, but he could hardly question Elijah Gordon about the murder without mentioning his wife's infidelity.

"Please, Inspector," Eleanor pleaded. She placed her hand on his forearm and looked into his face, her eyes shimmering with tears. Daniel knew it wasn't the love of her husband she feared losing, but her home and comfortable lifestyle. If Elijah decided to sue her for divorce, she'd be ruined and utterly disgraced. She'd likely never see her daughter or meet her grandchild.

"I'll see what I can do," Daniel muttered, and fled. He could easily see why Frank Darrow had chosen Eleanor over his own wife. Eleanor was a sensual and persuasive woman, but if she was right, then Frank had found a new love and, quite possibly, a new enemy.

Daniel had every intention of speaking to Elijah Gordon before continuing to Brentwood but changed his mind when he saw the man lumbering toward the outdoor privy. Elijah would most certainly have the strength to hold Frank down, but not to hoist him up on the wheel, not unless he had help. Frank had been at least a head taller than Elijah and as muscular as a pugilist. Elijah's girth would make it nearly impossible for him to climb onto the wheel, especially with a dead body in tow. Even if he knew of the affair between Frank and his wife, Daniel couldn't see Elijah Gordon choosing that method of murder. It'd have been much easier to knock Frank over the head and stuff him into a barrel, which could then be disposed of in various ways, such as dropping it into the river and letting it float away. By the time the body was discovered, no one would think to question Elijah Gordon.

Did he mark his barrels with some sort of symbol? If he didn't, then no one would be able to connect the barrel to him. And if he did, that was still not evidence, since anyone in Essex might have purchased a barrel crafted by Elijah Gordon.

Deciding to leave the conversation with the cooper for another day, Daniel drove into Brentwood. It was a beehive of activity. Numerous wagons clogged the streets as they made last-minute deliveries, and costermongers screamed themselves hoarse as they tried to dispose of their stock before the onset of the holiday. Daniel spotted several girls with trays slung around their necks, selling oranges and packets of sugarplums. The girls' noses were red, and their fingerless gloves revealed fingers that were bluish with cold. They must have been out there for hours already, starting as soon as the sun came up, their scuffed boots and threadbare shawls not nearly warm enough to keep the elements at bay.

Daniel stopped and purchased four oranges and two packets of sugarplums. The girls wished him a happy Christmas and walked off, their shoulders hunched beneath the weight of their trays. Daniel stowed his purchases under the seat and continued toward the address Sergeant Flint had written down for him.

Mr. Adler's house was on the outskirts of town, the red-brick Georgian mansion a quiet testament to prosperity. Despite its attractive façade, it had that look of neglect houses often got when their owners went away, leaving the windows to stare blankly at the street. The doors to the carriage house were firmly shut, and the curtains were drawn in the upper-story windows, giving the house a secretive appearance.

Daniel took himself to the servants' entrance and knocked. He was admitted by Mr. Grills himself, a thin, distinguished-looking man in his sixties whose erect posture and narrow-eyed gaze bespoke years in the army. The man was assessing the situation, much as Daniel was assessing him. Daniel introduced himself and showed his newly minted warrant card.

"Mr. Grills, I'd like to ask you a few questions about the break-in you reported."

"Of course, sir. Right this way," the butler said, and led Daniel to the butler's pantry, where he offered him the guest chair.

Daniel sat down and studied the neat rows of ledgers arranged on dustless shelves. This man was a pedant if he'd ever seen one, and pedants made the best witnesses.

"Can you tell me what happened on the night of December fourteenth?" Daniel asked, settling more comfortably in the stiff-backed cane chair.

"Of course. It had been a quiet day, what with the family away for a fortnight, so I gave the staff the evening off and locked up for the night. The servants' quarters are upstairs, but I have a room on the ground floor, on account of my dodgy knee." He smiled sadly, acknowledging his infirmity.

"You were in the military, if I'm not mistaken," Daniel said.

"Fought at Waterloo," Mr. Grills said proudly. "I was hardly more than a boy then. Saw the great man himself from afar. He was a sight to behold, Lord Wellington," Mr. Grills reminisced, his eyes clouding with memory. "I remained in the army for more than a decade after that but was discharged after taking a cudgel to the knee during a revolt in Sadiya."

Daniel nodded, mentally adjusting the man's age. If Mr. Grills had fought at Waterloo in 1815, he was probably somewhat older than Daniel had first assumed. "Please, go on," Daniel invited.

"It was around eleven when I heard a noise. I'm a light sleeper, you see. Any noise will wake me. I lay quietly, listening. It sounded like footsteps. Now, naturally, I assumed it was one of the maids going down for a cup of water or warm milk, but the steps seemed to be going toward the dining room. I didn't bother to light a candle—I see quite well in the dark—and went to investigate. I heard the clinking of metal coming from the dining room and rightly assumed that someone had got at the silver, so I grabbed a poker from the drawing room and crept up on the intruder. He had a sack laid out on the dining room table and was filling it with the family silver. He spun around when he heard me coming and grabbed one of the knives before lunging at me. I had the advantage over him, what with the poker in my hands, so I swung it with all my might and brought it down on his thigh."

"Why the thigh?" Daniel asked.

"I didn't wish to kill the man, only to incapacitate him. I thought I'd summon the constable once I had him disarmed."

"What happened then?"

"He let out a howl of pain, grabbed the sack of silver, and bolted toward the window, which was still open. He hurled himself out and hobbled off toward a wagon that had been waiting for him just down the street."

"Can you tell me anything about the man you wounded?"

"He wore a tweed cap pulled low over his eyes, but he was young, that I can say for certain. And thin. It was too dark to make out the color of his hair or eyes, but I don't believe he was fair. He was certainly agile, and quick to react. Had he hesitated for even a few seconds, I would have managed to stop him from getting out the window."

"And the man waiting with the wagon?"

Mr. Grills shook his head. "All I can tell you with any certainty is that he was heavy-set and wore a bowler hat."

"Was there anything in the wagon?"

Mr. Grills thought about that for a moment. "Yes. There was something in the wagon, but it was covered with a blanket or canvas."

"Mr. Grills, whom do you purchase coal for the house from?"

"Our coal?" Mr. Grills asked, confused by the change of subject.

"Yes."

"Graham and Sons."

"And did you have coal delivered on the day of the burglary?" Daniel asked, gratified by the look of understanding on the man's face.

"Yes. Yes, we did."

"And I suppose you had at least one chimney cleaned," Daniel continued, watching the man's face.

"Yes. The chimney in the library was smoking, and the master spends much of his time in there, so I instructed the man to clean that chimney immediately. The rest would be done at a later date, since they didn't have time to clean all the chimneys at once."

"How close is the library to the dining room?" Daniel asked.

"Just down the corridor."

119

"And do you know the name of the man who cleaned the chimney in the library?"

"I never thought to ask."

"Was he alone?"

"No. There were two lads with him. One of them stayed with the wagon while the other went up on the roof. Are you suggesting they were involved in the break-in?"

"I'm not suggesting it, Mr. Grills, I'm saying it straight out."

"But you haven't got them?" the butler asked.

"I'm afraid not, but your account has been most helpful as it confirms what I'd already suspected."

Mr. Grills looked disappointed. "What am I to tell Mr. Adler when he returns?"

"You are to tell him that the police are doing all they can to apprehend the intruders."

"I'm sure he'll be pleased to hear that, but what about the stolen silver?" Mr. Grills asked as he rose to his feet.

Daniel shook his head. "I'm sorry, Mr. Grills, but given that the break-in took place ten days ago, it's sure to have been disposed of by now."

"There were several items of great sentimental value taken," the butler persisted.

"I understand, and I really am sorry, but I doubt they can be retrieved at this stage."

"I see. Well, I have much to be getting on with, Inspector," Mr. Grills said, clearly upset.

"Of course. Thank you for your time, Mr. Grills."

Daniel stepped back outside and walked toward his cart, lost in thought. Mr. Grills certainly was a 'clever old sod,' as Sergeant Flint had described him, but not clever enough to have stopped the thief from getting away with the silver. Had he aimed for the man's head or stomach, the intruder would be in custody now. Or dead. But Mr. Grills' story supported Daniel's theory that Frank Darrow had cased the houses while cleaning the chimneys and left a window unlatched for whoever had carried out the burglary. Mr. Grills had said that the man had been young and thin. He could easily have been one of the Darrow boys, except that Daniel had seen them only yesterday and neither one had been injured. However, it was now ten days since the break-in, enough time for the injury to heal if it was superficial.

Mr. Grills had said the man driving the wagon had been heavy-set. Daniel wouldn't call Frank Darrow heavy-set exactly, but he had been a big man, and if he were sitting in a hunched position on the bench of the wagon, he might appear heavy-set to someone who was looking out the window. *Yes*, Daniel thought, excited that things were finally falling into place. Frank Darrow and his sons were responsible for the spate of burglaries, and Dickie Stokes had lied when he'd said Frank had only small items to dispose of. A sack of silver was hardly insignificant and would fetch a lot of dosh for both the thief and the duffer.

Unless, Daniel thought as he climbed into the cart, Frank and his accomplices were disposing of their ill-gotten gains through someone else, and Frank, being too cocky to worry about the fallout, had taken some items for himself and sold them through Dickie without his partners' knowledge. But if Frank had been using his sons to handle the actual break-in, that would mean that they had been his accomplices and might have killed him if their arrangement had gone sour. Daniel climbed back out and returned to the servants' entrance.

"Did you forget something, Inspector?" Mr. Grills asked as he opened the door.

"Mr. Grills, how hard did you hit the intruder with the poker?"

"I swung it with both hands and used all my strength to bring it down on the man's leg."

"Do you think you might have broken his leg?"

"I didn't hear a crack, but I know I drew blood. There was blood on the floor and the carpet and all over the windowsill and even down the wall. The maids weren't happy with having to clean it up."

"Having been in the army, I assume you have seen many a wounded man. Would you say the wound would have healed by now?"

Mr. Grills looked thoughtful, then shook his head. "Not completely. There would be bruising left, at the very least."

"And which leg did you say you'd hit him on?" Daniel asked.

"The right. I struck his right leg."

"Thank you, Mr. Grills. I won't be troubling you again today."

"You are most welcome, Inspector," Mr. Grills said, a genuine smile tugging at the corners of his mouth.

"Do you find something amusing?" Daniel asked, confused by the man's reaction.

"I'm just pleased they've finally hired someone with a bit of sense. You'll go far, Inspector. I always know an ambitious man when I see one."

"Why, thank you," Daniel said. He felt uncomfortably warm despite the chill of the day. "That's kind of you to say. Good day."

Daniel tipped his hat to the man and left. Again. There was only one way to prove that the Darrow boys were involved. Daniel climbed into the cart and headed toward the police station. The Darrows would be at work today but could be tracked down easily enough with the help of Robert Graham. If one of them had a fresh bruise on his right thigh, then he was the one Mr. Grills had assailed, which would in turn prove that the Darrows had been involved in the burglaries, right alongside their father. Even if they hadn't killed him themselves, they were sure to know who had.

Having explained the situation to Detective Inspector Coleridge, Daniel left his office and approached the front desk. Sergeant Flint was on duty again, his moustache twitching as he chewed a glob of tobacco.

"Sergeant, I am in need of a constable. Detective Inspector Coleridge has authorized the request."

"Pullman," Sergeant Flint hollered.

Constable Pullman emerged from a side room, where he'd no doubt been having his midday meal.

"You're with Inspector Haze."

"Yes, sir," Pullman said, his eyes lighting with excitement. "Is it another murder, sir?"

"No. I just need backup in case my hunch is correct, and the suspect tries to flee or fight his way out."

"I have my truncheon, sir," Constable Pullman said. He nipped into the other room and returned with his helmet. "Ready when you are, sir."

Chapter 21

The offices of Graham and Sons Coal Dispensary were quiet; several clerks were bent over ledgers, their faces pasty in the sunlight pouring through the window. There was no festive spirit here, only the scratching of nibs against paper.

"Can I help you, sir?" a middle-aged man with gray hair parted in the middle and whiskers to match asked Daniel as soon as he entered.

Daniel introduced himself and showed his warrant card. "I need to have a word with James and William Darrow. Where might I find them, Mr…eh?"

"Mr. Rippon, at your service," the older man replied. "I'm sorry, but I wouldn't know where the delivery wagons are. This office handles the clerical aspect of the business. You'd need to visit our distribution facility outside of town. That's where the wagons are loaded."

Mr. Rippon gave Daniel directions, wished him a pleasant day, and sent him on his way. Daniel climbed in next to Constable Pullman and they set off, with the constable now driving the cart. Daniel rubbed his hands together. His fingers were stiff despite the leather gloves he wore, and his feet were numb with cold. He inwardly congratulated himself on remembering to don his long woolen underwear. Thankfully, it wasn't a long ride. The distribution facility, which was nothing more than an ambitious name for the stone barn they found themselves in front of, was surprisingly close to the Pump House, where he'd visited Dickie Stokes only two days before.

Mere coincidence or a clue? Daniel wondered as he alighted. Surely Robert Graham wasn't in business with the likes of Dickie Stokes, but anything was possible. He wouldn't be the first legitimate businessman to dabble in prostitution or narcotics. Daniel couldn't be sure, having never been involved in either himself, but he imagined there was more money to be made in selling women or feeding someone's opium habit than purchasing coal from mines, bringing it to one's distribution center, then delivering it to individual customers. But then, people always needed more coal. They needed to keep warm more than they needed to lose themselves in the oblivion of the pipe. Or did they? And how much would someone like Robert Graham make off a sack full of stolen silver?

"What if it's Robert Graham behind the burglaries?" Constable Pullman asked, as if he'd read Daniel's mind.

"You reckon?" Daniel asked, curious to hear what had brought Constable Pullman to that conclusion.

"Well, it's the term *distribution center* that put me on to the idea."

"How so?" Daniel asked.

"Robert Graham can control the chain of distribution," Constable Pullman said. "He supplies the coal and the chimney sweeps, gains access to the house, robs the owners, then disposes of the stolen goods through his own channels, leaving out the middleman."

Daniel considered this scenario. "I would tend to agree with you, Constable, except for two reasons. It was Robert Graham who put us onto the robberies in the first place, and if his customers keep getting burgled, they're more likely to take their business elsewhere, leaving Graham in an unenviable position. As much as I like the notion of Robert Graham controlling this whole enterprise, I don't think he's our man," Daniel said.

"Yeah. You're right, guv. It was just a thought."

The doors to the warehouse were locked, so Daniel walked around the building until he found a side door and knocked. A youngish man with a mop of dark hair and skin darkened by coal dust informed him that Jimmy and Willy Darrow had been sent out to Squire Talbot's manor house just outside the village of Birch Hill to deliver a load of coal. Since there was only one road that led from Brentwood toward Birch Hill, they were sure to come across the wagon as it made its way back from making the delivery. Daniel thanked the man and left the premises, hoping he wouldn't spend the rest of the day chasing after the Darrows. If worse came to worst, he'd find them at home later in the evening. It was Christmas Eve, after all, but he'd hoped to go home himself and spend a few hours with Sarah before attending the midnight service at St. Catherine's.

"Where are we off to, sir?" Constable Pullman asked good-naturedly once Daniel returned to the cart. He seemed thrilled to be out and about instead of spending his day under the watchful eye of Sergeant Flint, who was sure to find something disagreeable for the constable to do, like cleaning the cells or hosing down the mortuary in preparation for its next client.

"Birch Hill," Daniel said as he settled next to the constable, glad Pullman had been the one available to come along rather than Constable Ingleby, who was thin as a reed. Pullman was stocky and solid, the kind of man you wanted by your side in times of trouble. He was fully aware of the purpose of their errand and was raring to go. Daniel had no doubt he'd acquit himself admirably should the Darrows decide to fight, but still felt a twinge of nervousness in his stomach. Desperate people did desperate things, and if James and William Darrow were guilty of their father's murder, they'd be facing the gallows. Given their predicament, they would be prepared to kill in order to escape.

It was nearly forty chilly minutes later that Daniel spotted the wagon coming toward them down the lane. Jimmy and Willy sat on the bench, their caps pulled down low, their eyes fixed on the road. Jimmy elbowed Willy in the ribs when he spotted the dogcart but said nothing, hunching his shoulders instead as if he wished to make himself invisible.

"Good day," Daniel said as the two wagons drew alongside each other. "A word, please."

"Good day, Inspector. Constable," Jimmy said. "Ye'd best make it quick. We 'ave one more delivery to make today, to the Chadwicks."

"Oh? Are they back, then?" Daniel asked conversationally. The Chadwicks had left for London soon after the inquest into the death of Alexander McDougal and had not been back since, presumably enjoying everything that a London Season had to offer despite the recent death of Colonel Chadwick, whose death they'd managed to keep out of the London papers, presumably to avoid the mandatory period of mourning. Were the Darrows scoping out Chadwick Manor for their next hit?

Jimmy shrugged. "Wouldn't know. They 'ave a standing order."

Daniel stored away that bit of information for later and fixed his gaze on Jimmy, who seemed to be the spokesman for the brothers. There was no easy way to ask two men to drop their trousers, especially on a frigid winter's day, but it had to be done, and the sooner the better.

Daniel climbed down from the dogcart and motioned for Constable Pullman to do the same. He reached for the bridle of the Darrows' horse, his other hand on his truncheon.

"What's this 'bout, then?" Jimmy asked, his gaze shifting from Daniel to the constable.

"Jimmy, Willy, I must ask you to drop your trousers," Daniel began.

"Is this some kind of joke?" Willy asked, looking to his brother as if he expected him to laugh.

"I'm afraid not. There's something I need to see, and I would ask you to cooperate," Daniel said. "It's only for a moment."

"Come on, Willy," Jimmy said. "May as well do as 'e asks."

He jumped down from the wagon, followed by Willy. The young men looked uneasy as they unbuttoned their trousers and let them pool around their ankles. Daniel sucked in his breath in frustration. Both sets of thighs were unblemished, the skin pale and sprinkled with coarse dark hair.

"Thank you. You may get dressed."

The brothers pulled up their trousers and buttoned their flies, their wary gazes on Daniel. "Care to explain?" Jimmy asked. He sounded angry, but also curious.

"The man who broke into Mr. Adler's house on December fourteenth was attacked with a poker and would have a wound on his right thigh," Daniel said.

"And ye think it were one of us?" Jimmy asked, his expression one of disbelief.

"Jimmy, your father cleaned the chimney at Mr. Adler's house the day it was broken into. The man seen inside the house was described as young, thin, and dark-haired, wearing a tweed cap. Surely you understand how that sounds."

"Well, that really narrows it down, then, don't it?" Willy scoffed.

Jimmy removed his cap and scratched his head, ruffling his dark hair in the process. "Inspector, I know our word means little to ye, but Willy and I were not in on the scheme. We never broke in to no 'ouses."

"I need your help," Daniel said, trying to sound more like a friend and less like an inspector who'd just made them drop their trousers in the middle of a lane. "I need to figure out why someone would want your father dead, and since you and Willy spent more time with him than anyone else, you might know something that could help lead me to his killer. If you were not his accomplices, then someone else was, and it is my theory that your father did something to upset the balance of that partnership."

"Upset the balance of that partnership," Jimmy repeated, imitating Daniel's tone perfectly. "How posh ye make it sound."

Daniel could hear the derision in Jimmy's voice but didn't rise to the bait. "You are the only people who might hold the key to this mystery. Surely you want your father's killer brought to justice."

"'Course we do," Willy exclaimed.

"We're happy to 'elp, Inspector," Jimmy said, clearly resigning himself to answering more questions. "Ask us anything, but do it while we're sitting in the wagon. My feet are frozen."

"Of course," Daniel conceded.

The two men resumed their seats and watched Daniel, waiting for him to begin.

"Was there anyone who might have held a grudge against your father? Anyone at all?"

Jimmy looked thoughtful for a moment, while Willy turned to his brother, as if waiting for guidance. "Mr. Graham was none too pleased with 'im," Jimmy said. "On account of the thieving and all, but 'e'd hardly kill 'im. All 'e 'ad to do was turn 'im over to the police."

"Why didn't he?" Daniel asked, interested in Jimmy's take on the situation.

"'E 'ad no proof," Jimmy replied. "Things 'ad gone missing. Little things. Who's to say they wasn't misplaced or broken by the maids? Who's to say they weren't discreetly sold to pay off a debt? Who's to say they'd been there at all?" Jimmy sounded convincing enough when he presented his argument, but Daniel could sense his distaste for the subject.

"Do you think Mr. Graham fabricated a charge against your father?"

"No, 'e didn't fabricate it, as ye put it. Da were thieving; we told ye as much. All's I'm saying is that Mr. Graham 'ad no proof."

"Your father was casing houses in the course of his duties. Who would he have passed the information on to?" Daniel asked, feeling desperate. He'd asked similar questions before, and the brothers had given him nothing to go on.

"Look, guv, as we've already told ye, Da wasn't a friendly sort of cove. 'E trusted no one," Jimmy said.

"Except Elijah Gordon," Willy piped in. "'E said 'e would 'ave trusted Elijah with 'is life."

Daniel grew still. They kept coming back to Elijah Gordon. Elijah, the lifelong friend. Elijah, the cuckolded husband. Elijah, the heavyset man whose apprentice had clearly been in pain the last time Daniel had seen him. Elijah, whose anger may have

129

boiled over, especially if Frank had done something to cheat him financially after helping himself to Elijah's wife.

"Could Elijah Gordon have been his accomplice?" Daniel asked softly.

"Why would 'e bother?" Willy asked, rolling his eyes. "Elijah does a thriving trade. 'E delivers his barrels all over God's green earth. 'E goes to London at least once a month, don't 'e, Jimmy. 'As customers at the London breweries and the docks."

Daniel considered this for a moment. What better way to transport stolen goods than to hide them in a shipment of barrels, and then dispose of them once in London? No one would ever trace the stolen items to a barrel-maker from Essex. Not when there were so many thieves in London.

"Had you noticed a change for the better in your father's fortunes?" Daniel asked.

"'Course we 'ad. 'E were flush these past few months, but 'e blew all 'is ill-gotten gains on 'imself. Never bought a new bonnet for Ma or a length o' muslin for Kitty. Poor girl never 'ad a new dress in 'er life. Always wore Ma's hand-me-downs." Jimmy's resentment was palpable, but Daniel could understand his anger. He held his father responsible for their reduced circumstances.

"Jimmy, would Elijah Gordon have what it takes to murder a man?" Daniel asked, feeling foolish for even putting the question to him, but Jimmy had known Elijah all his life, and he was a shrewd young man.

"'Course 'e would, 'specially if 'e knew Da had been popping 'is wife."

"You knew about that?" Daniel asked, shocked.

Jimmy shrugged. "She's a comely piece, Mrs. Gordon is. Dad were always saying 'ow she were charming and elegant, unlike Ma, who's like a sack of coal."

"That was cruel," Daniel said, unable to control his anger.

"'E were a cruel man," Willy said. "A tight-fisted sod, and a debau—"

"Shut up, Will," Jimmy hissed.

"Why?" Willy asked, looking perplexed. "It's the truth. We're free to do as we please now 'e's gone."

"And what is it you want to do?" Daniel asked.

"We're going to go to Liverpool. Sign on with a merchant ship or a passenger liner," Willy said, grinning happily. "See the world. We couldn't leave as long as—"

"As long as we 'ad to support the family," Jimmy cut across his brother. "But now that Kitty's employed and Da's no longer 'round to gamble away our wages, we can go."

"Will your mother and Kitty be all right on their own?" Daniel asked.

"Ma's a thrifty old bird, and Kitty makes a good wage. Lord Redmond, 'e's a generous cove, and surprisingly kind for a toff. I s'pose it's because 'e's American and weren't brought up with a silver spoon in 'is mouth. They'll be just fine, and we'll send 'em money any'ow. We'll look after 'em," Jimmy said defensively. "We always 'ave. 'Specially Kitty." His face softened at the mention of his sister. "We'll make sure she's properly dowered should she wish to wed."

"I'm sure you will," Daniel replied. He reached under the seat of the dogcart and took out a packet of sugarplums. "Happy Christmas."

He wasn't sure why he'd done that, but it felt like the right thing to do.

Jimmy weighed the packet in his hand and nodded in appreciation. "We'll save these for when Kitty comes 'ome on Boxing Day," he said. "She loves sugarplums."

"I like 'em too," Willy said petulantly.

131

"Ye can 'ave one," Jimmy said, giving his brother a grudging smile. "Happy Christmas, Inspector. If ye've no more questions, we must be gettin' on."

"You sure are fearsome, sir," Constable Pullman said as he turned the dogcart around. "Do you give sugarplums to all the suspects?" Daniel smiled sheepishly but didn't reply.

"Where to, then, guv?"

"Back to the station."

The station was quiet, nearly everyone having left for the day, but thankfully, Detective Inspector Coleridge was still in his office, reading a report. A pair of wire-rimmed spectacles were perched on his nose, and his ruddy cheeks were flushed, probably with indignation, if his frown was anything to go by.

Daniel knocked on the doorjamb to announce his presence. "Sir?"

Detective Inspector Coleridge set down the report and removed his spectacles. "What's the word on the Darrows?"

"Not our men, sir, but I would like to pick up Elijah Gordon and his apprentice. I have reason to believe they're behind the burglaries, and by extension, Frank Darrow's death."

"Oh? And you think they're a flight risk?" Detective Inspector Coleridge asked. He was probably eager to get home and spend Christmas Eve with his wife and children.

"Elijah Gordon is more cunning than I gave him credit for, sir, so I wouldn't put it past him. According to the Darrows, he has contacts in London, as well as in other port cities. It would be easy for him to simply disappear, and if he got word that we wish to question him, I've no doubt he'd make himself scarce for a time. If he is our man, then he must have enough dosh stashed away to live on comfortably for a very long time."

"He's got a wife, doesn't he?"

"A wife who'd been carrying on with Frank Darrow for years. I don't think leaving her would be a hardship."

"I see. All right, then. I trust your instincts, Haze."

Daniel turned to go, but DI Coleridge called him back.

"Daniel, go to the Three Bells, and get yourself a hot meal and a drink."

"I was going to go with the men to pick up Gordon and his apprentice."

"The lads will see it done. Your talents will be better utilized once we have those two in custody. Now, go get some dinner. That's an order, Inspector."

"Yes, sir," Daniel replied, smiling despite his desire to argue the point. It was nearly three in the afternoon, and he was hungry.

Daniel waited until Detective Inspector Coleridge gave the order, then took himself off. The Three Bells was a tavern just around the corner from the station. It had a cozy atmosphere and a nice fire burning in the grate. Daniel removed his coat and hat and settled himself at a table by the hearth. The proprietor's lady gave him a friendly smile from behind the bar and sauntered over.

"Well, good afternoon to ye, sir. What will ye be having, just a drink or a meal?"

"Both. What do you recommend?" Daniel asked.

"We have some nice mutton chops with a side of mash and peas and mint jelly. Will that do ye?"

"Oh, yes," Daniel replied, his mouth watering. "I thought you'd be closing early," he said, noting that the dining room and bar were far from empty.

"Oh, no, sir. Why, Christmas Eve and Christmas Day are two of our busiest days. No man wants to be alone on Christmas, and there's many as got no one to be with on the blessed day." She gave him a curious stare, then looked away, not wishing to put him on the spot.

"I'll be at home with my wife tomorrow," Daniel said wistfully. He wished he could be at home with Sarah now, but he'd be damned if someone else took over his investigation, even someone as senior as Detective Inspector Coleridge. He was going to question Elijah Gordon and his lad himself.

"I'll have a half pint of ale," Daniel said. He would normally frown at anyone who drank on the job, but he was tense, his shoulders hunched forward and his jaw clenched. He forced himself to relax and leaned back in his chair, fixing his gaze on the fire in the grate. Watching the orange tongues lick and caress the wood always calmed him, and he felt almost himself by the time his meal and drink arrived. The chops were delicious, and he ate with relish, not knowing what time he'd get home.

The publican's wife returned for his empty plate and nodded in appreciation. "Glad ye liked it, sir. Now, ye stay put. I 'ave something for ye."

She returned a few minutes later with a warm slice of figgy pudding. "I always make a dozen," she said, setting the plate before him. "Enough to go 'round. It's on the 'ouse, sir."

"Thank you," Daniel said, genuinely moved. He consulted his pocket watch. He had time to indulge, since it would be at least another half hour until the constables returned to the station with Elijah Gordon and his apprentice, and the familiar smell of the Christmas pudding was making him feel less alone this Christmas Eve.

Chapter 22

It was nearly an hour later that Sergeant Flint came to get Daniel at the Three Bells. He looked irritable and tired, and no doubt wanted nothing more than to finally go home for the night, but Daniel cared little for his mood. He'd never boxed, not even at a gymnasium, but at the moment, he felt like a boxer getting ready for a match, jumping from foot to foot, throwing practice punches in the air and weighing his opponent with a narrowed gaze to gauge if he might be intimidated. This was his first big case as an inspector, and it would make or break his reputation for the future. Rested and well fed, he was ready to face his opponent.

Detective Inspector Coleridge was just coming out of his office when Daniel returned to the station. He was wearing his hat and coat, the rich fur collar totally at odds with the dimly lit corridor and the faint smell of carbolic that had been used to wash the floor.

"Are you leaving, sir?" Daniel asked, surprised to see him dressed for the outside.

"If I'm not home in time to dine with the family, my wife will be serving my head for our Christmas dinner tomorrow," Detective Inspector Coleridge said good-naturedly. "I have every faith in you, Inspector Haze. Follow your gut. If you believe the men are guilty, charge them and lock 'em in the cells. They can cool their heels until Boxing Day, when we'll offer them the opportunity to seek legal counsel."

"Yes, sir. Thank you, sir," Daniel added, buoyed by the inspector's faith in him.

"Happy Christmas, Daniel," Detective Inspector Coleridge said as he lifted his walking stick from the stand.

"Happy Christmas, sir."

Daniel returned to the front desk. "Did you put the suspects in separate rooms?" he asked the desk sergeant.

"Of course, sir."

"Did they resist arrest?"

"The younger man was frightened, but his employer was calm as you please and told the lad they'd be home in time to attend the midnight service."

"I doubt that, but I admire his optimism," Daniel said. "What's the apprentice's name?"

"Silas Pike, sir. Aged seventeen."

"I'll speak to him first and let Mr. Gordon stew for a bit," Daniel said. "Constable Pullman, I'd like you to be present for the interview."

"Yes, sir," Pullman replied eagerly.

Flint nodded, looking intrigued despite his usual sneer. "Good luck, sir," he called after Daniel as he approached the first interview room.

It was a small, dingy room with a small barred window, in case the suspect decided to try to escape. Silas Pike sat behind the narrow desk, looking as if he'd just sucked on a lemon. Daniel hoped he wasn't going to be sick all over the floor. Constable Pullman must have had the same thought because he disappeared for a moment and returned with a bucket, which he set under the desk. He then took up a position by the door.

Daniel sat down across from the young man and pinned him with a piercing stare. "State your name, age, and occupation," he said once he felt the boy was sufficiently rattled.

"Silas Pike, seventeen, apprentice cooper, sir."

Daniel was glad to see that Sergeant Flint had left a notepad and a pen and ink on the desk. It was always more intimidating to scribble notes while interviewing a suspect, the inspector he'd worked under in London used to say. They'd think you had something on them, and once it was there, in ink, it was an indelible stain against their character. Daniel made a show of writing the information Silas Pike had provided, even though it wasn't that important.

"Silas, how long have you been apprenticed to Mr. Gordon?"

"Since I were fifteen, sir," Silas replied. Up close, he looked even younger than he had at the workshop, where Daniel had taken little notice of him.

"And has Mr. Gordon been good to you?" Daniel asked.

"Oh yes, sir. Mrs. Gordon has been very kind too," he added, blushing to the roots of his hair.

Daniel was taken aback by his reaction but decided to ignore that bit of evidence for the moment. The boy might have developed feelings for his buxom mistress, or perhaps Mrs. Gordon had found someone new to scratch that itch.

"Silas, I will now ask you to stand up slowly and remove your trousers. I need to see your thighs."

Silas blanched, the blush of a few moments ago replaced by a pasty pallor. "What? Why?"

"Please do as I ask. If you refuse to cooperate, Constable Pullman will be happy to assist you."

"No, please," Silas muttered. He stood and began to unbutton his trousers. Daniel waited patiently, watching the boy's hands. They were trembling.

When he finally lowered his trousers, a livid bruise was visible on his right thigh, a dark scab in the center where the blood had congealed and dried to form a thick crust.

"You may put your trousers back on," Daniel said.

Silas yanked his trousers up and slid into his seat. He looked terrified, which pleased Daniel to no end. He hoped Silas would make this easy for him.

"Silas, it is my supposition that you've been helping your employer, Mr. Gordon, to burglarize houses in the Brentwood area. In fact, you received that wound to your leg when Mr. Adler's butler came upon you as you were helping yourself to his employer's silver and struck you with a poker. He also told me that you had attacked him with a knife. That's attempted murder right there, Silas. Know what the penalty for that is?" Daniel didn't elaborate. Silas wouldn't be hanged just for brandishing a knife at a man who'd come at him with a poker, but he didn't know that.

Silas looked like he was about to weep but remained silent, fixing his gaze on his hands, which were clasped on the table.

"If you and Mr. Gordon are charged, Mr. Gordon will hire a lawyer to defend him. Will he do the same for you, especially if you're charged with attempted murder? Or will he simply get himself a new apprentice once he's released?"

The chatter of Silas's teeth filled the quiet that had settled on the room after Daniel posed his question.

"Silas?" Daniel tried again. "Are you willing to die to protect Mr. Gordon?"

Silas shook his head but didn't look up. "I didn't have a choice," he finally muttered. Daniel was surprised to hear that he'd picked up his master's educated pronunciation.

"Didn't you?"

Another shake of the head. "My mother borrowed and scraped to get me an apprenticeship. I wanted to go in for shipbuilding, but she didn't have enough. And I'd be far away from home where I couldn't visit," he added miserably. "My mother is sick. She's got consumption."

Daniel nodded, feeling sorry for the boy. He wondered who was there to take care of his mother and if they might have contracted the disease, but he thought it best not to ask. After all, that wasn't why they were there.

"So, how soon after you started working for Mr. Gordon did he ask you to help him burgle houses?"

"About a year ago. He said he was too big a man to fit through a window, but I was perfect. All I had to do was get in, get the silver, and get out. He didn't ever ask me to go upstairs to search for jewels or other valuables. Just the family silver."

"Why do you think that is?"

"He didn't want us to get caught. There was no one on the ground floor at night. The servants were upstairs, and the owners were away. It was safe enough, as long as I was quiet and got out fast. Also, jewelry is easy to identify," Silas continued, warming up to the topic. "Silver can be melted down or sold on without too much fuss, but a piece of jewelry can be traced to its owner."

"So, what did Mr. Gordon do once you got the silver?"

"He'd hide it in one of his barrels and take it to London. He had a man there who took it all and asked no questions."

"Did you go with him?"

"Sometimes. If there wasn't too much work."

"Would you be able to lead the police to this man's shop?"

Silas nodded. He looked green around the gills, but at this stage, he knew he was better off cooperating. Daniel took a moment to savor his triumph. If his tip-off to Scotland Yard led to an arrest, Daniel would not only earn the respect of Detective Inspector Coleridge, but of the commissioner, whom he had yet to meet.

"Have you met Frank Darrow, Silas?" Daniel asked.

"Yes."

"Did he come by often?"

"Once or twice. He and Mr. Gordon met mostly at the Queen's Arms."

"Did Mr. Darrow and Mr. Gordon get on?"

"They seemed to," Silas replied, clearly surprised by the question.

"So, there was no falling out between them, over the proceeds, say?" Daniel prompted.

"I wouldn't know, sir."

Daniel looked at the quivering young man. He wasn't about to get much more out of him, but he had one last question to pose to him.

"Silas, did you help Mr. Gordon kill Mr. Darrow and hoist him up on the mill wheel?"

Silas's head shot upward, his eyes huge with shock. "No, sir. Mr. Gordon would never do such a thing. He's a greedy bugger, I'll give you that, but he's no killer."

"Sure, are you?" Daniel goaded.

"Yes, I'm sure," Silas said, his tone becoming defiant. "Thieving is one thing, murder something else."

"But you would have killed Mr. Grills had it come down to it," Daniel said.

"No!" Silas cried. "I'd never have killed him. I was only trying to hold him off so I could make my escape. I would have never used the knife."

"So, you think it's wrong to kill, but not to steal," Daniel said, watching the young man squirm.

"Those people we took from have so much; they'd hardly miss their precious silver. They could just buy more."

"Did you get a cut of the profits?" Daniel asked, wondering if the young man had been compensated for taking the risk or simply blackmailed into it.

Silas sighed with resignation. *In for a penny, in for a pound*, Daniel thought as he watched him.

"I used my share to help Mother. She was worried about dying before she paid off the debt, and I wanted to put her mind at rest. At least she'd go in peace when her time came."

"Who takes care of your mother?"

"A widowed neighbor. Mother pays her to come 'round."

Daniel nodded. Silas was hardly a seasoned criminal. He was just a boy who'd been thrust into a bad situation by someone in a position of authority and motivated by his desire to help his mother. All too understandable, but still punishable under the law.

"Please, sir, don't tell Mr. Gordon I grassed on him," Silas pleaded. "He'll skin me alive."

"I doubt he'll get the chance to do that, but I won't tell him if I can help it."

"Thank you, sir. And please don't tell my mother. This'll kill her."

Daniel sighed. Mrs. Pike would no doubt find out what her son had been up to, particularly when the money stopped and she received a letter from prison.

"Constable, take Mr. Pike down to the cells, and then we'll have a crack at Mr. Gordon."

"Yes, sir."

Constable Pullman took Silas away, leaving Daniel to plan his strategy. If Elijah Gordon had never entered the houses, he couldn't be charged with breaking and entering or stealing. He'd made sure of that. The only thing Daniel could pin on him was the disposal of stolen goods, but with a good lawyer, Gordon could probably get a reduced sentence. What Daniel had really wanted was confirmation that Silas had helped Elijah Gordon kill Frank Darrow, but Silas Pike's horror at the suggestion had seemed genuine, and Daniel didn't believe he was that good an actor. Perhaps Elijah had had help from someone else.

"Ready when you are, sir," Constable Pullman said when he returned to the room.

"How's Mr. Pike?"

"Crying like a baby. Is it wrong to feel sorry for him, sir?" Constable Pullman asked.

"I feel sympathy for him as well," Daniel admitted, and collected his notes. "I don't expect we'll feel any pity for Mr. Gordon."

Chapter 23

Elijah Gordon looked surprisingly relaxed for a man who was about to be questioned by the police. He was leaning back in his chair, his bulk spilling over the sides of the seat as he studied his nails with nonchalance. He looked up when Daniel and Constable Pullman entered the room.

"Ah, Inspector, we meet again. And so soon," he added with a sly smile.

"You're in awfully good spirits," Daniel remarked.

"Why shouldn't I be? It's Christmas."

"I don't imagine Christmas in prison is very festive," Daniel said as he took a seat.

"I imagine you're quite right," Gordon agreed. "But what's that got do to with me?"

"Well, it seems you've been keeping busy these last few months. How many houses have you robbed? I know of at least three."

"I make barrels, Inspector Haze. That might seem dull to you, but believe you me, there's a high demand for a well-made barrel. Every brewery, fishery, cannery, you name it, uses barrels. It's a good trade."

"I've no doubt it is, but how many barrels would you have to sell to make the amount of money you would get for a silver set for twelve, I wonder?"

"I really wouldn't know."

"Oh, I think you would. It was clever of you to find yourself a thin, agile apprentice who has an ailing mother."

"Is she ailing? I didn't know," Elijah Gordon answered, shrugging smugly.

"Be that as it may, I have concrete evidence that you were responsible for the break-in at Mr. Adler's house on December fourteenth."

"Do you, now? I doubt that."

"Constable Pullman, organize a search of Mr. Gordon's workshop and residence. Quick as you can, before Mrs. Gordon has an opportunity to dispose of the stuff."

"You won't find anything, Inspector," Elijah Gordon said. "Because there's nothing to find. Even if I were fool enough to burgle those houses, do you honestly think I'd leave the evidence just lying around?"

"I don't know. Would you?" Daniel asked. "You had no reason to suspect I was on to you, so you'd have no reason to hide the stolen goods."

Gordon actually laughed at that, making Daniel want to slap the self-satisfied grin off his face. "I'd like someone to contact my lawyer. Mr. Jonathan Barrett. If you please," he added with mock politeness.

"Mr. Barrett will be informed of your arrest tomorrow. I expect he'll be too busy to come to you on Christmas Day."

"I doubt that. I think he'll have plenty of time for an old friend."

"As you say, Mr. Gordon," Daniel agreed. "Did you and Frank Darrow have a falling out recently?"

"I told you; we were the best of mates."

"Even though he cuckolded you with Eleanor?" Daniel asked, hoping to shock Elijah Gordon, but he failed utterly. The man smiled and shook his head.

"Eleanor can be demanding and clingy. I honestly didn't have much interest in her, not in that way. I found her constant need for affection off-putting. I was glad when she started meeting Frank. She was satisfied, and her contentment made my life easier."

"So, you didn't mind in the least?"

"Not at all."

Daniel studied the man across the table. What kind of man didn't mind his friend helping himself to his wife? Daniel would have been mad with jealousy if he suspected Sarah of infidelity, but Elijah Gordon seemed genuinely unaffected by his wife's betrayal. He didn't fit Daniel's notion of a molly; he expected someone effeminate and flamboyantly dressed, like Shawn Sullivan, but perhaps his marriage to Eleanor was just a sham to cover up his attraction to men. He'd done his husbandly duty long enough to produce a child, then turned away from the marriage bed, leaving Eleanor to seek affection elsewhere. Daniel doubted he'd admit to it if asked outright, since homosexuality was a punishable offense, but if Elijah Gordon was homosexual, then jealously would no longer be a motive for murder.

"Would you have minded if Frank Darrow cheated you out of your share of the proceeds for the stolen goods?" Daniel asked. "Was he helping himself to valuable items and selling them without your knowledge?"

Gordon shrugged. "What Frank did while at work had nothing to do with me."

"Really?"

"Frank has had a hard time of it, Inspector, so if he got a few extra coins in his pocket, I'd be glad of it."

"So, you didn't kill him?"

Elijah Gordon's reaction seemed as genuine as Silas's. "Why on earth would I kill him?"

"Because he'd cheated you."

"Frank Darrow and I had no financial dealings, so he couldn't have cheated me, and I already told you I didn't mind about my wife. He was welcome to her."

To his chagrin, Daniel believed him. He hoped the search would back up his assumptions and produce concrete evidence but held out little hope. The man was too clever by half. He'd never leave stolen silver lying around, especially not ten days after the robbery. Those pieces were long gone.

"Happy Christmas, Inspector," Elijah Gordon said cheerily as he was led away toward the cells. "I expect we'll be spending it together."

Not if I can help it, Daniel thought wryly. He collected his notes, closed the inkwell, and got to his feet. He was going home.

Chapter 24

"So, what are we doing for Christmas?" Cecilia asked. She sat across from Jason in the chair Daniel Haze normally occupied when he came to call, watching Jason from beneath her lashes.

"We'll have Christmas lunch," Jason replied noncommittally. "I'm sure Mrs. Dodson will make it a special occasion."

"I'd like to go to the service," Cecilia said. "Don't you insist that Micah attend church?"

"Micah is Catholic. He will attend Mass with Mr. Sullivan."

"Really, Jason. I can't believe you permit such division in your household," Cecilia said haughtily.

"What would you suggest?" Jason asked.

"If Micah is to reside with you for the duration, then he should attend the same church you do."

"I don't agree," Jason said, his voice flat. Cecilia was grating on him. He used to find her opinions refreshing, daring even, but in this instance, she was interfering in matters that were none of her concern. Jason would never demand that Micah abandon the religion he'd grown up with and attend a Protestant church.

Jason glanced toward the window, hoping against hope to see the outline of a carriage making its way up the drive. Where was Mary? What had happened to her? And what was he to do if she failed to turn up? Daniel had been correct in suggesting that the vessel might have been delayed. There were winter gales and currents that could set the arrival date back by a week or more. Jason refused to consider the alternative. There had been no mention of lost ships in the papers; he'd checked. Of course, news of a tragedy might not have reached Liverpool yet. The worst could still happen.

If Mary didn't arrive by the new year, he'd go to Liverpool and inquire at every shipping office, demanding to see their passenger manifests. If he could be sure that Mary had arrived in England, then he could mount a search for her, not that he'd even know where to begin. He supposed he'd have to check with every livery in the area to see if Mary had tried to hire a carriage to bring her to Redmond Hall. Perhaps she'd had the address wrong and went to a different part of the country. He supposed that was possible.

"Penny for your thoughts," Cecilia said coyly. "You seem very preoccupied."

"It's nothing," Jason replied. He had no wish to tell Cecilia about Mary, or anything else that was on his mind. He'd planned to attend the Christmas service just to see Katherine, but if Cecilia were to go with him, he wouldn't have the opportunity to speak to her privately. And he could hardly forbid Cecilia to go to church. Perhaps she'd find it helpful at this difficult time.

Jason cast a sidelong glance at his former fiancée. Despite her loss, Cecilia wasn't wearing black, or even shades of purple. She wore a beautiful silk gown in a rich shade of claret, a hue that went well with her dark coloring. Her full lips were pink, and there was a bloom in her cheeks that hadn't been there when she arrived. Jason looked closer. She was wearing rouge, he realized, on her lips and cheeks. Was it because she was trying to disguise her pallor or because she thought it would make her more attractive to him? And why wasn't she wearing mourning attire? It had been only four months since her husband and son had died. Surely, they deserved that little bit of respect.

"Cecilia, what are your plans?" he asked. He hadn't meant to broach the subject today, but the words spilled out unbidden.

"How do you mean?" Cecilia asked, her eyes widening in confusion.

"I mean, what do you plan to do after you leave here?"

Cecilia momentarily looked away, her blush deepening naturally this time. "I don't know," she whispered. "I think that rather depends on you."

"Does it?"

"Oh, Jason, please, don't make me spell it out," Cecilia cried.

"I think you had better," Jason replied. He hadn't been gunning for an argument, but now was as good a time as any to have this conversation. The one thing that was sure to make him lose his temper was the knowledge that he was being manipulated, and he was in no doubt that Cecilia had planned her whole trip solely for the purpose of stopping off at his new home.

"Miss Talbot," Dodson announced as he entered the drawing room.

Jason sprang to his feet, eager to speak to Katherine before she entered the drawing room, but Katherine was already there, her bonnet peeking from behind Dodson's shoulder. Jason groaned inwardly, wishing he'd had a chance to explain.

"Good afternoon, Miss Talbot," Jason said with exaggerated formality.

"Captain, I—" Katherine never finished the sentence. Her eyes widened in surprise and her cheeks reddened with embarrassment. "I'm sorry. I didn't realize you had company."

"Miss Talbot, may I present Mrs. Baxter. She's a friend from New York." Jason fervently hoped Katherine wouldn't make the connection between Mrs. Baxter and the woman he'd been engaged to, but his hopes were dashed when he saw realization dawning in Katherine's eyes.

"Mrs. Baxter, it's a pleasure to make your acquaintance," she said, her voice catching.

"Likewise, Miss Talbot. Jason has told me much of your good works. I do admire a woman who dedicates herself to the well-being of others," Cecilia said, smiling graciously.

Coming from someone other than Cecilia and delivered in a different tone, this statement may have been taken as a compliment, but Cecilia had meant to belittle, and her words had found their mark.

"I do what I can," Katherine said softly.

"And what is that you've brought for the captain?" Cecilia asked, studying Katherine as if she were an amusing distraction.

Katherine had been clutching two paper-wrapped parcels beneath her arm, but now she looked at them as if she'd forgotten they were there.

"I wager these are Christmas gifts," Cecilia exclaimed, clapping her hands. "How charming. Jason, did you get a gift for Miss Talbot?" Jason glared at her, but she ignored him. "Do show us, Miss Talbot. I hate to be kept in suspense."

"Cecilia," Jason said in a warning tone, but it was exactly the wrong thing to do. Katherine's head snapped up at the use of Cecilia's Christian name, and she backed away, clearly mortified.

"I'm sorry to have intruded," Katherine muttered. "Please, give this to Micah for me. I thought he might enjoy it. I ordered it from London," she added in a whisper. She didn't mention the second package, which must have been for Jason.

"That's very kind of you," Jason said with feeling. "Perhaps you'd like to give it to him yourself," he suggested.

"No, I really must be going. Father has organized caroling for this evening."

Cecilia clapped her hands. "How quaint. Will you be coming by? Jason, tell Miss Talbot they must come to Redmond Hall. I simply must hear you sing."

"We're going to the village," Katherine muttered.

"Nonsense. You must come here. Why, it's practically your duty to show us Americans how Christmas is done in an English village," Cecilia persisted.

"I'm sure it's not that different," Katherine replied, looking to Jason for help.

"Well, perhaps we'll go to the village. Jason, what do you say? We can even walk. Do you remember how we used to like walking in the snow? We had that snowball fight in Washington

Square Park." Her eyes danced with merriment. She was amusing herself at Katherine's expense and enjoying every minute.

"Have a pleasant evening." Katherine shoved the two packages into Jason's hands and fled, leaving Cecilia to smile after her triumphantly.

"Did you have to be so insufferable?" Jason demanded, turning on her as soon as he heard the door close behind Katherine.

"How was I insufferable?" Cecilia asked innocently. "It's not my fault she's such a mouse. My, how your tastes have changed. You used to have spirit, Jason Redmond."

"And you used to have breeding," Jason snapped.

Cecilia rose to her feet and fluffed out her skirts, looking at Jason as if he'd just wounded her gravely. "I think you need some time to yourself. You're obviously in a bad temper. Perhaps Miss Talbot's little gift will cheer you up."

She swept from the room, leaving Jason feeling angry and frustrated, mostly with himself for allowing Cecilia to seize control of the situation. She was carrying on as if they were a married couple, not two people who'd once been promised to each other but now had nothing further to talk about. His obvious displeasure was doing nothing to drive her away. If anything, she seemed even more determined to stay. Mrs. Dodson had advised him to do what he wished, but he couldn't bring himself to ask Cecilia to leave. His father had taught him to be respectful and kind, and never to humiliate a woman intentionally, not even in private. He'd want Jason to be chivalrous and to put his feelings aside in Cecilia's time of need.

But what of Katherine's need? Jason thought of going after her but didn't give in to the impulse. Anything he said to her now would only further embarrass her, and he had no wish to do that. Instead, he picked up the packages he'd set on the side table and made his way to the top floor, where Micah and Shawn Sullivan were in the midst of a geography lesson.

"I'm sorry to interrupt," Jason said as he entered the schoolroom.

"It's quite all right. We're finished," Mr. Sullivan said as he replaced the globe on its shelf and closed the book he'd been using for the lesson. "I think it's safe to say that Micah has no interest in the Byzantine Empire."

Micah scoffed but didn't comment. "What's that?" he asked, spotting the packages beneath Jason's arm.

"Miss Talbot brought this for you." He held out Micah's parcel and waited as Micah carefully undid the wrapping and extracted a book.

"*The Adventures of Alice in Wonderland*," he read. He made a face. "Is this for girls?"

"Oh, I've heard about that book," Mr. Sullivan interjected. "It's quite a story. You'll love it, Micah."

"Will I?" Micah asked, sounding dubious.

"Oh, yes. It's a magical tale."

Micah still looked unconvinced. The pages were uncut, so he reached for the book knife and cut the first few pages, leafing through them carefully until he came to an illustration. He bent his head, studying the drawing of a giant caterpillar smoking a pipe. "Well, this is odd," he mumbled, but his attention was engaged.

"I think you should write to Miss Talbot and thank her," Jason suggested gently.

"Okay," Micah said.

"We don't say 'okay.' We say 'yes, sir,' or 'yes, Captain,'" Mr. Sullivan corrected him.

Micah gave him a disdainful look. "Okay," he said again, frustrating the poor man.

"It's all right, Mr. Sullivan. Micah is just being contrary."

"I am not!"

"You are. Now, how about a game of chess?" Jason asked. "I think Mr. Sullivan has earned a break."

"Fine. I'll give you a game," Micah agreed, but his gaze strayed toward the book.

"If you'd rather read—"

"I'll save it for later," Micah said. "What's in the other package?"

"I don't know."

Jason unwrapped the second package to find a tin of mince pies. He was sure Katherine had baked them herself, possibly just for him. It would have been inappropriate to give him a gift, and this was as close as she could come without bending the rules of propriety.

"Can I have one?" Micah asked, peering into the tin.

Jason held out the tin, and Micah helped himself to a pie. "Mr. Sullivan, please have one," Jason invited.

Shawn Sullivan looked as if he were about to refuse but changed his mind and helped himself. "This is wonderful," he said as soon as he swallowed the first bite. "Made with love," he added sheepishly.

Jason felt his cheeks grow warm, so he fixed his attention on the pies. Mrs. Dodson had made a batch just that morning, but he hadn't tasted them yet. In fact, he'd never had a mince pie before and wasn't at all sure what to expect.

"Mm," he said after taking a bite. "Delicious."

Micah gave him a knowing smile. "Come. Let's have that game," he said. "Perhaps you can write a note to thank Miss Talbot," he added cheekily. "Or maybe you can thank her in person."

Jason set the tin of pies aside and followed Micah downstairs, leaving Mr. Sullivan to tidy up the classroom. Jason had offered him time off for Christmas, should he wish to visit his family in Dublin or perhaps see a friend closer to home, but Mr. Sullivan had politely refused. He seemed to be a lonely and isolated young man, and Jason felt sympathy toward him. Life couldn't be easy for him, especially in a remote village where he had no companionship aside from Micah and Jason, who did his best to make him feel like a part of the family.

Once in the library, Jason and Micah settled before the chess table, each taking his usual seat. Micah rearranged the pieces to his satisfaction, even though they had already been set out, and made the first move. He seemed pensive, his blue gaze anxious.

"Something on your mind?" Jason asked as his hand hovered above a black pawn.

"Why did you want to marry her?" he asked. Jason had no need to ask whom he was referring to.

"I was young. And foolish," Jason added, although he hadn't been that young. He'd been twenty-four to Cecilia's twenty when he'd proposed to her. "I suppose I was a different person then, and different things were important to me."

"She's what my pa would call a *bitseach*."

"And what might that be?" Jason asked, although he had a pretty good idea.

"It's the type of woman who'd pretend not to see a starving child or a cripple, but wrinkle her nose all the same, so as to make them feel even worse. She's someone who'd call me a mick, as if being Irish makes me worse than dirt on her shoe."

"Has she called you a mick?" Jason demanded.

"No, but she's said stuff about Mr. Sullivan," Micah muttered under his breath.

"What sort of stuff?"

"She called him a disgusting molly when speaking to Fanny. What's a molly?"

Jason sighed. He didn't want to have to explain to Micah that Shawn Sullivan was homosexual, but perhaps it was better if he knew. "A molly is a derogatory term for a man who prefers men to women," Jason said.

Micah stared at him, uncomprehending. "Prefers them for what?"

"For love."

Micah's brows furrowed in confusion. "I don't understand."

"Micah, Mr. Sullivan is a good man and a competent tutor, and I trust him. That's all you need to know."

Micah nodded. "I used to want to grow up," he said, his hands folded in his lap as if he had lost interest in the game. "I thought it'd be grand to be my own master and do as I pleased."

"And now?"

"And now, I think being grown up is not so easy. Nothing is what it seems, and people are not who they claim to be."

"Some people are."

Micah shrugged in response and reached for his knight. It seemed he no longer wanted to talk.

Chapter 25

Jason had considered attending the Midnight Mass but changed his mind after Katherine's visit. He had no desire to spend any more time with Cecilia than necessary, nor did he wish to come face to face with Katherine when he was in no position to speak to her openly. Instead, he retired close to eleven and turned out the lamp, looking at the starry sky as he lay in bed, his arms folded behind his head.

Strange how life works, Jason thought as he gazed into the face of the nearly full moon. He'd never expected to still be in England come December. He'd only meant to stay for as long as it took to dispose of his grandfather's estate. And here he was, nearly seven months later, weak with longing for Katherine Talbot, assisting the Essex police, and playing at being an amateur sleuth. All in all, a definite improvement on last year, Jason decided. He hadn't thought he'd ever feel at peace again after what he'd seen on the battlefields of the Civil War, nor had he thought he'd recover from Cecilia's betrayal, but he had. The nightmares had subsided, a new love had been kindled in his heart, and he felt a sense of purpose he'd lacked since returning home to New York after the war years. Life went on, and he was ready to look to the future.

Jason closed his eyes as his body relaxed, the tension flowing out of him as he breathed deeply, allowing his mind to wander as it succumbed to sleep. He wasn't sure if he'd been asleep for mere minutes or hours when the door to his bedroom flew open and the light of a single candle shone in his face.

"Captain! Captain, wake up!" Fanny cried. "Please, come quick!"

"What is it?" Jason asked as he exploded out of bed. "Is it Micah?"

"No. It's Kitty. Please, come."

Jason pulled on his trousers and shirt and ran after Fanny, his bare feet slapping against the wooden floor. She led the way to the upper floor, her candle casting strange shadows on the whitewashed walls.

"Fanny, tell me what happened," Jason demanded.

"I was getting ready to leave for the midnight service. Kitty said she didn't want to come. She 'adn't felt well earlier and decided to go to bed. When I passed 'er door, I 'eard 'er crying. She sounded like she was in pain."

Fanny didn't have time to tell him the rest. They'd reached the landing where Mrs. Dodson and Henley were standing outside Kitty's door, their faces tight with worry. Mrs. Dodson was wearing her Sunday best, her bonnet obscuring part of her face, while Henley clutched his bowler in his hands, staring at Kitty's door as if he could see right through it. His coat was still buttoned.

"We were just about to leave when we heard Fanny calling," Mrs. Dodson said. "Dodson's downstairs," she added to explain her husband's absence.

Kitty's agonized cries filled the dim corridor. Jason knocked on the door and called out, "Kitty, I'm coming in."

The room was dark aside from the moonlight streaming through the dormer window. Jason set the candle he'd taken from Fanny on the bedside cabinet. Kitty was lying on the bed, curled into a fetal position, her forehead pressed to her knees. She was moaning and shivering, and when she looked up, her eyes were glazed with pain. Jason closed the door behind him to block out the curious stares of the other servants and sat down on the side of the bed. Kitty let out a desperate cry and buried her face in her hands.

"Kitty, look at me," Jason said as he pressed his hand to her forehead. She wasn't fevered. Her skin was clammy and cold, her lips bluish in the light of the candle.

"Kitty," Jason tried again. "Tell me where it hurts."

"Stomach," Kitty whispered hoarsely. "It hurts so bad."

"I need to examine you."

"No. Please," Kitty cried desperately. "Please, don't touch me." Her fear was palpable, so Jason drew his hand away, not wishing to upset her.

"Kitty, I'm not going to hurt you," he assured her. "I only want to make sure you don't have an inflamed appendix."

"I don't," Kitty hissed through clenched teeth.

"It feels just like a stomachache," Jason tried to explain. "But it can be quite serious."

"Please, let me be," Kitty moaned, her desperation mounting.

"Kitty, I can't leave you like this. Please, let me help."

Kitty shook her head. Jason could see her throat working as she tried to get a handle on her pain, which had to be extreme. He was just about to try to reason with her again when she drew her legs up even higher and let out a low and urgent cry. It seemed to come from someplace deep inside her, and brought unbidden memories of men who'd been torn apart by cannon fire, their bodies in unbearable agony before shock set in. Kitty's cry went on and on, her whole body convulsing as she wrapped her arms about her middle as if she were trying to hold herself together. And then, Jason felt something hot and sticky through the leg of his trousers. He jumped up and pulled back the blanket that had been covering Kitty's legs. Thick, dark blood was pooling beneath her hips.

"Dear God," Jason muttered as he looked on helplessly.

Kitty was shaking now, her lips clamped together as she tried to stifle the screams. Jason grabbed a towel that hung on the back of the door and quickly wrapped up the fetus that had slid out onto the blood-soaked mattress. He was about to check for signs of life when Fanny burst in with his bag, panting with the effort of running up the steep stairs. Jason blocked the child from view, hoping Fanny hadn't already seen it. Mrs. Dodson and Henley peered into the room, and Jason saw Dodson's pale face, and Cecilia's angry one, her arms crossed in front of her defensively. Thankfully, Micah was still in his room, hopefully, fast asleep.

"What's going on?" Cecilia demanded as she pushed her way to the front and tried to enter the room.

"Get out," Jason snapped.

Cecilia opened her mouth to protest, but he shut the door in her face.

Jason turned back to the bed and looked down at the severely premature child, his eyes stinging with tears. It was still alive, if only just, its narrow chest rising and falling as it struggled for breath. Its eyes were tightly shut, and its hands balled into fists. Jason leaned against the door to make sure no one came in and closed his eyes for a moment, desperate to block out the devastating scene. There was nothing he could do as a medical man to keep that baby alive. Given its size and stage of development, he'd say it was a twenty- to twenty-two-week fetus. It stood no chance of survival and the sooner it died, the better off it would be. And given the way Kitty had looked at him when she'd birthed it, he was sure she didn't want it to live.

Jason took a deep breath and opened his eyes, ready to deal with the aftermath of Kitty's miscarriage. She was still moaning and shaking, but seemed calmer now, her limbs somewhat looser than they had been a few minutes ago. The worst of the pain had passed. Jason wrapped the child in a towel, relieved to see that it was no long struggling. He carefully placed it on the end of the bed, then sat down and stroked Kitty's cheek, giving her a few moments to rest. She looked at him, her gaze unseeing.

"I'm sorry, yer lordship," she whispered. "I'm so sorry."

"There's nothing to apologize for," Jason said gently, still stroking her hair. "There now. The worst is over."

"Is it—?" Kitty whispered.

"It's gone," Jason said.

"Was it a boy?"

"It was a girl," Jason said softly.

"What will happen to it?" Kitty asked. He could see the worry in her eyes and sense her innate fear of him. He had the power to ruin her life.

"I will see to it," Jason said. "You needn't worry. No one need ever know."

"Really?" Kitty asked, her voice lifting with hope.

"You have my word."

"The mattress is ruined," she suddenly said.

"Don't worry about the mattress. Can you tell me what happened?"

Kitty shook her head and closed her eyes. She was exhausted, but Jason couldn't leave her lying in a pool of blood. Nor could he leave the now-deceased child where it was.

"We need to get you cleaned up," Jason said. "I'll examine you tomorrow to make sure there's nothing left inside. If there is, it might fester."

"It still hurts," Kitty muttered.

"Once we get you clean, I'll give you a few drops of laudanum to help you rest. You'll feel better in the morning."

"Thank ye, my lord."

"Kitty, who's the father of your child?" Jason asked gently.

"No one."

"He's not in any trouble. Neither are you. I thought he might like to know that you're all right."

Kitty didn't reply, so Jason turned his attention to the child. He laid a finger on its chest just to make sure it was truly gone, then wrapped it more securely and carefully laid it inside his medical bag. It didn't fully fit, so he left the top open, hoping no one would look at the bag too closely once he left the room. He then opened the door and looked at the assembled servants until his gaze settled on Fanny.

"Fanny, please help Kitty get cleaned up and into a fresh nightdress. We'll put her in one of the unoccupied rooms since her mattress is ruined. Come get me when you're ready, and I'll carry her to bed."

Fanny nodded. "Yes, sir."

"Kitty is all right," Jason said in his most reassuring tone as he stepped out of the room and closed the door behind him. "An attack of appendicitis. Please, continue with your plans."

"Appendicitis?" Cecilia asked, her voice shrill. Jason hadn't even realized she was there. "There was blood everywhere."

"Cecilia, please return to your room," Jason said sternly.

She gave him a knowing look but seemed to think better of arguing with him. Everyone trooped down the stairs. They still had time to make it to church before the service began if they hurried. Jason returned to his bedroom and removed the child's remains from his bag. He'd assured Kitty that he would take care of everything, but now that he was faced with the tiny corpse, he wasn't sure what to do. The child could obviously not be buried in the graveyard, not having been baptized, and not if Kitty wished to keep her pregnancy a secret. It could be buried somewhere on the estate, but if the grave wasn't deep enough, someone was sure to come across it, or animals would get at the remains. And it was too cold to dig a deep grave without attracting attention to what he was doing.

He would have to cremate it, but he could hardly use the range in the kitchen or one of the fireplaces. Fanny or even Kitty might see fragments of bone when they cleaned out the ashes. He would have to deal with it later, but until then he had to keep it out of sight. Jason felt terribly guilty as he wrapped the child more securely and deposited her at the bottom of his trunk. It seemed wrong to treat her remains with such disrespect, but he couldn't think of another alternative.

Jason didn't pray often, but he bowed his head and said a prayer for the little girl whose life had been snuffed out at birth. And for Kitty, who he was sure had suffered, not only physically but emotionally. She was only fourteen. Still a child. Whether she had lain with someone willingly or had been forced, she had been too young and too vulnerable to deal with the consequences alone. No wonder she hadn't wanted to remain at home, where her mother might have noticed the changes in her body. Kitty hadn't been obviously showing, but a woman who'd given birth to three children was sure to notice something.

There was a soft knock on the door. Fanny stood outside, the dress she'd changed into for the service smeared with blood. "Kitty is ready to be moved, sir."

"I'll see to it," Jason said. "I'm sorry about your dress, Fanny."

"It's all right, sir. Nothing a soaking in cold water won't take care of."

Jason nodded and followed Fanny back upstairs. Kitty was wearing a clean nightdress and wrapped in a shawl, her shoulders stooping with fatigue. She sat on the unsoiled part of the mattress, her back against the wall, her head drooping, but she was awake.

"How do you feel?" Jason asked.

"Tired."

"Is there pain?"

"A bit."

Kitty's uterus would continue contracting for a few more hours at least, and she'd bleed for days to come. He hoped Fanny had provided her with some menstrual rags but didn't want to embarrass her by asking. He lifted Kitty into his arms and carried her to one of the empty bedrooms on the second floor, then added a few drops of laudanum to a glass of water and held the glass to her lips.

"I'm sorry," Kitty said again. She was still pale, her gaze anxious over the rim of the glass. She was looking at him, but Jason was sure she wasn't speaking to him. She was speaking to the child she'd lost, to her daughter. He tried to think of something reassuring to say, but Kitty's eyes were already closing, her head rolling to the side as the laudanum took effect.

Covering her with the counterpane, Jason left the room, closing the door softly behind him. Instead of returning to his own room, however, he went up the stairs to the servants' quarters. The door to Kitty's room was closed, and a good thing too, since the interior still looked like an abattoir. The mattress would need to be disposed of as well as the bedding and the woven rug that was splattered with blood. Jason shut the door and turned to face the room, his gaze going to the small bedside cabinet. There was nothing on top, so he opened the drawer and scanned the contents. There was a half-burnt candle, a small box of tooth powder, and a hairbrush.

Jason brought the candle closer so he could see the back of the drawer, but there was nothing there. He then went through the pockets of Kitty's skirt and apron but didn't find anything either. Looking around, he spotted an embroidered purse with a tarnished brass clasp beneath the chair. He lifted it off the floor and opened it. Inside were a few coins, a handkerchief, and a small brown bottle. Jason unscrewed the lid and sniffed. An unpleasant, musty odor confirmed his suspicions. Pennyroyal. Kitty's miscarriage had not come about naturally.

Chapter 26

Having returned to his own room, Jason spent a fruitless two hours trying to get back to sleep. Thoughts of Kitty occupied his mind, and unanswered questions kept him awake. Giving up, Jason pulled on his dressing gown and ventured downstairs, hoping a glass of warm milk would calm him enough to rest. It hadn't been a conscious thought, but when he saw the oil lamp burning in the kitchen, he realized he'd been hoping to encounter Mrs. Dodson. She was still dressed for church, her hair neatly parted and pulled into a tight knot at the back. Jason was accustomed to seeing Mrs. Dodson in the linen cap that she used to cover her hair while preparing food, or in the bonnet she always wore to church. Looking at her now, he realized she was probably younger than he'd originally thought, closer to forty-five than fifty.

"How was the service?" he asked as he took his customary seat at the pine table.

"Oh, it was lovely," Mrs. Dodson replied.

"Can I trouble you for a glass of warm milk?"

Mrs. Dodson nodded and went to the larder to fetch the jug of milk. She poured some into a warming pan and set it to heat on the range, which was still hot from the tea she'd made for herself.

"There's nothing you could have done," Mrs. Dodson said as she set the glass of milk before Jason and settled across from him. She was a woman of the world and knew exactly what she'd witnessed tonight. Jason could only assume that the rest of them did as well.

"Mrs. D, you've worked alongside Kitty for three months now. Had you noticed anything? Does Kitty have a young man?"

Mrs. Dodson shook her head. "If she does, it's news to me. The only times she left the house were when we all went to church and when she went to see her folks on her afternoons off, and even then, I think she would have preferred to remain here. Reluctant, she was, to go home."

"Why do you think that was?"

"Young girls often don't see eye to eye with their parents, but I wouldn't have said that of Kitty. She's so docile, so obedient."

"Someone got her with child," Jason said, shaking his head in dismay. "She's hardly more than a child herself. Had she carried that baby to term, her life would have been ruined."

"She wouldn't be the first," Mrs. Dodson replied. "But I wouldn't have thought if of Kitty. She's not the type."

"Is there a particular type?" Jason asked, surprised by the remark. "I would have thought any young woman could be susceptible to being charmed."

"There are girls who court that kind of attention, who play with fire," Mrs. Dodson said vehemently. "Kitty is a mouse of a lass. I can't see her ever encouraging a young man or going off with him on her own."

Jason took a sip of milk. It warmed and comforted him despite the horror he'd witnessed tonight. "Kitty was about four months gone, which means that she was already with child when she came to Redmond Hall," Jason theorized.

"I doubt she knew it though."

"Was she ill at all?" Jason asked.

"No. Only the last two days. I thought she was distraught over her father's death. She loved him. She was always asking after him, every time her brothers came to collect her."

"Perhaps he was the only man who made her feel safe," Jason said. "I thought she feared me because of my social station, but maybe she feared me simply because I'm a man. Maybe she thought I'd take advantage of her. How was she with Dodson and Henley?"

"She seemed fine," Mrs. Dodson said, her gaze thoughtful.

"Did Kitty have another position before coming here? Could she have been desperate to get away from someone?"

"No, this is her first situation. She was at home with her mother before this."

"So, not a previous employer or a member of staff," Jason mused. "It would have happened over the summer. Perhaps some local boy?"

"I couldn't tell you," Mrs. Dodson replied. "I've never seen her with anyone except her brothers."

"And she is all right with them?" Jason asked.

"Oh, yes. There's genuine affection between those three. Her brothers are very protective of her."

"Perhaps they have a reason to be," Jason said.

"You think she was raped, don't you?" Mrs. Dodson asked, watching him intently.

"Raped, or coerced. I'm going to speak to her as soon as she wakes up."

"Go easy on the poor girl," Mrs. Dodson said. "She's likely mortified enough as it is, having the lord of the manor witness her pain and humiliation and know her darkest secret can't be easy."

"It is not my intention to humiliate her, Mrs. D. But I will get to the bottom of this. In this house, Kitty is under my protection, and if someone's hurt her, then there will be hell to pay."

"Oh, I'm sure there will. I wouldn't want to get on the wrong side of you, Captain."

"Am I so frightening?" Jason asked, smiling for the first time that evening.

"You're not frightening, but you're a man who won't tolerate injustice, and that makes you a force to be reckoned with."

"I suppose I can live with that description of my character," Jason said, and pushed away the empty glass.

"Get some rest. Tomorrow will not be an easy day," Mrs. Dodson said.

"Because of Kitty, you mean?"

Mrs. Dodson shook her head, giving him a knowing look. "Because of the awkward position you got yourself into," she replied cryptically and slid out of her seat. "I'll wish you goodnight, then."

"Goodnight, Mrs. Dodson," Jason said. He did feel better for talking to her and thought he could finally go to sleep. Mrs. Dodson was right—tomorrow, or technically today, would be a difficult day.

Jason walked up the stairs and let himself into his room. Getting into bed, he stretched out on the cool sheets and allowed himself to sink deeper into the mattress. He was tired, both physically and emotionally, and tried not to think of the poor baby that lay at the bottom of his trunk. He'd deal with the remains tomorrow, or the day after.

Chapter 27

Jason woke with a start, suddenly aware of another body in his bed. At first, he thought it was Micah. He used to come into Jason's bed all the time when he had a bad dream, but since coming to England, Jason had been firm in his resolve that Micah should remain in his own room. It didn't do for an eleven-year-old boy to be sleeping with his guardian.

But it wasn't Micah. Now fully awake, Jason found himself gazing into Cecilia's face as she straddled him, leaning down low, her breasts brushing against his bare chest. She brushed her lips against his, then ran her tongue over his bottom lip, her eyes glowing with desire.

Jason took hold of Cecilia's hips with the intention of pushing her off, but she took it as consent and brought her mouth down on his, kissing him hungrily. His traitorous body instantly responded, his reaction further encouraging her. Cecilia began to move her hips slowly, seductively, grinding against him until he thought he'd explode with need. And that was all it was—need, not desire, and certainly not love. He'd never been unfaithful to Cecilia, who'd been a virgin and would have become his wife in the true sense on their wedding night.

Not even when the soldiers had found willing women in the towns they'd passed through had he given in to his urges. It was only several months after getting back from Andersonville that he'd gone down to the docks in search of female companionship. There were several brothels close to the port, catering to incoming sailors and soldiers. He would have felt dirty and guilty before but coming face to face with death did things to a man. He was alive, but he hadn't felt as if he were living. He'd been caught in limbo, his healing body in the present, his mind in the past, and he'd needed to bring the two halves together. He'd needed to feel like a man.

The experience had not been as sordid as he might have imagined. The woman had been close to his own age and surprisingly tender. He'd seen her several more times before leaving for England and had given her a tidy sum as a parting gift, one that would help her start a new life if she wished to. But that had been seven months ago, and his body remembered only too well what it had been missing.

Sensing his hesitation, Cecilia pulled down the side of her nightdress, exposing one creamy breast. She reached for his hand and pushed against his palm, arching her back until her breast was cupped in his hand. Jason lowered his hand and gently pushed Cecilia off him, pulling up her nightdress as she sat next to him, staring at him in confusion.

"Cecilia, I can't," he said huskily.

"Why not? It's clear you want me," she protested.

"Please, go back to your room," Jason said, hoping she would do as he asked, but Cecilia was not a person to take no for an answer. It was clear she hadn't made the decision to come to him easily, and now that she was here, she wouldn't be sent to her room like a little girl.

"I'm not asking you for anything. I've been so lonely, Jason. Mark and I… Well, it wasn't a happy marriage. We weren't well matched, not in temperament and not in the bedroom. I'm offering myself to you. Please, don't reject me."

Jason felt like the worst sort of cad, but he shook his head. "Cecilia, I know you feel lost and lonely right now, but that's all the more reason for me to refuse. It's not me you want. You will regret this come morning."

"It is morning," Cecilia said bitterly. "It's that Miss Talbot, isn't it?" Cecilia hissed, anger bubbling to the surface. "You feel as if you would be betraying her."

The words hit home. She was right. He would be betraying Katherine. They weren't promised to each other, but in his heart, he belonged to her. If he hoped to make a life with Katherine, and he did, he couldn't begin it with a betrayal.

"Cecilia, please return to your room, and we'll pretend this never happened," Jason said quietly but firmly.

"We'll pretend this never happened?" Cecilia cried, her voice shrill. "Are you joking?"

Jason didn't want to have this conversation, especially not in bed when they were both nearly naked, but it served to harden his resolve. Yes, he'd been tempted, but for just a moment. He didn't want Cecilia, not even if this proved to be a one-time occurrence and she left, never to be seen again. He didn't want to lie with just any woman. He wanted to lie with a particular woman, and he would have her or no one at all.

Jason got out of bed, grabbed Cecilia by the ankles, and dragged her to the edge of the bed, where he could easily scoop her up. She let out a strangled cry and tried to yank her ankles out of his grasp, but he was not only stronger but also driven by a seething anger. Jason lifted her into his arms and strode from the room, just barely managing to open the door without dropping her. He carried her down the corridor, pushed open the door to her room, and dumped her unceremoniously on the bed, walking out just in time to nearly collide with Shawn Sullivan, who was clad in his dressing gown and held a cup of water in his hand.

"Mr. Sullivan," Jason said solemnly.

Shawn Sullivan took in his state of undress, disheveled hair, and angry scowl, and wisely chose not to comment. "Captain," he said, nodding curtly.

The two men parted ways and returned to their respective rooms. Riled as he was, Jason was sure Shawn Sullivan would never mention the incident to anyone.

Chapter 28

Monday, December 25

Despite his nearly sleepless night, Jason woke early. It was still dark outside, but a thin ribbon of pinkish light was just visible on the horizon, heralding the arrival of a new day. Jason washed, dressed, and crossed the hall, carefully opening the door to Kitty's room. She was awake, her face a pale oval in the near darkness.

"Good morning, yer lordship," she whispered. Her hands clutched the counterpane.

"How are you feeling?"

"I'm all right," Kitty lied. Given the events of last night and her appearance this morning, *all right* was clearly not an adequate description of her state.

"Are you in any pain?" Jason asked as he touched her forehead. It was cool, which was a blessing.

"Are ye 'ere to examine me?" she asked, her voice shaking with terror.

"Would you allow me to examine you?" Jason asked, already knowing the answer.

Kitty shook her head. "I c-can't. Please," she begged. She looked so terrified, Jason decided that to persist would probably do more harm than good.

He'd make up a vinegar douche for her to flush out any traces of the fetus or the placenta that might have remained in the womb and could cause an infection. But, just then, Kitty was embarrassed enough as it was, and he had no wish to cause her further distress.

"I won't touch you, Kitty, but you will have to follow my instructions if you want to avoid complications. Can you do that?"

Kitty nodded vigorously, clearly relieved. "Will it 'urt?"

"No. Not at all."

Kitty breathed a sigh of relief. "Thank ye, my lord, for everything ye've done for me. I never imagined it'd be so awful."

"Few women do," Jason replied.

He sat down on the edge of the bed and studied her for a moment, taking in the still-childish face and the huge, frightened eyes. He did not think for a moment that this girl was sexually aware. She was a child, inside and out, a child who'd been interfered with. Jason laid a hand over her small, cold one and felt her stiffen. She was afraid of him, terrified he'd do something to hurt her. Jason instantly withdrew his hand and stood. He had no wish to intimidate her. Instead, he pulled up a chair and settled at a respectable distance from the bed.

"Kitty, I am going to put forth a theory and I want you to tell me if I'm on the right track. Will you do that?"

"What's a theory?" she asked, staring at him with those anxious eyes.

"It's a guess. Or an assumption, if you will."

"All right," Kitty agreed hesitantly.

"I don't believe you have lain with someone willingly. Someone has forced himself on you and got you with child," Jason said softly, watching her face for a reaction.

Kitty looked as if she were going to be sick but lowered her eyes and nodded miserably.

"Was it someone in this house?" He believed Kitty must already have been pregnant when she'd come to Redmond Hall, but he could be wrong in his estimation. He was not an obstetrician and hadn't had much experience with premature births. Of course, to think that one of the men at Redmond Hall had raped Kitty was daunting. He could never suspect Dodson, which left Roger Henley, Joe Marin, and Shawn Sullivan. Shawn was not interested in the opposite sex, at least not as far as Jason could see, which left Joe Marin and Roger Henley. Jason liked Joe. He was taciturn at times but came off as strong and capable, someone one could trust.

Could my valet have forced himself on the girl? Jason asked himself. Roger Henley had a drinking problem and often looked the worse for wear in the mornings, but Jason had never noticed any signs of aggression or violence in the man. He was handsome though, in his own way, and could perhaps appeal to a trusting young woman. Could he have seduced her, maybe while drunk? Would he even remember?

"Kitty," Jason prompted when she failed to answer. "Was it someone in this house?"

"No, yer lordship."

"Can you tell me who it was?"

"No, yer lordship."

"Did this person furnish the pennyroyal you took?" Jason asked.

"No, yer lordship."

"Who gave it to you, then?" Jason asked, not really expecting her to fess up.

"I can't tell ye, yer lordship."

"Kitty, I can't help you if you won't talk to me," Jason said, leaning forward in his agitation.

Kitty instantly drew back, alarmed. "Am I to be dismissed?"

"Do you wish to be?"

"No. Please, don't send me 'ome. I want to stay 'ere."

"I'm not going to send you home. Your position is safe, but you are to rest for at least two days."

"It's Christmas, yer lordship. Mrs. Dodson needs my 'elp."

"Mrs. Dodson will manage without you. You are not to worry about anything."

"Thank ye, yer lordship. Ye're very kind," Kitty said softly. "I feel safe 'ere with ye."

"Kitty, promise me you'll talk to me if you ever feel threatened. I will never hold you accountable for someone making you feel unsafe."

She nodded and looked away. Jason took that as his cue to leave. He'd learned as much from her as he was likely to.

By the time Jason came downstairs, thin morning light filtered through the dining room windows. He helped himself to bacon and eggs from the dishes set out on the sideboard and took a seat at the table, grateful for a few moments of solitude. Fanny bustled into the dining room, a silver pot of coffee in her hands.

"Here ye are then, yer lordship. And happy Christmas to ye."

"Thank you, Fanny. Happy Christmas to you too."

"Shall I fetch ye some toast?"

"If it's not too much trouble."

Fanny beamed at him. "Of course, it's not too much trouble, sir."

"Fanny, have you ever seen Kitty with a young man?" Jason asked.

It was common knowledge that servants knew everything that went on above and belowstairs. Mrs. Dodson might have missed the signs, but maybe Fanny had seen something. Jason had a knot in his stomach as he posed the question he couldn't have put to Mrs. Dodson. Roger Henley was her nephew; she'd feel honor-bound to protect him.

"Has Henley been paying court to her?"

"Lord, no," Fanny sputtered. "Roger likes a bit of sport, to be sure, but Kitty's just a child. I hear Moll from the Stag is sweet on him."

Jason nearly laughed out loud. Moll was sweet on anyone who wore trousers and was younger than seventy. "Does Roger return her affections?"

"Oh, I'd say," Fanny said, lowering her voice even though there was no one else about. "He's smitten."

"Well, I wish them joy of each other," Jason said, hoping for Roger Henley's sake that he knew what he was about and could identify signs of the clap before he acquired it. Moll was not a woman who'd been saving herself for her future husband, and given the number of travelers who'd passed through the Red Stag, the odds were high that Moll had been busy.

"I'll get that toast for ye, sir."

"Thank you," Jason said. He poured himself a cup of coffee, added a splash of milk, and stirred in two sugars. The first sip was always the best, especially when his mind was dulled by lack of sleep. An ugly thought was taking shape in his mind, but he'd have to find proof of his suspicions before he voiced his concerns to Daniel Haze.

Jason looked up as Cecilia swept into the dining room. She looked tense, her chin held at a defiant angle. Cecilia poured herself a cup of coffee and fixed Jason with a questioning look.

"Good morning," Jason said, acting as if their encounter last night had never happened. "Did you sleep well?"

"As well as can be expected," Cecilia retorted, bright spots of color blooming in her cheeks.

"Cecilia," Jason began, but she silenced him with her hand.

"Please, don't," she choked out.

Jason gave her a curt nod by way of reply. Cecilia held the cup of coffee with both hands and studied him over the rim.

"Something you'd like to ask me?" Jason said, wishing he'd been able to finish his breakfast in peace.

"Have you sacked that little hussy yet?"

"Excuse me?"

"If any servant got herself in the family way in my household and put on a display like that, she'd be out on her backside before the day was out."

"It was an attack of appendicitis," Jason replied. "And she's feeling better, just in case you were wondering."

"I wasn't, and it wasn't. I was the daughter and wife of a doctor long enough to know a miscarriage when I see one. And I wager it wasn't a sad event, as the repressed people of this country like to refer to it. She self-aborted the brat as sure as today is Christmas."

"I'll thank you to keep that opinion to yourself. Kitty is only fourteen, and she'd been forced," Jason replied, hoping that bit of information would shut Cecilia up. He was becoming fed up with her self-righteous ways and unwelcome presence.

"That's what she wants you to believe," Cecilia replied. "Bring me some toast and fruit compote," she ordered Fanny imperiously when the servant walked through the door.

"I'm afraid we don't 'ave any compote, madam," Fanny said. "Would orange marmalade do?"

"I suppose," Cecilia replied ungraciously. "And ask the cook to make a fresh pot of coffee. This one's nearly empty."

"Yes, madam," Fanny replied, and left.

"I'd like it very much if you would accompany me to church this morning," Cecilia said, softening her tone. She could tell Jason was annoyed and was trying to backtrack into his good graces. "This is my first Christmas without them," she whispered, her eyes misting.

"I'm sorry. I know it must be difficult for you," Jason said, feeling guilty for his lack of compassion. He was sure that Cecilia was trying to draw his attention first to Kitty, and now to her bereavement to distract him from recalling last night.

"I know I've been...well, difficult, I suppose, but I'm just not myself these days," Cecilia said, gazing at Jason with a pleading expression on her face. "Forgive me?"

"There's nothing to forgive. Everyone deals with grief in different ways."

"I feel anger, and sorrow, and rage at the injustice of it, and I can't seem to stop weeping," Cecilia said, dabbing at her dry eyes delicately with a handkerchief.

"The only thing you can do now is take life day by day. It will get easier," Jason assured her.

"Yes, I suppose it will. Thank you for being so patient and kind, Jason."

"Think nothing of it. I want to help."

Did he? Jason stole a glance at Cecilia, who was sipping her coffee. Was he quick to anger because Cecilia's betrayal prevented him from truly sympathizing with her? Was he really that selfish? Would he feel more kindly disposed toward her if she were weepy and sad? Perhaps. But he'd seen grief in all its forms and knew that it often manifested itself as anger and irritability. Cecilia was simply trying to cope in the only way she knew how and was using him to fill the void Mark and Georgie had left behind.

Even if she and Mark hadn't had a good marriage, he'd still been her husband, the father of her child. She had to have loved him at least a little to have married him so quickly after Jason had left. Perhaps she'd harbored hopes of working things out, but now it was too late. She'd never get the chance to say the things she should have said, or make amends, for Jason was in no doubt that whatever rift there had been between Cecilia and Mark, it had been caused by Cecilia herself.

"I'm sorry I haven't been supportive," Jason said, reaching across the table to cover her hand with his own. "You deserve better."

Cecilia smiled at him, her eyes alight with hope. "Can you ever forgive me, Jason? For marrying Mark?"

"I forgive you," Jason replied, even though he wasn't sure he meant it. He was grateful when their conversation was cut short by the arrival of Micah and Shawn Sullivan.

"Merry Christmas!" Micah cried, his gaze searching as he smiled at Jason.

Jason chuckled to himself. "Your gift is in the conservatory."

"The conservatory?" Micah echoed, confused. "Did you get me a plant?" he asked, his face drooping with disappointment.

"Of course, I didn't get you a plant," Jason replied, amused by Micah's reaction. "I simply put it there because I think that might be the place to put it to good use. There's something for you as well, Mr. Sullivan," he added.

"Can we go see?" Micah pleaded with the tutor. "Can we?"

"Why don't we breakfast first and then go open our gifts," Mr. Sullivan suggested. "I'm sure his lordship would appreciate your company this morning."

Jason caught a glint of amusement in the tutor's blue eyes, but Shawn quickly looked away, probably not wishing to cause offense.

Micah looked contrite. "I'm sorry, Captain. Of course, I want to have breakfast with you. Can you tell me what the present is? Please," he pleaded. "I'll be on pins and needles all through breakfast if I don't know."

Jason chuckled at Micah's impatience. Micah's family had been too poor to get the children proper gifts for Christmas, so Micah wasn't accustomed to getting something every year. The first time he'd received a store-bought gift had been last Christmas, and he had been awed and overwhelmed by Jason's generosity. This year, Jason had got him something he knew would take Micah's breath away.

"All right, if you'd rather ruin the surprise," Jason said, hoping Micah would opt to wait, but Micah nodded vigorously, his head bobbing up and down. "It's a telescope," Jason said.

Micah let out the breath he'd been holding. "A telescope?" he whispered. "You mean I'll be able to see the stars and the moon up close?"

"Well, not up close, exactly, but much closer. Maybe even other planets," Jason suggested, enjoying Micah's barely contained excitement. He glanced at Mr. Sullivan, who jutted out his chin toward the chafing dishes on the sideboard.

"Breakfast first," he said. "You won't be able to see anything now anyway. Not until dark."

"Fine," Micah moaned, disappointed. "But I'm staying up all night tonight," he warned the tutor, who rolled his eyes in amusement before quickly rearranging his expression to one of solemn respectability.

Micah filled a plate for himself and sat on the other side of Jason, casting a baleful look at Cecilia. He didn't like her, and the feeling seemed mutual. Cecilia glared at Micah and Mr. Sullivan, who'd taken some eggs and kippers and sat at the table. Cecilia's look clearly proclaimed that the tutor was too lowly, and Micah too young, to share their breakfast table. Jason supposed she'd expected them to eat in the schoolroom.

"Was someone ill last night?" the tutor asked as he poured himself a cup of tea. "There was a commotion around eleven."

Fanny came into the dining room and set a fresh pot of coffee before Cecilia with unnecessary force. "Yer coffee, madam."

"Thank you," Cecilia said, remembering her manners. "Just an attack of appendicitis," she replied smoothly to Mr. Sullivan's question. "The patient is much better this morning."

"Who was it?" Micah asked through a mouthful of egg.

"Kitty was taken ill," Jason said.

Micah looked crestfallen. Given his tender feelings toward Kitty, he would have wanted to be there to comfort her had he known. "She's had a hard time of it," Micah said suddenly.

"How do you mean?" Jason asked.

"Well, she was feeling ill and wanted her mother, but was too frightened to go home."

"When was this? And why was she frightened?" Jason asked, sitting up straighter.

"This was a few weeks ago," Micah said. "I came across her puking. She was afraid of her father. I asked her if he beat her, but she said he'd never laid a finger on her, not in that way at least."

"What *did* he do?" Cecilia asked, her curiosity getting the better of her.

"He had her work at the mill. She didn't like it there. She didn't want to go."

"But the mill is closed," Jason said. "What sort of work did he have her do?"

"It is closed, but she said he still had hopes of turning things around and had her clean the place once a fortnight. There were rats and mice, and spiders," Micah said, grinning. "She's such a fraidy cat."

"And what did her father do while she was cleaning?" Jason asked, his voice low.

"I don't know," Micah replied. "But she didn't like to be alone with him. I could see it in her face."

Jason set down his cutlery and rose to his feet. "If you will excuse me," he said, and strode from the room and directly outside, crossing the frosted cobblestones of the yard toward the stables.

"Joe, get the carriage ready," Jason said. "And happy Christmas," he added belatedly.

Jason returned to the house, donned his coat, hat, and gloves, and stepped outside to await the carriage.

"Where to, sir?" Joe asked once he brought the brougham around.

"To the Haze residence," Jason said, and climbed into the carriage. It was exceedingly bad manners to call on Daniel so early in the morning and on Christmas Day, but what Jason had to say couldn't wait.

Chapter 29

"Lord Redmond to see ye, sir," Tilda announced. "I told 'im ye're at breakfast," she added self-righteously. Daniel bolted out of his seat.

"Daniel, wait," Sarah called out. "Invite him to join us."

"I don't think he's here to eat," Daniel replied as he hurried from the room.

"I'm sorry to call on you so early, and on Christmas of all days, but I needed to speak to you," Jason said, looking apologetic.

"Please, come in. Can I offer you some refreshment?"

"No, thank you. I'm not staying long," Jason said as he followed Daniel into the drawing room. He looked as wound up as a coil, his expression tight.

"What happened?" Daniel asked.

Jason didn't bother to take off his hat or unbutton his coat. "I don't think Frank Darrow was killed because of his criminal activities, despite all evidence pointing in that direction."

"What makes you so sure?" Daniel asked. He was standing across from Jason, his hands in the pockets of his trousers.

"Kitty Darrow suffered a miscarriage last night," Jason said, his expression pained. "I found a vial of pennyroyal in her room. I think she was hoping to abort the child while everyone was at the midnight service but hadn't realized how truly awful it was going to be. She'd been unable to keep from crying out."

"But she's only fourteen," Daniel sputtered, appalled.

"I questioned her this morning, and she admitted that she'd been forced, but she wouldn't tell me who the culprit was or who'd given her the remedy."

"What are your thoughts?" Daniel asked. He felt an overwhelming desire to pace. It always helped him think more clearly.

"Mrs. Dodson had intimated that Kitty was reluctant to go home, and Micah said that Kitty feared her father. It seems Frank made her go to the mill every other week."

"Why? It's deserted," Daniel said.

"According to Mrs. Dodson, Kitty never left the house on her own. The only time she went out was when they all went to church or when she went home on her afternoons off. Her brothers came to collect her and then brought her back."

"So?" Daniel asked, confused.

"So, it's unlikely that she would have been accosted by a stranger, or even someone from the village. She was never alone long enough. And she had been about four months along, given the size of the fetus, which means she was already pregnant by the time she came to Redmond Hall."

"Which means she could have been raped by someone in Elsmere. Who's to say she didn't go out alone before taking up the position at Redmond Hall?"

"No one, but she feels compelled to protect her attacker. She wouldn't give me his name."

"Perhaps she doesn't want this getting out. If you make a public accusation, her life will be ruined," Daniel pointed out.

"I think to some degree her life is ruined already. She'll never forget what she's suffered. Micah said that when he asked if her father beat her, she said her father never laid a finger on her, at least not in *that way*, but he was sure she feared being alone with him."

Daniel's mouth hung open as he tried to comprehend what Jason was suggesting. "Are you saying her father is the one who got her with child? Jason, that's grotesque."

"Grotesque, but not impossible. There was a case at the hospital when I was a medical student. A young girl had been strangled by her father. She had been interfered with and had been pregnant at the time of her death. Her mother went to the police and told them that her husband had been abusing the girl for years and had killed her in a fit of rage when she tried to refuse him. The man confessed while in police custody. The mother hanged herself after the trial."

"That's a horrible story. Are men really capable of such evil?"

"That and worse," Jason replied sadly.

"What about the brothers?"

"Mrs. Dodson said she'd never noticed any tension between Kitty and her brothers. Kitty was always pleased to see them and went off with them willingly."

"That doesn't mean anything," Daniel said, sickened by the very idea of a father or a brother having their way with the girl. "Look, perhaps it was someone she'd grown up with, someone she trusted. She wouldn't be the first girl to fall in love and be led astray, believing her lover would make everything all right should the worst happen. And the fact that she went to the mill with Frank is hardly evidence."

"In theory I agree with you, but there's a sick feeling in the pit of my stomach that won't go away. I may be totally wrong, but something tells me that whoever killed Frank was avenging Kitty."

"I need to speak to the Darrows," Daniel said. "Today."

"I'm coming with you," Jason said.

"There's no need," Daniel protested, feeling guilty for taking Jason away from home on Christmas.

"There's every need," Jason protested. "My carriage is just outside."

"I'll just make my excuses to Sarah," Daniel said, dreading having to tell her he might not be there to take her to church. Sarah was more understanding than most wives, and she was so proud of him for making inspector, but even she had her limits, and her condition was making her overly emotional.

Sarah glared at him over her teacup when he told her, but didn't admonish him, for which he was grateful. "Mother and I will attend the service. Perhaps you can meet us there. If not, I'll see you back here for Christmas lunch," Sarah said pointedly.

"I will do my best, my dear," Daniel promised, and made his escape.

The day was sunny and brisk, the carriage modern and comfortable. Daniel might have enjoyed the ride through the frosty countryside had his mind not been teeming with questions and futile arguments.

"If what you're proposing is correct and Frank was responsible for Kitty's pregnancy, who do you reckon killed him?" Daniel asked.

"James and William."

"But he was their father," Daniel protested. "Surely they wouldn't have been able to do what they did. I mean, the manner of his death..." Daniel's voice trailed off as his mind returned to the night of the Christmas ball and Frank's cold, lifeless body strapped to the wheel, his stiff member sticking straight up from the thicket of hair between his legs. No son could do that to his father, even if he had been driven beyond the point of endurance. Could he?

"They wished to destroy him, in every way possible," Jason replied. "If I'm correct in this, he'd committed an unforgivable offense, a trespass so grotesque he had to be punished, even in death. Exposing him that way belittled him as a man and made him a laughingstock. People will forget what manner of man he'd been, but they'll still talk about his swollen cock pointing at the moon."

All too soon, the carriage pulled into the Darrows' yard. Daniel and Jason alighted and went to knock on the door. The dog didn't even bother to yap, just lay there staring at them as if they weren't worth the bother.

"Let me start," Jason said. Daniel nodded, since he wasn't sure how to phrase the questions he needed to ask.

Sadie Darrow opened the door. She looked even more haggard than the last time they'd seen her, and her gaze was wary. "It's Christmas," she said bitterly.

"We're sorry to trouble you again, Mrs. Darrow, but there are some things we need to discuss," Jason said, his tone unyielding. "May we come in?"

Sadie Darrow stepped aside to let them in, and they stepped into the warm interior of the house. Sadie appeared to be alone, a plate with the remnants of her breakfast still on the table, her tea cooling in a flower-painted cup.

"May as well sit," Sadie said ungraciously.

Daniel took a seat, but Jason remained standing, his hat in his hands.

"Mrs. Darrow, I attended on your daughter last night," Jason said.

Sadie's gaze flew to Jason's face, her eyes filled wish anxiety. "Is she all right, my girl?"

"She's going to be fine. She's resting."

"Oh, thank God," Sadie breathed.

"You didn't ask me what was ailing her, but then, you already knew, didn't you?" Jason asked.

"She's been under the weather." Sadie averted her gaze. "She was always a sickly child."

"Mrs. Darrow, Kitty suffered a miscarriage last night, brought on by a dose of pennyroyal. Where did she get it?" Sadie's lack of surprise only confirmed Jason's suspicions.

"It were mine," she replied, her voice barely audible. It wasn't until she'd spoken the words that Daniel realized that despite her haggard appearance and gray hair, she was still of childbearing age.

"So, you gave it to her and told her how to bring about a miscarriage?" Jason asked, his voice edged with accusation.

"She's only fourteen," Sadie moaned. She was wringing her hands in her lap, her gaze fearful as she glanced at Jason. "It would 'ave ruined 'er life. She'd 'ave lost 'er position."

"Who's the father of her child?" Daniel asked, pinning the woman with his gaze.

"I don't know," Sadie whispered. "She were a wicked girl. Wicked," she reiterated.

"Mrs. Darrow, Kitty admitted she'd been raped. She was not wicked. She was a victim of someone she felt the need to protect," Jason said. Daniel could hear the anger in his voice. What Jason had witnessed last night had affected him more than Daniel thought possible.

Sadie began to cry, her head bowed in shame. "She begged me," she said softly. "She begged me to 'elp 'er."

"Who was the father of her child?" Jason asked again. He'd come a little closer to Sadie Darrow, and she looked up at him, fear evident in her eyes.

"A boy from the village," she finally said. "A boy she's known all her life. She didn't want to bring trouble to 'is door."

"I don't think that's the case," Jason said, his gaze boring into her like a drill.

"And who do ye think it was as got her pregnant?" Sadie cried. "What is it ye're not saying, yer lordship?"

"I believe your husband's death has something to do with Kitty," Jason stated, his voice flat now.

"And why would ye think that?" Sadie demanded.

"Because whoever killed your husband wanted to punish him, to humiliate him, to emasculate him, even in death."

"Emasculate," Sadie said softly, as if savoring the word. She likely had no idea what it meant, but she got the gist of Jason's suggestion.

"Where are your sons, Mrs. Darrow?" Daniel asked.

"They're asleep upstairs," Sadie said. "Ye leave my boys out o' this."

"I'm afraid we can't do that," Daniel replied. "Did they kill their father to avenge Kitty?"

Sadie's head shot up, and her eyes filled with hatred. "'E weren't their father."

"He wasn't?" Jason asked, exchanging a look with Daniel.

"Frank was my 'usband's brother. My James died before Kitty were born. An accident at the mill. At least that's what I always thought. 'E bled to death."

"You don't think his death was an accident?" Daniel asked, his perspective on the case shifting again.

Sadie shook her head. "Frank was the younger brother, so the mill would never 'ave come to 'im. It would 'ave gone to my Jimmy, but Jimmy were too young when 'is father died. Just a boy," Sadie said miserably. "Frank offered to take over till the boys were old enough to step up. 'E were kind and thoughtful and made me feel safe and cared for." She was crying softly now, her head drooping like a flower after the rain. "I trusted 'im. I thought 'e'd be a good father to my children. But 'e never wanted me or the kids. 'E wanted the mill and the money James left for our upkeep; 'e admitted it once, when he were roarin' drunk. 'E might not 'ave killed 'is brother outright, but 'e let 'im bleed to death. 'E never went for 'elp, just watched 'im die. 'E took everything that 'ad belonged to my James and 'e burnt through it all—gamblin', drinkin', whorin'."

"And Kitty?" Jason asked softly.

"'E were always kind to 'er. I thought 'e loved 'er. 'E took her on outings and bought 'er treats."

"Did you ever suspect his interest in her wasn't purely paternal?" Jason asked.

Sadie shook her head. "It weren't till the Sunday before Frank's death that Kitty came to me. She thought she were ill. She were frightened."

"But you recognized the symptoms," Jason said.

Sadie nodded. Tears rolled down her nose and dripped onto the bodice of her dress. "She told me then what 'e'd been doing to 'er up at the mill. 'E said 'e wanted to keep the place tidy. Maybe sell the lot. I never thought—"

"And you told your sons," Daniel said, watching Sadie. He felt a deep pity for this woman. Her decision to marry her husband's brother had cost her everything, most importantly her children. Regardless of the reason for their crime, her sons would hang.

Sadie nodded again. "I couldn't stop cryin' after Kitty left. I were so distraught. I'd failed 'er. I'd failed all three of them. Frank 'ad lost our livelihood. 'E'd squandered James' savings. And 'e'd debauched my girl."

Now the manner of Frank's death made perfect sense. Jimmy and Willy had been judge and jury. And they had been the executioners. They'd avenged not only their sister, but their mother and father as well. They'd risked their lives to mete out justice.

Daniel's head whipped toward the window. A heavy *thunk* was followed by a muted scream and the neighing of horses. He yanked open the door and felt the air driven from his lungs as a wooden cudgel came down on his ribs. Jimmy Darrow, barefoot and wearing only trousers and a shirt, loomed before him, his face a mask of murderous rage.

Daniel sank to his knees, gasping for breath, but Jimmy wasn't satisfied. He brought the cudgel down again, striking Daniel's shoulder. The sheer force of the blow drove Daniel downward, his face sinking into the thick mud of the dooryard. Out of the corner of his eye, he saw Jimmy take a swing at Jason's head. A dull thud was followed by a howl of pain and what might have been a scuffle, but Daniel couldn't find the strength to get up, or even move his head.

"Jason," Daniel moaned, but there was no reply.

Daniel's vision was blurred by tears of pain, but he could just make out the sleek body of the carriage careening down the lane, James and William Darrow on the box, their hair whipping in the wind. The vehicle swayed from side to side, its black form a stark contrast to the glare of the morning sky. Daniel closed his eyes and curled around his throbbing middle. Even that small motion caused him unbearable pain, and he whimpered like a child, wishing his mother were there to comfort him. Every breath he took was absolute agony, his ribs like sharpened spikes that pierced his lungs.

He heard the crunch of boots on the icy mud, but bright, colorful orbs were exploding before his eyes, and he couldn't bring himself to care about anything but keeping the pain at bay. There was a dragging sound and a deep masculine voice, but he couldn't make out the words over the loud hum in his ears. The colorful bursts vanished as suddenly as they had appeared and were replaced by impenetrable darkness. Daniel felt it beckon to him and gave in, desperate not to be in pain any longer.

Chapter 30

Daniel woke to find himself stretched out on the floor of the Darrows' house, Jason looking anxiously down at him. Jason had a bruised cheek and his lip was split, but he seemed otherwise unharmed. Joe, on the other hand, had a bandaged head, the linen soiled with fresh blood. He sat on the floor, leaning against the wall, his eyes closed against the sunlight that streamed through the window.

"Daniel, can you hear me?" Jason asked softly as he bent over him.

"Yes."

"You have three broken ribs and your collarbone may be fractured," Jason said. "I've bandaged the ribs, but you will need to remain on bedrest for several weeks."

"I want to go home," Daniel moaned. "I want Sarah."

Jason smiled kindly. "Sadie Darrow has gone for help."

"Or she's run off to join her sons," Daniel said hoarsely.

"She'll be back. I told her that assisting the police might help her sons' case, should it get to court."

"Those devils are long gone by now," Daniel muttered. He felt pressure on his bladder but could hardly tell Jason he needed the pot. "It hurts," he said instead.

"I know. I don't have anything with me to relieve the pain," Jason said. "Joe's hurting too. They nearly cracked his skull."

Jason sank down to the floor and sat next to Daniel, leaning against the wall. He put his hand to his face and winced when he touched the bruise.

"You'd best marry soon, or no woman will have you. Not if you go on like this," Daniel said, alluding to the faint scars that marred Jason's cheek. The livid bruise bloomed right above them, and a trickle of blood oozed from his swelling lip. Jason's chuckle turned into a groan.

Daniel wasn't sure how much time had passed, but eventually two burly men appeared, followed by Sadie Darrow, who looked ashen. The men followed Jason's instructions for lifting Daniel and carried him to an open wagon, where they laid him in the back and covered him with a moth-eaten blanket. They helped Joe climb in next to Daniel, and he sat down, his head in his hands. Jason joined the driver on the box and instructed him to drive them to Redmond Hall.

By the time the wagon pulled up in front of the Georgian façade of the hall, Daniel was nearly insensible with pain. Every sway and jolt felt like someone had taken a hammer to his ribs and shoulder. He could not recall ever feeling such agony. Jason jumped down from the bench and helped Joe down from the wagon.

"I'll just be a moment," he told Daniel. "I know you're in great pain."

Jason reappeared a few minutes later, having passed Joe into the capable hands of Mrs. Dodson. He held a tin cup to Daniel's lips, and the familiar sickly smell of laudanum assaulted his senses, but he welcomed its potent power. Daniel felt a pleasant heaviness settle into his limbs as the opium did its work, and the sharp edges of the pain dulled as if by magic and then receded into nothingness. He closed his eyes and gave himself up to the drug-induced sleep, grateful for its oblivion.

Chapter 31

Having returned home, Jason checked on Joe, who'd have a devil of a headache for the next few days, then went up to his bedroom, changed out of his filthy clothes, and cleaned his own wounds with alcohol. His lip stung and his cheek throbbed, but aside from colorful bruises, he wasn't badly hurt. He came downstairs just in time to meet the church party.

"Dear God, what happened to you?" Cecilia exclaimed when she saw him.

"It's nothing. Henley, I need you to deliver an urgent message to Detective Inspector Coleridge of the Brentwood Constabulary. If he's not there, give the message to the desk sergeant on duty."

"Yes, sir," Roger Henley replied without much enthusiasm. He'd probably been looking forward to Christmas lunch, not a windswept gallop to Brentwood.

"Captain, are you all right?" Micah asked softly as he followed Jason into the drawing room. "Can I pour you a drink?"

Jason tried to smile. "I'm fine. I feel a lot better than I look. Can you do me a favor?"

Micah nodded.

"Keep a lookout for Henley and let me know when he's back. You can use your telescope," Jason suggested casually.

"I will. You can count on me, Captain," Micah exclaimed, and hurried from the room.

"You look awful," Cecilia snapped as she swept in in a flurry of skirts. "Why do you get mixed up in business that's best left to those qualified to handle it?"

"And why do you sound like you're my wife?" Jason snapped.

"You never change, do you, Jason?" Cecilia admonished as she continued with her tirade. "Always throwing yourself headfirst into danger. Had you not given in to your noble instincts and joined the army, everything would have been so different," she said, her voice tearful now. "And why do you insist on people calling you Captain Redmond? You are no longer in the army, Jason, or even in the country where your rank is recognized," Cecilia exclaimed. "You are an honest-to-goodness lord. A nobleman. Start acting like one."

Jason took a deep breath to steady himself. Cecilia was not only grieving but reeling from his rejection. She was angry and upset and needed to vent her feelings, but he wouldn't be her punching bag. Not now, not ever.

"How I choose to style myself is my own business, and had you loved me, even a little, you would have at least waited to make sure I was dead before marrying my best friend."

"Jason, I was grieving for you," Cecilia cried. "Mark was there, grieving right alongside me. It was our love for you that brought us together. If I could turn back the clock—"

"Well, you can't. What's done is done," Jason said, forcing himself to moderate his tone. "You no longer have a claim on me, Cecilia. I'll thank you to remember that."

"How could I possibly forget?" Cecilia hissed under her breath. "You made it abundantly clear last night. And had you loved me," she added spitefully, "you'd have a little more compassion, a little more forgiveness in your heart. You left me first, Jason."

"But you left me last," Jason said quietly. "You made your choice, Cecilia, and now I will make mine. Now, if you don't mind, I'd like to be alone for a while."

"As you wish."

Cecilia left the room, shutting the door behind her and leaving a peaceful silence in her wake. Jason sat down and rested his head against the back of the chair, closing his eyes and allowing himself to sink into the rejuvenating embrace of solitude. He was relieved that the ordeal was over and everyone had survived, in the physical sense at least. Daniel would take several weeks to recover, but he'd be all right and with a good result under his belt. Not a bad way to begin his career with the Essex Police. But Kitty…

Jason sighed when he considered the poor girl resting upstairs. She was the true victim in this crime, and although her body would heal, she might never recover from the pain her family had inflicted on her. With Frank dead, she was free of him at last, but if her brothers failed to get away, it'd be the gallows for them, and she would have to live with the knowledge that they had died to avenge her. Jason wondered if Kitty had known the truth of the murder all along, but he doubted it. He didn't think Kitty would ever allow her brothers to risk their lives for her sake. She'd managed to get away from Frank by coming to live at Redmond Hall. No wonder Sadie Darrow had been desperate to get her daughter situated in a great house. She wanted her safe. And with Jimmy and Willy taking her to and from work, she was never alone with her stepfather.

But the solution had come too late. Kitty had already been with child, a fact she probably hadn't been aware of until the last few weeks. The poor girl must have been in hell, trying in vain to keep her secret while desperate for help. How many times had Frank forced himself on Kitty before her eventual escape from his clutches? Jason rubbed his eyes as an unbidden image sprang to mind. He hoped Frank hadn't been violent with her. As it was, those memories would haunt Kitty forever and possibly affect her future relationships with men. No wonder she had been frightened of Jason. As the lord of the manor, he was in a position of power over her, and with her living under his roof, she'd be at his mercy had he chosen to take advantage of her. Jason hoped she wouldn't think badly of all men. Maybe, in time, she'd learn to trust again.

And then there were the Darrow boys. The law was the law when it came to murder, but some small part of Jason hoped that Jimmy and Willy would manage to escape. They'd done what they had done out of love and guilt. They'd failed to protect their little sister from a predator who had lived under their roof. How could they have known? They were hardly more than boys, and Frank Darrow had been their father since they were small. And Sadie.

Had she suspected all along, or had Kitty's pregnancy come like a lightning bolt out of the blue, striking down hard and burning down everything it had touched? She'd had pennyroyal on hand, Jason reminded himself. How many children had she aborted since marrying Frank?

How cruel people could be to each other, Jason thought sadly. How thoughtless and unrepentant. Frank Darrow had been a thief, a liar, an adulterer, and a debaucher of innocence, a man who didn't deserve any consideration in life or in death, but the law would not take his character into account when sentencing those boys. The law would come down like a hammer on an anvil, striking with brutal finality.

"Dear God, have mercy on their souls," Jason whispered.

He wished he could talk things over with Katherine, but he hadn't seen her since she'd stopped by with the gifts and he'd allowed Cecilia to belittle her. What must she think of him? Probably no less than he thought of himself for allowing the woman he loved and respected to be treated badly and sent off without a word of recrimination. He would see Katherine tomorrow, no matter what. And he would attend to Kitty's child.

Having made the decision, Jason finally allowed himself to rest. The strain of the past few hours had caught up with him, and he felt like a limp puppet, its strings pooled around its limbs as it lay broken on the makeshift stage. He closed his eyes and allowed sleep to claim him.

Chapter 32

When Jason woke, the bright light of day had been replaced by the muted shades of a winter twilight. The first stars were already twinkling in the sky, and the moon hung over the trees, its light as silvery and mysterious as the glowing orb itself. Jason sat up. He had a crick in his neck and was ravenously hungry. He consulted his watch. It was just past four. He was just about to go in search of something to eat when Micah came into the room, his expression anxious.

"Are you okay?" Jason asked, using the American expression that only Micah and Cecilia would understand. "Did Henley not come back?"

"He came back an hour ago," Micah said. "But you were asleep, and I didn't want to wake you. He's delivered the message, as you asked."

"So, why the long face?"

"A carriage just turned in through the gates," Micah said. "Are you expecting anyone?"

"No," Jason replied, not sure why Micah was upset. Perhaps he was worried Jason would leave again.

"I don't want you to get hurt," Micah confessed, his expression one of a worried mother. "You're all I've got."

"Micah, I will spend the rest of the evening in this chair. Well, after I get something to eat, that is. I will not budge from this spot. If you'd like to bring in the chess set, I can even give you a game."

"I don't much feel like playing," Micah said. "I'm waiting for it to get fully dark so I can go look at the stars through the telescope. Do you think there's really a man in the moon?"

"I don't, but it's your scientific duty to find out," Jason replied.

"I will, but only after I see who's come to call."

"Sounds like a reasonable plan," Jason replied.

He was secretly glad that Micah was in no mood to play chess. His head was throbbing, and his stomach growled with hunger. He briefly wondered what had become of his carriage and if he'd ever get it back, but the sound of wheels on gravel drew him toward the window. Micah followed, practically pressing his nose to the glass.

A boxy black carriage pulled up to the house. Its exterior was dented and scratched, and the black paint was flaking off the wheels, showing dark wooden spokes. The driver, who looked grizzled and bad-tempered, jumped off the box and hurried to open the door. For a moment no one alighted, and then, a thin red-headed girl in an unbecoming black coat and an old-fashioned bonnet carefully stepped out, her face pale and frightened as she clutched her bundle to her chest and gazed up fearfully at the imposing façade of Redmond Hall.

A cry of astonishment tore from Micah's chest, and he took off, running out of the drawing room, through the foyer and out the door. The girl was momentarily startled, and then her lower lip began to tremble as tears slid down her cheeks. Micah wrapped his arms about her middle, then pulled back, startled, staring at the bundle in surprise. A small hand emerged from the wrappings and grabbed a stray curl, pulling hard enough to make the girl wince.

Jason abandoned his spot by the window and hurried outside. Micah turned to face him, and the look in his eyes brought tears to Jason's eyes. There were no words to describe the joy he radiated, nor the gratitude in his gaze.

"Captain, it's Mary," he cried, his voice breaking. "It's Mary," he repeated, softer this time.

The girl's blue gaze, so like Micah's, turned to Jason, and he found himself grinning like an imbecile, happy to have been able to facilitate this reunion.

"Welcome, Mary," he said. "Come inside. It's cold out here."

"Thank you," Mary mumbled. "Eh, the driver…"

"Dodson, please pay the man and offer him a meal and lodging for the night," Jason said to Dodson, who'd appeared at his elbow as if by magic, his face as impassive as ever.

"Of course, sir."

"Mary, this is Captain Redmond," Micah gushed as he pulled her by the hand. "He took me in after Pa and Patrick died. Where have you been? We looked all over for you. Well, never mind, you can tell us later. You must be hungry, and tired. And he—she?—looks like it's about to cry."

The child scrunched up its face but seemed to change its mind as the gas light fixture in the foyer distracted it from giving in to the impulse. It stared at the light, its tiny mouth opening in wonder. Mary stopped in the middle of the foyer, seemingly overwhelmed. Micah pulled her by the hand, towing her into the drawing room.

"Come and sit by the fire. Are you hungry? I can ask Mrs. Dodson to fix you some food."

"Micah," Mary said softly, reaching out to stroke his orange curls. "Oh, Micah."

Jason thought he should give the brother and sister a moment, but Mary looked so out of her element, he decided to step in.

"Mary, it's a pleasure to make your acquaintance. I'll have a room prepared for you, and I believe there's a cradle in the nursery. It'll be brought down to your room. What's this little one's name?" he asked carefully, trying to get a better look at the baby. It looked to be about nine months old. The child had the same wide-eyed stare as Mary, but its hair was dark and wavy.

"Liam," Mary said, finally getting hold of herself. "After our father," she explained.

"Are you married, then?" Micah asked. "Where's your husband?"

Mary hesitated and looked away, her gaze fixing on the leaping flames in the hearth.

"Micah, I'm sure Mary would like to rest," Jason said. "You two will have plenty of time to talk later."

Mary threw him a grateful but curious look. She probably wondered why the lord of the manor looked as if he'd just been in a bar brawl, but wisely said nothing.

"Yes, I would like to rest," she said quietly. "It's been a long journey from Liverpool, and Liam's been fussing."

"I'll have hot water and refreshments brought up for you. If there's anything you need, please, don't hesitate to ask," Jason said.

"Just some milk for Liam, please," Mary said softly.

"Of course. Mrs. Dodson will warm it up for you."

Mary followed Jason toward the stairs, where Fanny was waiting, agog with curiosity, to see her to her room. Mary followed Fanny meekly, her head swiveling on her thin neck as she took in the splendor of the hall and the sweeping grandeur of the staircase, which was lined with paintings, their subjects made all the more splendid by the polished gilded frames and the sheer size of the canvases.

"Dodson, I'll take tea in the drawing room. And bring some sandwiches too—real ones," Jason clarified. A bite-sized cucumber sandwich would not feed his hunger. "I'm famished."

"Of course, sir. Real sandwiches. For two?" he asked, eyeing Micah.

"I only want tea cakes," Micah replied. He was obviously still in shock, but Micah wouldn't be Micah if he wasn't up for cakes.

"Dodson, please make sure Miss Mary has everything she needs."

Dodson gave him a scathing look, and Jason tried to hide his smile. Dodson would see to everything. He always did and didn't need to be reminded.

"I'm sorry. I'm just thrilled to have Mary here at last," Jason offered by way of an apology.

"I know, sir. Wonderful Christmas gift for Master Micah."

"Indeed, it is," Jason agreed, and followed Micah into the drawing room to await their tea.

Chapter 33

Christmas dinner was a subdued affair with a chastised Cecilia keeping a low profile, Micah thrumming with impatience to spend time with Mary, and Jason worrying about Daniel and wishing he could have seen Katherine, if only for a few minutes. Only Shawn Sullivan seemed his usual ebullient self but, given the general mood around the table, he wisely decided to keep quiet. Jason was relieved when the meal was finally over and Micah and Shawn left the dining room, eager to make use of the telescope.

"Will you allow her to stay?" Cecilia asked as she followed Jason into the drawing room and sat across from him, eager for a nightcap.

"Who? Mary?"

"Who else?"

"Of course. Why wouldn't I?" Jason asked, wishing he'd gone directly upstairs. He wasn't in the mood for another confrontation.

"I'd bet my bottom dollar that child is a bastard," Cecilia said spitefully. "Are you now running a home for wayward children and orphans?"

"I'm certainly not running a home for bitter ex-fiancées," Jason snapped, and got to his feet.

"Ouch!" Cecilia said, putting a hand to her heart. "That was unnecessarily cruel."

"Cecilia, I didn't want to do this today, of all days, but I think it's best if we don't see each other again. Given that my carriage has been stolen, I will make alternative arrangements to deliver you wherever you wish to go. After that, my responsibility to you ends."

"Jason, really! There's no need to get so offended on behalf of those micks. You know I mean them no harm. I just don't see why you feel responsible for them, that's all. Surely, we can kiss and make up?" she asked, pouting in a way that would have softened his heart a few years ago.

"Cecilia, this is not about Mary and Micah, and I would thank you not to refer to them as micks ever again or you will find yourself forcibly expelled from this house. This is about your arrogant, self-serving insistence that we still mean something to each other. Our association ended the moment you accepted Mark's proposal. Or did he accept yours?" Jason asked, suddenly wondering if Cecilia had been the one to cross the line between friendship and romance. "You made a choice, and now you must deal with the consequences of that decision."

"Jason, please, don't evict me. I know I've been horrid, but I'm still grieving. Surely you can understand grief," Cecilia moaned theatrically.

"I'm sorry for your loss; truly, I am, but coming here uninvited and installing yourself in my house will not bring your loved ones back, nor will it win me over. Now, I'm going up to bed. I suggest you do the same. You have much to do tomorrow, seeing as you're leaving. Goodnight, Cecilia, and best of luck."

With that, Jason left a tearful Cecilia and strode from the drawing room, feeling not a smidgeon of remorse. That was one situation dealt with. Only half a dozen more to go.

Chapter 34

It was well past midnight when Jason heard the soft crying of the child, followed by timid footsteps. He pulled on his dressing gown and stepped out into the corridor, coming face to face with Mary, who was barefoot and clad in nothing but her nightdress and a plain woolen shawl.

"Are you all right?" Jason asked.

"Liam is hungry," Mary said. "And so am I," she admitted shyly.

Jason smiled at her reassuringly, or as reassuringly as he could with a bruise on his cheek and a bloody scab on his lip. "Why don't you get Liam and we'll go raid the pantry," he suggested.

Mary looked momentarily scandalized, but nodded and nipped back into the room, emerging with a squirming Liam. The baby looked wide awake, his blue eyes staring at Jason as if he were deciding whether he should bother crying or not waste the effort.

"Does he take any solids?"

"Some," Mary replied.

She followed Jason down the stairs and through the green baize door. They descended to the dark kitchen, and Jason lit the oil lamp Mrs. Dodson kept on hand for her nocturnal visits.

Jason got the range going, then sliced some bread while the milk for Liam heated. He pushed the crock of butter toward Mary.

"I think I can find some strawberry jam," he offered.

Mary nodded enthusiastically and buttered a slice of bread for Liam. Jason found a jar of jam and set it on the table before turning his hand to making chocolate. Mary looked like she could use something decadent, and caloric. She was way too thin. Jason had instructed Mr. Hartley to pay for a first-class cabin, but Mary didn't have the look of a woman who'd just enjoyed a luxurious trans-Atlantic voyage. She spread a bit of jam on the bread and handed it to Liam, who grabbed it with both hands and began to eat hungrily, jam smearing on his pale cheeks.

"Now, let's see what we have," Jason said once he'd poured two cups of chocolate. "Real food or cake?"

"Cake," Mary replied without hesitation.

"Cake it is, then." Jason found the remains of a plum pudding, several mince pies, and a dish of pear compote, and brought them to the table. "Will this do?"

Mary nodded eagerly and reached for a pie. She took an experimental bite, nodded in appreciation, and stuffed the rest of the mince pie into her mouth. "Good," she said as soon as she swallowed.

Liam, who'd finished his bread, reached out and grabbed a fistful of plum pudding. He stuffed it in his mouth, looked momentarily surprised by the unfamiliar flavor, then swallowed and reached for more. Despite the pallor of his skin, he appeared to be a healthy child who was a good size for his age and developing appropriately, from what Jason could tell. He'd spotted at least six teeth when Liam opened his mouth for more sweet. His hair was lustrous and his skin clear.

"He's beautiful," Jason said softly, wishing he could hold the baby.

"I wish his father had seen him," Mary said.

"Where's his father, Mary?"

Mary set down the spoon and her head drooped, her thin neck like the stem of a wilting flower. "Gone. Dead."

"Who was he?"

She exhaled sharply and looked up, her gaze meeting Jason's across the pine table. "Thank you for bringing me here, Captain Redmond. I don't know what I would have done had Mr. Hartley not found me. It's been so awful." She sighed. She seemed to draw in on herself, hunching her shoulders and instinctively using her body to shield Liam, as if there were some unseen danger lurking in the kitchen.

"Tell me," Jason invited. He genuinely wanted to know, but also worried that Mary's tale might upset Micah and wanted the chance to talk things over with her. At eleven, Micah was still an innocent, and had immediately assumed that Mary had married and the child had been born within wedlock. Jason had his doubts. He hated to agree with Cecilia, but there was a good chance she was right in her estimation of Liam's paternity.

"I begged Pa not to enlist," Mary began, a faraway look in her eyes. "We'd only just lost Ma, and I didn't want to be left alone at the farm, but Pa was all fired up, and so were the boys, especially Micah, who thought it'd be a grand adventure. He saw them as heroes who would fight for the country that had given us a home and a chance at a better life. And it had been a good life, before it all went wrong." Mary swallowed hard, her throat working as she tried not to cry.

"Before Pa and the boys left, Pa hired a farmhand to help me. I couldn't have managed on my own. Brendan was the son of our neighbors, the McCauleys. He was strong and fit, but hard of hearing, so the Army wouldn't have him, and it was a source of great shame to him. It made him feel like he wasn't the man everyone else was."

"And how did you and Brendan get on?" Jason asked carefully, wondering if Brendan was Liam's father.

"Brendan was to be paid a percentage of the grain and produce I sold, so he had a vested interest in doing a good job," Mary explained. "And he did. He was a hard worker. And a good friend."

"Just a friend?"

Mary nodded. "It was never like that between us. We'd known each other nearly all our lives, and to me, Brendan was like a brother." Mary sighed heavily. "Brendan could have stayed at the farm. There was plenty of space, but he went home in the evenings to see his parents, so I was left on my own. I had taken to sleeping in the barn because I was scared to be in the house alone."

Mary shifted Liam as he tried to grab for the cup of chocolate. She took a sip and continued. "We managed all right for a while, Brendan and I, but then in August of sixty-four, a battle was fought close by, at Folk's Mill." She waved her hand in a dismissive gesture. "The name wouldn't mean anything to you, of course."

"Go on," Jason said, praying all the while that Mary hadn't been a victim of marauding soldiers.

"I was in the barn on the night of August second, when I heard something down below. I peered through the gap in the wood and there was a man, a soldier. His uniform was filthy and covered in blood, but I could see it was light gray, not the blue of the Union army. I didn't know what to do. I was so scared. I lay quietly for the rest of the night, afraid to make a sound, but I needn't have bothered. He was so weak and delirious he wouldn't have stirred had I done a jig right next to where he lay."

Mary sighed and smoothed Liam's silky hair. His lids were growing heavy now that his belly was full.

"I felt sorry for him. What can I say?" Mary said defensively. "He was young and scared and desperate. I helped him into the house before Brendan came and settled him in one of the back rooms. Brendan never knew he was there."

"What was his name?" Jason asked quietly.

"Clayton. Clayton Overton from Mobile, Alabama. An awfully posh name for a kind and simple lad. He'd been shot in the stomach," Mary said, her eyes filling with tears. "I thought for sure he was going to die, and no one should die alone, like a dog." She sniffled and wiped her damp cheeks with the back of her hand. "I thought I'd at least make his last days more comfortable."

"But he didn't die," Jason guessed.

Mary shook her head. "It took over a week for him to start improving, but once he was on the mend, he got better every day and was eventually able to get out of bed."

"What happened, Mary?" Jason asked. When he and Micah had gone back to Clarke's Pointe, the farm had been burned down to the ground, and no one in the settlement seemed to know what had become of Mary Donovan.

"I was stupid, that's what happened," Mary cried, startling a sleepy Liam. "I grew careless. One day Brendan came in and saw two dirty plates and cups in the basin. I had been too tired to wash up after supper the night before. It didn't take him long to put two and two together, and he tore through the house, looking for Clayton. He found him asleep in my bed, naked and defenseless."

"What did he do?"

"I thought he was going to go for Clayton, but he didn't. He just left, but the look he gave me as he walked out the door was warning enough. He told his parents and they told everyone else. That night, a mob showed up at the farm. They had torches and were demanding that I give up Clayton or I'd come to harm."

"But you didn't give him up," Jason said. If Mary was even half as plucky as Micah, she'd have stood her ground.

"I made sure Clayton was safe. There was a place Micah and I used to hide when we were children. It was an old cabin in the woods. The wood was rotted, and the inside smelled of dead things, but it was shelter, and no one ever went there. I took Clayton there as soon as Brendan left and told him to wait for me for two days. If I didn't come, he was to leave."

Mary sighed heavily and stroked Liam's head. The child was fast asleep, his mouth open and his lashes fanned out against his cheeks.

"I told everyone the soldier had gone, but they didn't believe me. They called me names, and some even went for me. They were so angry, so ready to tear me to shreds. These were people I'd grown up with, sat next to in church, but they would have killed me had the priest not stepped in and told me to tell the truth if I hoped to be spared. So, I cried and told them the soldier had forced his way in and threatened to kill me if I told anyone."

"But they didn't believe you," Jason said, his voice flat. No mob would.

"No, they didn't believe me. They forced their way in, and when they didn't find Clayton, they fired the house. I was left with nothing but the clothes on my back and the bundle of food and clothes I'd given Clayton. Once it was safe, we left and made our way south. Clayton wanted to go home, and I had no home to return to, so I went with him. It took us more than a month to get to Alabama, but we made it. Got there by the end of October. Well, his folks were thankful to have their son back, I can tell you that," Mary said bitterly. "But they wanted no part of me. Clayton told them he loved me, and we were going to get married as soon as the war was over."

Mary lowered her head as silent tears rolled down her pale cheeks. "His father said it was his duty to return to his regiment. He promised they'd look after me until Clayton came back, but he didn't. He was killed two months later, in Virginia. Mr. and Mrs. Overton turned me out as soon as they heard the news."

"Did they know about Liam?" Jason asked. The promise of a grandchild might have softened their hearts.

Mary shook her head. "I never bothered to tell them. What was the point? As soon as it was safe, I went back north, but I couldn't bring myself to return to Clarke's Pointe, so I kept going. I wound up in New York, first in Hell's Kitchen, then Five Points."

"How did Mr. Hartley find you there?" Jason asked, amazed that the inquiry agent had been able to locate Mary in the antheap that was Five Points. It was a miracle Mary and Liam hadn't been carried off by cholera like so many who lived in the densely populated area that was home to countless poverty-stricken immigrants.

"I had a friend in Clark's Pointe. Anna McKendrick. I wrote to her once I was settled, just in case someone came looking for me. Anna heard that Mr. Hartley had been asking after me and wrote to him. That was in September. He came looking for me as soon as it was safe and the epidemic had abated. He said you'd been looking for me all this time and had offered to pay for my passage," Mary said, swallowing hard. "I thought I'd died and gone to Heaven, to discover that Micah was alive, and I'd see him again. Thank you," Mary said. "Oh, thank you, Captain, for bringing us together again."

"Mary, you are welcome to stay here indefinitely. I will be happy to have you and Liam, but if you wish to return to the States, just say the word. I will see to everything, and neither you nor Micah will ever want for anything. You'll never have to struggle again."

Mary nodded, her eyes luminous with hope. "Can I stay? For a while, at least? I've nothing to go back to, and Micah loves you so. I can tell."

"For as long as you like. Stay forever," Jason said, smiling at her. "I lost my family too, so you'd be doing me a kindness."

"I'd best get him to bed," Mary said, looking lovingly at her son. "He's getting heavy."

"Mary, why don't you tell Micah you and Clayton were married," Jason suggested. "It'll make it easier for him, and for you, I think. No one need know Liam was born out of wedlock."

Mary raised her face, looking at him with wonder. "Would that not be a sin?"

"I don't think so, and it sounds like Clayton would have wanted you to do whatever it took to make life easier for you and his son."

Mary nodded. "All right, then. Mary Overton it is," she said. "Never thought I'd be respectable."

"You don't need to be married to be respectable. Come, time for bed."

Mary heaved Liam onto her shoulder and waited for Jason to put away the remnants of their feast. He turned out the lamp, and they made their way upstairs in companionable silence.

Chapter 35

Tuesday, December 26

The day dawned sunny and bright, with a sky so blue it might have been high summer. After a leisurely breakfast, Jason left Micah and Mary talking quietly in Mary's room, their coppery heads bent together as they shared their painful experiences of the past few years. It was mild enough out to walk, so Jason set off in the direction of Daniel's house, eager to check on his patient. He found Daniel awake and alert, with Sarah by his side, feeding him a breakfast of soft-boiled eggs and toast.

"When can I leave my bed?" Daniel grumbled.

"When it no longer hurts like hell," Jason replied, and instantly regretted his choice of words. "I do beg your pardon," he said to Sarah, who smiled tearfully.

She stood and picked up the tray. "I'll leave you two to talk. Captain, can I offer you some refreshment?"

"Thank you, no."

Sarah left the room and Jason shut the door behind her.

"How do you feel?" Jason asked. "Really?"

"Could be worse. Nothing hurts as long as I don't breathe." Daniel suddenly grinned, the smile lighting up his usually serious face. "I got him, Jason."

"Whom did you get? Not Jimmy and Willy?"

Daniel shook his head and instantly winced. "Detective Inspector Coleridge sent Constable Pullman with a message yesterday evening. The search of Elijah Gordon's workshop didn't turn up any of the stolen items, but Sergeant Flint spotted something when they searched the house. It's called a kiddush cup, and Mrs. Gordon had decided to use it to display her poinsettias. The cup belongs to Mr. Adler—Mr. Grills identified it—and even has an inscription on the base. It was a wedding gift from his father-in-law. The inscription says, 'To Hannah and Isaac Adler. May your cup overflow.'"

"That's wonderful news, Daniel," Jason exclaimed. "He won't get off so easily now, not even with Jonathan Barrett representing him."

"He isn't. He turned down the case. Seems his house had been burgled as well," Daniel said. "The audacity of it. To rob your own lawyer."

"I don't suppose Elijah Gordon thought he'd get caught."

"No. To be honest, I never would have suspected him had it not been for Mr. Grills' account. Had he not managed to wound Silas Pike, there'd be nothing to connect Gordon to the break-ins."

"Any word on the Darrows?"

"Not yet," Daniel said. "They could have gone anywhere. I think you'll need to order a new carriage," he added.

"I think you might be right. And speaking of carriages, Mary arrived last night, with a baby."

"Did she?" Daniel exclaimed. "Where has she been all this time?"

Jason spent a half hour chatting with Daniel, then bid him and Sarah a good day and set off for the vicarage. His heart hammered in his chest as he reached for the brass knocker. He probably should have waited until his face looked more presentable, but he couldn't wait another moment to speak to Katherine.

She looked surprised to see him when she opened the door, her mouth opening in shock when she took in his battered countenance and tense expression.

"What in God's name happened to your face?" she exclaimed. "Are you all right? How badly were you hurt?"

"I'm fine, really. This is the worst of it," Jason assured her. "May we speak privately?" he asked when she failed to invite him inside.

"Father is not at home," Katherine replied.

"I'm not here to see your father."

"We can't be alone and unchaperoned," Katherine replied primly.

"I can hardly say what I've come to say on the doorstep," Jason replied.

"You're not leaving us, are you?" she asked, her expression growing anxious.

"Would it upset you if I were?"

"Yes," she said, and finally stepped aside to allow him to come in.

As soon as they were in the sitting room, Jason turned to face her. "Katherine, I know you have concerns about your father, but you have my word that I will see to your father's needs. I will gladly hire a housekeeper, an entire staff if I have to, to make sure you're free to live your life without the weight of responsibility you've been carrying since your mother passed."

Jason took a shaky breath, grateful she hadn't stopped his outburst yet. "I don't want to be without you, not ever. You are everything that's good and beautiful and true, and I want to spend every day trying to make you happy."

He stopped talking and looked at her, his insides twisting with nervousness. Katherine looked up at him, her eyes bright behind her spectacles. A sweet blush bloomed in her cheeks.

"And the woman you have installed in your house? What is she to you?"

"Cecilia is my past. You are my future. I love you, Katherine," he exclaimed desperately. "Won't you give me an answer?" he pleaded.

Katherine tilted her head to the side, a ghost of a smile tugging at her lips. "You haven't actually asked me anything," she reminded him gently.

211

Jason could have kicked himself for being so crude in his proposal. He sank down on one knee and reached for her hand, which she gave willingly. "Katherine Talbot, will you do me the great honor of becoming my wife? Please," he added, making her laugh.

"Yes," she said, her voice barely audible. "Yes," she said louder, and laughed as tears shone in her eyes. "Yes!"

Jason stood and picked her up, twirling her around the room until she cried that she was dizzy. He set her down and held her close until she began to relax, a look of wonder passing over her face as she looked up at him.

"I love you too," she said softly. "I think I've loved you since the first time I saw you in the Chadwicks' drawing room. You looked so dashing. And so vulnerable," she said softly. "I knew it was silly, but some part of me just wanted to comfort you."

"You did," Jason said, recalling their conversation that night. "And you made me feel less alone."

He cupped her cheek, and she raised her face to his. Their lips met in a kiss both sweet and urgent, their bodies melding together as Jason pulled her closer. It was at that moment that his future father-in-law decided to make an appearance, his face turning puce with anger.

"Katherine!" he roared. "For the love of God. What do you think you're doing, girl?"

"Father, Captain Redmond has asked me to marry him," Katherine announced. "And I said yes," she added hastily before her father could come up with any objections.

Reverend Talbot cleared his throat, his eyes blazing with indignation as he nailed Jason with his gaze. "You might have asked me first, sir," he said. "Or is it not customary to ask a father's permission in America?"

Chastised, Jason nodded in acknowledgement of the reverend's rebuke. "Please accept my apology, Reverend Talbot. You are absolutely correct. I should have given you the respect of asking for your permission," Jason said in his most appeasing tone.

His heart fluttered and his stomach muscles clenched with nervousness. Given his reluctance to part with Katherine, the reverend could refuse permission just to be spiteful, but the stubborn tilt of Katherine's chin made it clear that she wouldn't accept anything less than a blessing.

"Reverend, I love your daughter and humbly ask for permission to marry her. I hope you will give us your blessing," Jason added, reminding the man that Katherine had already accepted him and didn't need his permission.

Reverend Talbot glared at him for a moment, but then his expression softened, if the unpursing of the lips could be described as such. "I don't suppose I have much choice in the matter," he replied. "You have my permission."

Katherine's face fell as she watched and waited. When the reverend didn't say anything further, she asked, "But not your blessing?"

The reverend looked as if a war was waging inside him, but whatever paternal feelings he had for Katherine finally won. "And my blessing," he added. "I wish you a lifetime of happiness."

"Thank you, Father," Katherine said, visibly relieved.

"Thank you, sir," Jason said. "I'll take good care of her."

The reverend nodded. "I'll be ready to dine in five minutes, Katherine," he said and left the room.

Katherine beamed at Jason and he smiled back, swallowing his irritation with the reverend for treating his daughter like a skivvy. In a few months, they'd be married, and then she'd never have to take care of the man again. Jason would see to that.

"I love you," Jason said softly. "And I can't wait for our life together to begin."

Katherine stood on her tiptoes and pressed her lips to his, all her feelings there in the sweetness of her kiss.

Epilogue

May 1867

Jason was woken from a deep sleep by Liam, who was squealing like a piglet, his feet pounding down the carpeted corridor as he made his escape. Jason pulled the pillow over his head and tried to get back to sleep, but it was useless. He'd have to speak to Mary about moving Liam upstairs to the nursery and maybe engaging a nanny so she could get some rest from the little devil. Now that he was walking, Liam was running poor Mary off her feet.

Micah's piping voice cut across Liam's squeals as he joined Mary in the corridor. Jason could hear them talking together, and it made him smile. Micah had been so happy since Mary arrived nearly five months ago, his faith in the world nearly restored. Jason waited until the siblings went downstairs, then got out of bed and poured some water into the basin, running his hand along his jaw. He really didn't feel like shaving. Perhaps he should grow a beard. It might look smart for the wedding. The thought of the wedding made him smile hugely. Only a few more weeks. He could hardly wait. And then he and Katherine would be off on their wedding trip to Italy for a whole month. What bliss! And maybe by the time they got back…

No, he wouldn't jump ahead of himself. He couldn't help it though, could he? He had babies on the brain, mostly because Sarah had asked him to attend on her during her pregnancy. There was a new physician in Birch Hill, a Dr. Parsons, but Sarah had taken an instant dislike to the man and refused to see him ever again. Jason couldn't say he blamed her. The man had the bedside manner of an army drill sergeant.

Sarah was due any day now, and Daniel was growing progressively more unhinged, dancing attendance on his wife whenever he was at home as if she were the first woman to ever have a baby. Jason could understand his anxiety, particularly since he spent so much time working new cases. There hadn't been anything as dramatic as Frank Darrow's murder, but Daniel was kept plenty busy.

Jason's carriage had been eventually found near the Southampton docks, which had led police to believe that James and William Darrow had signed on to a vessel and were long gone. They would be arrested if ever they set foot on English soil again, but they hadn't been foolish enough to turn up thus far, or if they had, they'd used aliases. Those lads weren't nearly as stupid as Robert Graham had led Daniel to believe.

Kitty was as quiet as ever, but she did seem less pensive whenever Jason saw her and had even been known to smile from time to time. He held out great hope for her, as he did for Sadie Darrow, who, by all accounts, was a much happier woman since her husband had been so unceremoniously disposed of, and looked the part. Neither mother nor daughter had ever asked what became of Kitty's baby, and Jason had never volunteered the information. He'd buried the body in the woods, having given up on the idea of cremation, and marked the spot with a makeshift cross, just in case Kitty ever felt the need to visit her child's resting place. Jason hoped she wouldn't. It could only cause her pain. And she'd suffered enough. News of her brothers' guilt had been splashed all over the papers, and even though Daniel had managed to keep Kitty's name out of the sheets, there were some reporters who'd managed to glean nearly the whole story, and the newspaper headlines screamed:

REVENGE MURDER.

DARROW KILLED FOR DESPOILING A YOUNG GIRL.

Jason had made sure that no papers were left lying around for Kitty to see and usually tossed them on the fire as soon as he was finished reading. He was sure Kitty knew all the same though and carried not only the blame for Frank's murder but the guilt for her brothers' exile. She had, however, become quite close with Mary, who'd been a great comfort to her and told her time and again that she was not to blame. She had been the victim, not the instrument of revenge.

The papers made much of the method of the murder, rehashing Frank's final act and almost praising the Darrow boys for their creativity in displaying the body, but Katherine had a different theory.

"Don't you see?" she'd said, eyeing Jason over her spectacles as they slid adorably down her nose. "They reenacted St. Catherine's wheel."

"How do you mean, Katie?" Jason had taken to calling Katherine "Katie" once they'd become engaged. Her mother and sister used to call her that, and she associated it with love and security, and he felt honored to be included in such esteemed company.

"Kitty's full name is Catherine, and St. Catherine was broken on a wheel as a punishment for her refusal to compromise her virtue. Jimmy and Willy, in essence, broke Frank on a wheel as a punishment for violating their sister and stealing her virtue. It was their way of meting out justice."

"I agree that killing Frank was a sort of poetic justice, but I doubt they had Scripture on the brain when they stripped him naked and hoisted him up on that wheel."

"Say what you will," Katie said, a smile tugging at her lips, "but lessons from the Bible are never far from a devout Christian's mind."

Jason was glad she made no mention of St. Cecilia, who was the patron saint of musicians. It seemed that Cecilia had met someone while traveling in Italy, a musician, as it happened, and planned to be wed as soon as her year of mourning for Mark and George was over. Jason did not see this as divine intervention, but Katie had romanticized the coincidence, possibly because she was relieved to know that Cecilia wouldn't be paying Jason any more unannounced visits.

"All I can say is that I hope you never decide to revenge yourself on me should I do something to displease you. I shudder to imagine what that curious mind of yours will come up with," Jason joked, reaching for her hand and planting a kiss on her palm.

Katie's smile grew wider. "I suppose you'd better behave, then," she replied, and cupped his cheek tenderly.

"I plan to," Jason promised, and absolutely meant it.

Jason Redmond had nearly finished breakfast when Dodson appeared, looking as exasperated as ever. He still hadn't forgiven Jason his refusal to hire proper staff and thought their unorthodox household was probably the butt of the county gossip.

"Inspector Haze is here to see you," Dodson intoned, his nostrils flaring with indignation.

"Show him in here and ask Fanny to set another place," Jason said.

"There's no time for that." Daniel Haze's voice came from behind Dodson's shoulder. He sounded tense and upset.

"What's happened, Daniel?"

Daniel's shoulders seemed to sag under the weight of the news. "It's Imogen Chadwick, Jason," he said quietly. "She's been murdered. I need you to accompany me. Examine the body. I left Constable Pullman to keep watch."

"How was she killed?" Jason asked, as he pushed away his plate and stood, shoving the chair back so hard it scraped against the floor.

"Garroted. The killer nearly took her head off."

"Right. Let's go, then," Jason said, steeling himself for a new investigation.

The End

Please turn the page after the Notes for an excerpt from
Murder in the Caravan: A Redmond and Haze Mystery
Book 4

Notes

I hope you've enjoyed this installment of the Redmond and Haze mysteries. I have several more planned.

I'd love to hear your thoughts. I can be found at irina.shapiro@yahoo.com, www.irinashapiroauthor.com, or https://www.facebook.com/IrinaShapiro2/.

If you would like to join my Victorian mysteries mailing list, please use this link.

https://landing.mailerlite.com/webforms/landing/u9d9o2

Excerpt from Murder in the Caravan

Redmond and Hazy Mysteries Book 4

Prologue

Glowing rays of the morning sun sliced through the thick canopy of leaves, dappling the dewy grass with patches of sunlight. The meadow sparkled beneath a cloudless blue sky, the birds performing their arias as if for a rapt audience. Luca never tired of watching the world come to life, nor did he question the nomad lifestyle of his ancestors. Most people dreamed of living their lives tied to a piece of land, toiling endlessly and passing their woes to future generations, but Luca loved life on the road, the promise of new places, fresh sights, and unexpected loves.

He smiled broadly as he recalled last night. That had certainly been unexpected, but all the more wonderful for it. He took one last look at the sleeping woman in the bed and closed the caravan door softly behind him before cutting across the meadow toward his own caravan, all the way at the far end. Borzo came trotting toward him, pushing his wet nose into Luca's palm.

"Good morning, dog," Luca said, and patted the mutt on its head. Borzo looked all set to follow Luca to his caravan but changed his mind when Luca's mother stepped out of his parents' caravan, ready to get breakfast started. Borzo instantly turned tail and ran off.

"Traitor," Luca said under his breath before greeting his mother, who gave him a knowing look. He ignored it and skipped up the steps of his caravan. He pulled open the door, stepped inside, and nearly crashed headlong onto the floor when he tripped over something that lay in his path.

Luca grabbed the doorjamb for support and moved sideways, allowing the morning light to illuminate the dim interior.

He gasped and took a step back, nearly tumbling backward down the steps. A young woman was stretched out on the floor, her face pale as marble and just as stony. Her eyes were wide open, a grimace of pain and fear etched into her lovely features. He hadn't noticed it at first, but a thin line ran across her throat, the cut so deep it must have nearly severed her head. A pool of congealed blood glistened darkly beneath the woman's head, forming a gruesome halo.

 Stumbling outside, Luca ran toward his parents' caravan. His father would know what to do.

Chapter 1

Wednesday, May 8, 1867

Jason Redmond scraped the razor across his lean cheeks and watched in the mirror as his valet, Henley, went about laying out his clothes. Henley was often bleary-eyed and pale in the mornings, given his love of strong drink, but today was different. He didn't appear hungover, just worried and sad, emotions that were completely at odds with his good-natured personality.

"Are you all right?" Jason asked as he wiped the remaining soap off his face and approached the man.

"Yes, sir."

Jason cocked his head to the side. "Are you ill?"

"No, sir. Just worried, I suppose."

"What about?" Jason asked as he picked up the shirt Henley had prepared.

"Moll Brody never came home last night," Henley said, inadvertently revealing that he'd been at the tavern until closing time.

"From where?"

"No one knows, sir. Just went out in the afternoon and never came back. Davy Brody is mad with worry," Henley said.

Jason dressed in silence, his mind on Moll Brody. He'd known her for nearly a year now, having met her when he'd first arrived in Birch Hill from New York to claim his late grandfather's estate. Moll was a fixture in Birch Hill, but Jason didn't really know anything of her life beyond the fact that she helped her uncle run the Red Stag tavern. Moll's lush beauty and sharp tongue often gave people, men in particular, the wrong idea, and she had something of a reputation in the village for being loose.

Many years ago, in medical school, a friend of Jason's had been fond of sharing his theory about women's libido with his fellow students over a pint. Chett Bleaker had said that women could be divided into three categories. The first were those who would gladly choose celibacy if it didn't have the unfortunate side effect of spinsterhood. The second, respectable women who enjoyed the attentions of their husbands but didn't display any appetites that would be considered unnatural. And the third, those rare women whose desires could match those of any man and who were clearly cut out only for whoring. Jason hadn't much liked Chett or agreed with his opinions but thought that most people would slot Moll into the third category. She was so overtly sensual, it was impossible not to feel an answering desire when confronted with such frank interest.

Despite many thinly veiled invitations, Jason had managed to resist Moll's charms, but he wondered if Moll might have found herself a fancy man and was with him right now.

"I'm sure she'll turn up," Jason said as Henley expertly tied his cravat. "Moll is clever and resourceful. Perhaps she had an argument with her uncle and decided she needed a bit of space."

Henley's eyebrows lifted in astonishment. "And gone where to get it, sir? She has no other family or friends she can stay with."

"Please inform me when she returns. I'd like to know she's safe."

"Yes, my lord," Henley replied.

Jason made his way downstairs and entered the dining room. Most mornings, he found Mr. Sullivan, his ward's tutor, already at breakfast, but this morning Jason appeared to be the first to come down.

"Morning, sir," Fanny greeted him cheerfully as she entered the dining room. "The usual?"

"Please." Jason's brain didn't operate at full capacity until he'd had at least two cups of coffee. Mrs. Dodson always sent up two fried eggs, a rasher of bacon, grilled tomato and some mushrooms with toast and butter for his breakfast, which he quite enjoyed. Jason reached for a freshly ironed newspaper that Dodson had left for him and scanned the headlines as he waited for his meal.

He had nearly finished breakfast when Dodson himself appeared, looking as exasperated as ever. He still hadn't forgiven Jason his refusal to hire proper staff and thought their unorthodox household was probably the butt of the county gossip. Jason didn't much care. Being American, he preferred to do things his own way and saw no reason to have twenty people look after the needs of four.

"Inspector Haze is here to see you," Dodson intoned, his nostrils flaring with indignation.

"Show him in here and ask Fanny to set another place," Jason said.

"There's no time for that." Daniel Haze's voice came from behind Dodson's shoulder. He sounded tense and upset.

"What's happened, Daniel? Is it Sarah?"

Sarah Haze was due to give birth any day now, and Jason had intended to be on hand during delivery should any complications arise. He'd performed a cesarean section on a village woman last autumn and had saved her and her baby from certain death, earning Sarah's complete trust. She was wary of the new doctor, whom she thought old-fashioned in his methods and unpleasant in his manner. Since she was correct on both counts, Jason was more than happy to step in.

"No, Sarah is well," Daniel replied.

"Is it Moll Brody?" Jason asked carefully.

"No. Why would you ask that?"

"Henley said Moll never came home last night. Davy is worried sick."

"And how would Henley know that?" Daniel asked.

"I can only assume he was at the Red Stag last night. Thankfully, he managed not to overindulge. But never mind that. What has happened?"

Daniel's shoulders seemed to sag under the weight of the news. "It's Imogen Chadwick, Jason," he said quietly. "She's been murdered."

"Imogen Chadwick?" Jason repeated, unable to fully accept what Daniel was telling him. "Are you certain?"

"That it's Imogen or that she's been murdered?" Daniel asked wearily.

Imogen Chadwick had recently married Harry Chadwick, one of the wealthiest men in the county, and was the daughter of Squire Talbot, who owned most of the village and ruled it as if it were a medieval fiefdom, much as his ancestors had done since the Crusades, when they had settled in these parts and claimed the land for their own. Imogen was quiet and shy, and despite her typical English prettiness was the type of young woman people tended to overlook on account of her demure disposition. Having to now share a house with her widowed mother-in-law, Caroline Chadwick, a woman one should only cross at one's own risk, and her two sisters-in-law, Arabella and Lucinda, Imogen couldn't have been having an easy time of it after being sheltered and doted on by her parents. They'd arranged the marriage to their closest neighbor long before Imogen was at the age of consent in the hopes of binding the two houses in a union of material bliss, made even sweeter by the combined social power the two families wielded in the county.

The very notion that someone would wish to harm Imogen seemed utterly preposterous and unexpectedly personal. Jason had assisted Inspector Haze and the Brentwood Constabulary on several cases, but this was the first time he'd known the victim.

"I'm afraid so, on both counts. I need you to accompany me, Jason. Examine the body. I left Constable Pullman to keep watch."

Jason pushed away his plate and stood, shoving the chair back so hard it scraped against the floor.

Dodson was already in the foyer, Jason's coat, hat, and gloves at the ready. Fanny, who must have overheard the conversation and hurried upstairs to fetch Jason's medical bag, held it out to him, her gaze filled with anxiety. Jason didn't think he'd be needing any medical supplies, given that Imogen was beyond his help, but he thanked Fanny for her thoughtfulness and followed Daniel out the door.

"I brought the dogcart," Daniel said as they stepped into the glorious May morning. "It's quite a ways."

"Where exactly was she found?"

"At the encampment. One of the travelers tripped over her this morning."

"Can you kindly translate that?" Jason asked.

"Sorry. You wouldn't know what I mean, of course. Every year, around this time, Romani Gypsies set up camp in Bloody Mead. Imogen was found in one of their caravans."

"Bloody Mead? Did someone die there after overindulging in tainted mead?" Jason asked. The English had a creative if somewhat peculiar way of naming things, and he quite enjoyed learning the history behind the monikers, since the names usually went back generations and were always meaningful to those who'd lived in the area.

"It's named after a wildflower, actually," Daniel replied. "Bloody Cranesbill, or some such. It quite pretty. When it blooms, it's like a purple quilt spread over the meadow. Mead is short for meadow," he added.

"What would Imogen Chadwick have been doing in a Gypsy caravan?" Jason asked.

"That's what I mean to find out," Daniel replied as he guided the horse down a narrow track through the woods.

"So, are you here as Inspector Haze of the Brentwood Constabulary or as the former Birch Hill parish constable? I was under the impression that all legal matters pertaining to the village fell to Squire Talbot."

"Bloody Mead lies outside the parameters of Birch Hill, so Squire Talbot has no legal jurisdiction over the Romani, and given that the victim is his daughter, it's best for everyone if the investigation is handled by a professional police force."

"Has Squire Talbot been informed?" Jason asked.

"Not yet. Detective Inspector Coleman wanted us to confirm the identity of the victim and examine the body before informing the next of kin."

"Who reported the crime?" Jason asked.

"The Romani sent a boy to the station."

"That's very civic minded of them," Jason observed.

Daniel shrugged. "Normally, the Romani avoid the police like the proverbial plague, since the law is rarely on their side, but in this instance, they probably decided that it was in their best interests to get ahead of this situation."

"I don't see how this will help them," Jason said. "Reporting a body found in one of their caravans is practically admitting that one of their own is responsible."

Daniel shrugged. "I won't argue with you there, but had they decided to dispose of the body, the investigation would focus on them anyway, seeing as they are strangers and are always treated with suspicion and resentment, and such an action would only convince the police they have something to hide. Ah, we're nearly there."

Chapter 2

Jason looked ahead, his mouth opening in surprise when the trees parted and Bloody Mead, liberally dotted with the flower it was named after, came into view. He'd never seen a Gypsy camp before, and the sight came as something of a surprise. He supposed he'd expected a handful of makeshift tents and rickety wagons, but what he saw had an almost magical quality. There were about ten caravans grouped around the meadow, the bright exteriors embellished with beautiful designs that had been skillfully painted. Each dwelling was a work of art, unique in color and design.

Several people were about. The men sat around, talking quietly, while the women, who were dressed in colorful skirts and wore gold jewelry, tended their cooking fires and kept an eye on the children, who ran around barefoot and shouted to each other in a language Jason didn't understand. Several horses grazed in the meadow, the breed unfamiliar to Jason. They were smaller and stockier than the horses he was used to and were black and white in coloring, almost like cows. Long fringes covered the bottom of their legs, the feathery hair blowing in the breeze.

A bulky wooden police wagon stood beneath the trees, the horse munching lazily on the grass. Ned Hollingsworth, a crime scene photographer recently hired by the commissioner of the Brentwood Police Constabulary, stood leaning against the wagon, his camera and tripod on the ground next to him where he could keep an eye on them. He lifted a hand in greeting but made no move to approach the dogcart. Having finished what he'd come to do, he was clearly ready to leave but needed a ride back into town. Ned was a taciturn man who didn't mix with the coppers, but unlike his predecessor, who had sold copies of the photographs to the newspapers, Ned was trustworthy and efficient. He would have the photographs ready by the end of the day, but for now, all Daniel Haze had to work with was the actual crime scene and his own instincts and observations.

The two men alighted from the dogcart and were approached by an older man, who appeared to be the leader. He wore a white linen shirt and wide black trousers paired with a colorful waistcoat and a red kerchief tied around his neck.

"Good morning," Daniel said politely. "I am Inspector Haze of the Brentwood Constabulary, and this is Lord Redmond, our police surgeon."

The man nodded, his expression grave and his shoulders stooped in defeat. Most people were astounded that a nobleman would act as a police surgeon, but the man didn't seem to care, clearly having more important matters on his mind.

"We mean to cooperate with the police," he said hoarsely. "We hope you keep that in mind, Inspector."

"May I know your name?" Daniel asked.

The man hesitated. "My name is Bogdan."

"Is that a surname?"

"No, it's my given name. We're not much used to using surnames."

"Do you have one?" Daniel persisted.

"Lee. It's Bogdan Lee."

"Thank you, Mr. Lee. I will need to interview everyone at the camp. Please inform them of my intention. Where is Constable Pullman?" Daniel asked, looking around for the burly policeman who was nowhere to be seen.

Bogdan gestured toward a green-painted caravan parked at the edge of the meadow. "Your man is inside with the body. He prefers the company of the dead to us," the man said with obvious bitterness.

Daniel ignored the comment. "Shall we?" he said to Jason.

Jason and Daniel approached the caravan but stopped before going in, taking time to examine the scene. Unlike the other caravans, whose doors were turned toward the center of the meadow, the green caravan was partially turned away, the door facing outward toward the surrounding forest.

"What do you think?" Jason asked after several moments.

"There is no sign of a struggle, and the door doesn't seem to have been forced. There are also no footprints, since the caravan is parked on the grass."

"The grass hasn't been flattened, which means the body wasn't dragged here."

"My thoughts exactly." Daniel walked up the wooden steps and opened the door. Jason followed. Inside, the caravan was as lovely as it was from the outside. It was painted in fanciful patterns and decorated with rich fabrics and colored glass baubles. Every space appeared to serve its own purpose and was well organized.

Constable Pullman sat on a velvet-covered bench, his shoulders stooped, his helmet in his hands. Sweat glistened on his brow even though the interior of the caravan was pleasantly cool. Constable Pullman breathed a sigh of relief when he saw Daniel.

"Thank the Lord you're here, Inspector," he said. "I was beginning to think I'd be keeping her company all day. 'Tis a gruesome sight, this is."

"You can step outside now, Constable," Daniel said. With the body on the floor, there was hardly any space for the men to stand, especially if the constable remained inside the caravan.

Constable Pullman sprang to his feet, sidestepped the body, and stepped outside, sucking in the fresh air with as much gratitude as if he'd been trapped underwater. "I'll just be by the police wagon," he said, and trotted off.

"Should I wait outside while you examine the body?" Daniel asked.

"It is rather a tight squeeze," Jason said. "You can watch through the door."

Jason positioned himself next to the body, which lay on the floor between the bench Constable Pullman had just vacated and a round-bellied stove whose pipe extended through an opening in the roof. The gold-tasseled curtains were drawn, but the interior was still light enough to see an ornate bed built into the rear wall of the wagon, several cabinets, and a polished table draped with a damask cloth of pale blue. There was a jug of fresh flowers, a violin in a battered case that lay atop one of the cabinets, and several plates and cups arranged neatly on built-in shelves. The ceiling was low and curved, making Jason feel uncomfortably boxed in. He pulled open the curtains, allowing the morning light to shine onto the young woman at his feet.

Imogen lay on her back, her blue eyes bulging slightly, her mouth open as if in a silent scream. A deep, razor-thin gash encircled her throat, and there were livid scratches on both sides of her neck. Her face was cold to the touch, and her limbs had already begun to stiffen, rigor mortis having set in. Jason examined the front and back of the body, then inspected each hand in turn. All fingers except the thumbs were cut to the bone, the incision even and of the same width as the wound on her neck. Jason peered beneath the fingernails before moving on to a more intimate examination. Daniel stood on the top step of the caravan, blocking the entrance, so that Jason had complete privacy and Imogen's remains weren't exposed to idle curiosity from the travelers who were watching the wagon in rapt silence. Daniel looked away respectfully as Jason pushed Imogen's thighs apart to examine her more closely.

Having known Imogen, Jason felt a trifle guilty for taking such liberties with her person. She would have been mortified by the intrusion and would have most likely refused such an intimate examination had she survived the attack. Jason rearranged the skirts to cover her most private areas and moved downward, focusing on the calves and ankles, then the feet, still clad in silk stockings and dainty kid slippers.

"Well?" Daniel asked at last.

Jason got to his feet and leaned against one of the cabinets, wishing he could leave the confined space and step outside into the fresh air, but they needed to speak privately, and there were too many people hovering nearby.

"Has she been violated?" Daniel asked. He looked angry and tense, and deeply embarrassed at having witnessed Jason's thorough examination of the body.

"No. There are no signs of rape. Her underclothes were not in disarray, nor are there any obvious wounds save the ones on her neck and hands. I think she came to the encampment of her own volition and entered the caravan willingly, but she did fight for her life. Her nails are torn, and there's blood and tissue beneath them—her own, I presume. She tried to insert her fingers beneath the garrote, hence the scratches on her neck, and it nearly sliced her fingers off. The killer nearly decapitated her, possibly because he or she used a thin wire that sliced through skin and muscle."

"You're sure she was garroted with a wire?" Daniel asked.

"I am. The diameter of the cut is too thin for it to have been anything else."

"When was she killed?"

"I can't give you a precise time, but based on the level of rigor, I'd say she was killed yesterday evening. She's lain here all night."

"How is that possible?" Daniel demanded. "You'd have to climb over her to get to the bed. Did no one sleep here last night?" Daniel shook his head in dismay. "Do you think the Chadwicks will agree to a postmortem?"

"I seriously doubt that," Jason replied. "Nor do I think it will tell us much more than we already know. The cause of death is obvious."

Imogen had been young and healthy, and seemed to have suffered no internal injuries. Jason had palpated her belly but couldn't tell if she might have been pregnant. At this stage, he wouldn't be able to know for certain without dissecting the womb. Normally, he would advocate for a postmortem, but he saw no reason to cut Imogen Chadwick up. Or perhaps it was his own reluctance to perform an autopsy on someone he'd known personally.

"Let's get the body in the wagon, and I'll have Constable Pullman take it to the station. The Chadwicks can collect the remains once we're ready to release the body. Once Pullman is off, I'm going to start interviewing the suspects," Daniel said.

"Are they all suspects, then?"

"I have to work under the assumption that they are until I can rule some of them out, which might prove difficult, as the Romani are not known for being truthful or straightforward, not that I can blame them. People are generally not well disposed toward them."

Jason stepped out of the caravan, relieved to be in the open air. No matter how beautifully appointed, the small space made him anxious. He returned his unopened medical bag to the dogcart, while Constable Pullman and Daniel carried Imogen Chadwick's remains to the police wagon and arranged the body inside. His only contact with the dead through the lens of his camera, Ned Hollingsworth made no effort to help and climbed onto the bench, ready to leave as soon as Constable Pullman was ready to go. The constable looked like a man sprung from jail as he pulled away, eager to be away from the campsite where he'd spent the past few hours with only a dead woman for company.

The Gypsy tribe was gathered in the meadow, most people silent and watchful as Jason and Daniel approached. There were eleven men, eight women, and at least a dozen children of varying ages, whose expressions ranged from open-mouthed curiosity to obvious hostility.

Daniel addressed Bogdan, who came toward him. "May I use one of your caravans to conduct the interviews?" he asked.

"You can use mine," Bogdan said. "It's the red one." He pointed to one of the larger caravans. "Would you care for tea?"

Daniel seemed taken aback by this gesture of hospitality but instantly rearranged his features. "Yes, thank you. That's very kind."

Bogdan gestured to an older woman who had to be his wife, and she nodded in acknowledgement. "I will bring it inside," she said.

"I'd like to speak to the person who found the body first," Daniel said.

"Would you like me to be present during the interviews or wait out here?" Jason asked.

"Please, come inside. I would appreciate your point of view in this matter," Daniel replied, holding the door open for Jason.

Reluctantly, Jason entered the caravan and settled on a bench beneath the window. Thankfully, this wagon was a bit wider, and the windows on both sides made it feel less coffin-like.

A swarthy young man appeared in the doorway, his dark gaze defiant. "I found her, Inspector."

Daniel gestured for him to step into the caravan and take a seat at the round table. "Name?"

"Luca."

"Surname?" Daniel asked.

"Lee. Bogdan Lee is my father," the young man said. He couldn't be more than twenty-two, and although he wasn't traditionally good-looking, there was something charming about his youthful face.

"Please, tell me what happened, Mr. Lee," Daniel invited.

Luca closed his eyes for a moment, as if trying to visualize what he'd seen, then began to speak, his voice low and melodious. "I returned to my vardo just as the sun came up. Vardo is a caravan," he clarified. "The curtains were drawn, so it was dark inside, and I nearly tripped over her. At first, I thought she'd fallen asleep, but when I shifted away from the door and the light fell on her face, I knew she was dead."

"What did you do?"

"I roused my father and told him what had happened. He sent one of the boys to fetch the police."

"You did not sleep in your caravan last night?" Daniel asked.

"No, I spent the night with a friend," the young man said, a sly smile spreading across his face. He didn't need to clarify that his friend was a woman.

"Do you live in the caravan alone?" Jason asked.

"For now."

"What does that mean?" Daniel inquired.

"I hope to be married soon, then I'll share the caravan with my wife," Luca explained.

"And when did you leave your caravan yesterday?" Daniel asked, watching the young man intently.

"Just before breakfast."

"So, it had been left empty for approximately twenty-four hours?" Jason asked.

"That's right."

"Where did you go?" Jason asked.

"Some lads and I had business to attend to," Luca replied, his gaze sliding away and fixing on the ornate bed carvings.

"What sort of business?" Daniel asked.

"We went to look at some horses we considered buying," Luca replied. He looked too shifty for Daniel to believe him, but Daniel made no comment. He wasn't here about horses, either bought or stolen.

"Did you know the deceased?" Daniel asked instead.

"Not to talk to, but I've seen her around."

"Have you, indeed?" Daniel asked, pinning Luca with his gaze.

"Look, Inspector, I was born in this meadow and have come back every year since. We don't have much to do with the villagers, but we do know them by sight, and I have seen that one before. Last summer."

"She came to the camp?" Daniel and Jason asked nearly in unison.

Luca nodded. "You need to speak to Zamfira. She'll be able to tell you more. She does some *dukkerin* for the *gorjas*."

"I beg your pardon?" Jason said, his face a mask of incomprehension.

"Fortune telling for the locals," Luca explained.

"Can you send her in, please?" Daniel said, making a note in his little notebook.

"Are we done here?" Luca asked.

"For now."

Luca left the caravan, and a young woman stepped inside. She was one of the most beautiful women Daniel had ever seen. With riotous dark curls, eyes the color of black coffee, and full, rosy lips, she looked foreign, and her colorful clothing and dangly gold jewelry made her appear even more exotic. Daniel cleared his throat and consulted his notebook, needing a moment to compose himself. He had a heavily pregnant wife at home; he had no business admiring other women's beauty, even if the observation had been dispassionate.

"Eh, name please," Daniel said, his pencil suspended over a clean page.

"Zamfira Lee," the young woman replied.

"Are you Luca's sister?"

"Sister-in-law," Zamfira corrected him.

"Did you know the deceased?" Daniel asked, studying her through the lenses of his spectacles, which magnified her already huge eyes.

"Yes. She came to the encampment last year. To have her fortune told."

"And she came to have her fortune told yesterday?"

"She did."

"Did you charge her?" Daniel asked.

"Of course. Why wouldn't I?" Zamfira asked, clearly surprised by the question.

"Did you tell her she was about to die?" Daniel asked, immediately ashamed of the sarcasm in his voice. "Did you see it?"

"I saw she wasn't long for this world, Inspector, but I had no way of knowing she'd die just after she left me. And no, I didn't tell her."

"So, what did you say to her?" Jason asked, curious how Zamfira handled dire predictions.

"I told her she'd live a long and happy life," Zamfira said smugly, her eyes flashing with amusement.

"Is that what you tell all the gullible young women who come to see you?" Daniel demanded.

"No, not all, but seeing as she wasn't going to be around long enough to disprove what I told her, I thought I'd let her die happy."

"What time did she come to see you?" Daniel asked.

Zamfira shrugged. "I don't own a watch, but if I had to guess, I'd say close to four. Maybe a bit later."

"And what did she do after the reading? Did she speak to anyone else?"

Zamfira made a show of thinking. "No, she silvered my palm, thanked me, and walked away."

"And what did you do after she left?" Jason asked.

"I went inside to nurse my baby," Zamfira replied. "Once I got him to sleep, I came back out to help my mother-in-law with supper."

"So, you didn't see Imogen Chadwick enter Luca's caravan?" Daniel asked, his gaze fixed on the young woman before him.

"No, I didn't."

"Thank you. That will be all," Daniel said. He sighed and called for the next person to enter.

Two hours later, Daniel and Jason finally emerged from the caravan. Daniel had a massive headache, and Jason looked like he was about to be sick.

"I don't like closed spaces," Jason said, breathing deeply as he walked toward the dogcart, the greenish tint fading from his skin and normal color reasserting itself.

"You should have said," Daniel replied, and climbed onto the bench, taking up the reins.

Jason gave a dismissive wave, his expression thoughtful as he settled next to Daniel. The Romani had kindly fed and watered the horse while he interviewed everyone in the tribe.

"So, what do you think?" Daniel asked. "Sounds like they'd all rehearsed their story before we got here."

"Either they rehearsed it or it's true. Have they ever murdered anyone that you know of?" Jason asked.

"Not murdered, as such, but there have been thefts, numerous incidents of illness, and general bad luck."

"And you think they're responsible?" Jason asked, clearly incredulous.

"I really couldn't say. I try to keep an open mind, but given that none of them have steady employment and spend their lives gallivanting from place to place, you have to wonder where their income comes from. How much can you make telling fortunes and selling baskets in the market? No doubt you've noticed how richly the caravans are decorated and what good horses they have. Finery doesn't come cheap."

"No, I don't suppose it does," Jason said, but he didn't sound convinced. "Where to now?"

Daniel sighed heavily. "Before we do anything, we must inform the next of kin."

Jason tilted his head to the side, a speculative gleam in his eyes. "Daniel, does it not strike you as odd that Imogen Chadwick has been deceased since yesterday evening, possibly late afternoon, and no one has reported her missing? Surely the Chadwicks would have noticed she wasn't at dinner."

"Perhaps not," Daniel replied. "I can't imagine she'd have told anyone she was coming to the Gypsy encampment. Perhaps she pled a headache, or some other illness, and everyone just assumed she'd retired early. Many married couples don't share a bed, so it's quite possible no one has realized she's not in her room." Daniel pulled out his pocket watch and consulted it. "It's nearly eleven. I wager the family is just now starting to suspect that something is wrong." He exhaled loudly. "Perhaps it's best if you don't come with me," he said. "Having you there will lead to awkward questions about the examination of the body."

"Drop me off at the gate. I'll walk home."

"Perhaps you can do me a favor," Daniel said, wishing with all his might that he didn't have to be the one to relay the heartbreaking news to the family. "Stop in at the Red Stag and see if Moll's come back."

"Do you think Moll's disappearance is relevant to the murder?" Jason asked.

"Don't you?"

"I suppose it's possible," Jason conceded.

"And speak to Matty Locke. Very little gets past that boy. Maybe he noticed something unusual."

"Like what?"

"Like a stranger arriving in the village," Daniel suggested. Given the nature of village life, anyone who wasn't a local would immediately become a suspect.

"Of course," Jason agreed, but he seemed distracted. "I'm curious about the dog."

"What?"

"I saw a dog. There might be more than one. Would they not have barked if a stranger had walked into the camp?" Jason asked. "Besides, what reason would a passing stranger have to kill Imogen Chadwick, and why on earth would he do it in a Gypsy caravan?"

Daniel shook his head, mystified by the whole business. "I honestly have no idea, Jason. No idea at all."

Chapter 3

The Red Stag was virtually empty except for a few regulars who were nursing their tankards despite the early hour. Dust motes danced in the shafts of light coming from the mullioned windows, and the smell of spilled alcohol permeated the air. Davy Brody stood behind the bar, his expression vacant. He always reminded Jason of a pugilist who was about to enter the ring, but today he looked as if he'd already been defeated, the match lost. Jason walked up to the bar.

"Good day, Mr. Brody," Jason said.

The man inclined his head in acknowledgement.

"Has Moll come home?" Jason asked without preamble. There seemed little sense in beating about the bush.

"She has not. What's it to ye, yer lordship?"

"A young woman was found dead this morning," Jason began, and instantly regretted his thoughtless words.

Davy paled as his mouth opened in shock. "Is it…?"

"No. No," Jason hurried to reassure him. "It's not Moll, but given what happened, Inspector Haze is concerned for Moll's well-being."

"She's not 'ere," Davy said hoarsely. "She went out round three yesterday afternoon and never came back."

"Where did she go?"

"Said she needed some air," Davy replied. "Went for a walk." Davy averted his gaze, focusing it on the mug he was wiping.

"Where does she normally walk?" Jason inquired.

Davy shrugged. "I don't know."

"Did you look for her?"

Davy shook his head. "Full 'ouse last night. Couldn't leave the premises." Davy set the empty mug down with a hollow thud and glared at Jason. "I'll organize a search party. We'll find 'er."

"I think that's an excellent idea. No doubt Roger Henley will wish to help."

"I'd rather 'e didn't," Davy growled. "Always sniffing around 'er like she were a bitch in 'eat. She's a good girl, Moll. No matter what ye lot think."

"I have the utmost respect for Moll," Jason replied. That wasn't strictly true, given that Moll had brazenly offered herself to him on several occasions, but he did like her and hoped she was safe.

"Moll's my only family," Davy said softly, his gaze sorrowful. "I do care for 'er," he added.

"Of course," Jason replied. "Please send word to Constable Haze if you find Moll." *Alive or dead*, Jason added inwardly.

"Who was the lass that died?" Davy asked.

"I'm not at liberty to say," Jason replied. The news would reach the Red Stag soon enough.

"Can ye tell me 'ow she died, at least?" Davy persisted.

"She was garroted."

"Where?"

"In one of the Gypsy caravans."

"Lord 'ave mercy on 'er soul," Davy exclaimed. "Did she suffer, guv?"

"It would have been quick," Jason lied. Imogen would have known what was happening, would have had time to feel panic, and terror, and pain, but he saw no reason to share that with the publican, not when his niece might have suffered the same fate.

"Did Moll ever visit the Gypsy campsite?" Jason asked. He thought Davy would be surprised or even outraged by the question, but he seemed to draw in on himself, pulling his head in like a turtle.

241

"She always went to see them, as soon as they came," Davy said morosely. "She were drawn to them."

"Why?" Jason prompted.

Davy looked away, fixing his stare on St. Catherine's Church through the front window, its solid shape distorted by the wavy panes. Davy seemed to be wrestling with indecision. Then he suddenly slapped his hands on the bar and nodded, as if he'd come to some inevitable conclusion. "Come with me," Davy said, beckoning to Jason to follow him to the small office behind the bar, where he kept his more valuable stock and tavern ledgers. He gestured toward the rickety cane chair he kept for visitors and sat down behind the desk, practically falling into the seat, which creaked ominously beneath his bulk.

Jason remained silent, waiting for Davy to speak.

"I may as well tell ye, given what's happened, but I'll 'ave yer word as a gentleman that this goes no further than Inspector Haze." He stared at Jason belligerently, daring him to refuse.

"You have my word, Mr. Brody," Jason said, wondering what on earth Davy was about to impart.

Davy exhaled loudly and stared at his splayed hands for a moment, as if still unsure if he should speak. This was obviously difficult for him, and he would no doubt regret what he was about to share, but his affection for Moll finally won out.

"My sister, Rachel, took up with one of the travelers when she were fifteen. 'E were a fine-looking cove, turned 'er silly 'ead with words of love and little trinkets 'e lifted from honest folk. My father, 'e put an end to it right quick when 'e found out, but not before she got with child. Now, my father, 'e were an 'ard man, but 'e loved 'is Rachel. Couldn't bear to see 'er earning 'er keep as a dollymop."

"Sorry?" Jason interjected, unfamiliar with the term.

"A whore," Davy clarified angrily. "'Ave ye never been to a dollyshop, man?"

Jason didn't reply. "Please, go on," he said instead.

"My father put the word out that Rachel were to wed one of the farm 'ands, and she would 'ave, but the man done a runner before the banns were called. Didn't appreciate being my father's tool. My father, oh 'e were angry, but 'e'd done what 'e set out to do. Made everyone think the scoundrel got Rachel with child and run out on 'er. There was still talk, mind ye, but Rachel was young and sweet, and soon enough the gossip died down. Rachel, she doted on Moll. Loved the life out of that girl, 'cause she loved the father, ye see. Never got over losing 'im," Davy said sadly.

"What happened to Rachel?" Jason asked softly.

"Rachel died when Moll were seven. Our parents weren't far behind. So I sold the farm, bought this place, and took Moll in. Some might say different, but I love 'er in my own way."

"I've no doubt you do," Jason said.

"Ye know what it's like to love a child that ain't yers," Davy said, nodding his understanding. "I seen the way ye look at that Irish lad. 'E's the son ye never 'ad."

"Micah and I have a stronger bond than many fathers and sons," Jason agreed. He had no wish to elaborate. What he shared with Micah was private and had nothing to do with the case. "Did Moll know who her father was?"

"I never told 'er, and she never asked."

"Do you know his name?" Jason asked, wondering if Moll's father had been of the same tribe as the one camped out in Bloody Mead.

"Andrei Lee." Davy spat out the name as if it were something foul.

"And did this Andrei Lee know Moll was his daughter?"

"Aye, 'e did. Came for 'er after Rachel died. Said 'e'd cared for Rachel and would be glad to be a father to 'is girl, if we'd let 'im. My father chased 'im off. Nearly shot the poor bastard's 'ead off."

"Do you think any of the Lees told Moll she was a relation?" Jason asked, still trying to absorb the fact that Moll was half-Romani. He hadn't expected that.

Davy shook his head. "Moll never said nothin', and I think she would 'ave had a lot to say 'ad she found out. She's not one to keep 'er feelings to 'erself, if ye know what I mean. They was always kind to 'er, though," he added. "Made 'er feel welcome. Well, I best be getting on. I 'ave a search party to round up."

Jason nodded. "I hope you find her, safe and sound."

Having left the Red Stag, Jason walked a few paces to the stable yard, where Matty Locke was filling a trough with water.

The boy smiled in welcome. "Hello, guv."

"Hello, Matty," Jason said. "How's the leg?" Matty had broken his leg a few months back, but there was no sign of the injury now.

"Right as rain, yer lordship. I can't thank ye enough for looking after me," Matty said. "Is there aught I can 'elp ye with?"

"Matty, have you seen any strangers in the village over the past few days?" Jason asked.

Matty looked heavenward as he considered the question. "Well, I don't know if they's strangers, exactly."

"Whom did you see?" Jason asked, eager to get Matty talking.

"Well, the Gypsies, of course. They came 'bout three days since, but they do every summer," he said.

"Anyone else?"

"Sir Lawrence arrived on Sunday afternoon."

"Sir Lawrence?" Jason asked, trying to recall where he'd heard the name before.

Matty nodded enthusiastically. "Sir Lawrence Foxley. 'E 'as a fine carriage," Matty said dreamily. "And a lovely pair of grays."

244

"Where is he staying, Matty?" Jason asked, hoping to focus the boy's attention on the matter at hand.

"Chadwick 'All, of course, seeing as 'ow 'e's Miss Lucinda's intended."

Now the name fell into place. He'd heard Lucinda Chadwick was betrothed, and given the number of times her mother had uttered the words "Sir Lawrence Foxley, Baronet" within hearing distance, he should have remembered.

"Did Sir Lawrence come alone?" Jason asked.

"Well, 'e 'ad 'is coachman, of course, and 'is valet," Matty replied, giving Jason a look of bafflement that said that being a nobleman himself, Jason should know better than to ask such a foolish question.

"Right. Thank you, Matty." Jason tossed Matty a coin, which the boy deftly caught, and headed toward the vicarage, cutting across the village green.

Made in the USA
Columbia, SC
24 July 2021